D0871646

DISCARD

Heft

**Center Point
Large Print**

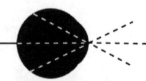

**This Large Print Book carries the
Seal of Approval of N.A.V.H.**

HEFT

Liz Moore

Farmington Public Library
2101 Farmington Avenue
Farmington, NM 87401

CENTER POINT LARGE PRINT
THORNDIKE, MAINE

002000348651

This Center Point Large Print edition is published
in the year 2012 by arrangement with
W. W. Norton & Co., Inc.

Copyright © 2012 by Liz Moore.

All rights reserved.

The text of this Large Print edition is unabridged.
In other aspects, this book may
vary from the original edition.
Printed in the United States of America
on permanent paper.
Set in 16-point Times New Roman type.

ISBN: 978-1-61173-450-8

Library of Congress Cataloging-in-Publication Data

Moore, Liz, 1983–
Heft / Liz Moore.
pages ; cm.
ISBN 978-1-61173-450-8 (library binding : alk. paper)
1. Life change events—Fiction. 2. Self-realization—Fiction.
3. Overweight men—Fiction. 4. Friendship—Fiction.
5. New York (State)—Fiction. 6. Domestic fiction.
7. Large type books. I. Title.
PS3613.O5644H44 2012b
813'.6—dc23

2012008668

For my mother, Christine

Acknowledgments

Many thanks to Seth Fishman, Jill Bialosky, Alison Liss, and Dave Cole;

to Bergen Cooper, Adriana Gomez, and Vani Kannan;

to Jessica Soffer, Alex Gilvarry, Peter Carey, Nathan Englander, Colum McCann, and my classmates at Hunter;

to Dr. Mark Davis, James Lawson, Chris Pohl, Dr. Matthew Rivara, and Jon Shehan;

and to Mac Casey, Christine Parkhurst, Stephen Moore, and Rebecca Moore.

Contents

Arthur

The first thing you must know about me is that I am colossally fat. When I knew you I was what one might call plump but I am no longer plump. I eat what I want & furthermore I eat whenever I want. For years I have made very little effort to reduce the amount that I eat for I have seen no cause to. Despite this I am neither immobile nor bedridden but I do feel winded when I walk more than six or seven steps, & I do feel very shy and sort of encased in something as if I were a cello or an expensive gun.

I have no way of knowing exactly what I weigh but I estimate that it is between five and six hundred pounds. The last time I went to a doctor's office was years ago and back then I weighed four hundred eighty pounds & they had to put me on a special scale. The doctor looked at me & told me I was very surely on a path toward early death.

Second. In my letters to you these two decades I have been untruthful by omission. For shortly after I last saw you a variety of circumstances combined to make it impossible for me to continue my academic career. About this—

about many things—I have been unforth-coming. My references to former friends and colleagues are memories. I have not worked as a professor for eighteen years.

Last & most important: I no longer go out of my house.

Fortunately it is a very nice house & largely I am proud of it. I did not purchase it; it was bestowed upon me. It is 25 feet wide. Very wide for this block. & once it was very lovely inside and out, decorated very nicely, O this when I was a small boy. But now I fear I have allowed it to fall into a sort of haunted dis-repair. Only scraps of its loveliness remain: the piano (I played when I was a boy); the book-shelves around the fireplace; the furniture, which once was what they call high-end, but at this point has been sinking slowly toward the floor for forty years because it has borne the weight of me on its back. There are nice things on the upper floors I suppose but I haven't seen them in a decade. I have no reason to go up there. I couldn't if I tried. My bedroom and everything I need are on this floor, my little world, & outside my window is the only view I need. The state of the house is one of the things I'm most ashamed of, for I have always loved the house, & sometimes when I am sentimental I feel the house loves me as well.

Because I no longer go outside, I have become very good at ordering whatever I need online. My home sometimes feels like a shipping center; every day, sometimes twice a day, somebody brings something to me. The FedEx man, the UPS man. So you see I'm not entirely a shut-in because I must sign for these things. And what leaves my house does so in garbage bags that I toss to the curb from my top step, very late at night, when it's dark out.

There are companies now for everything. One for bringing you your books and news-papers and magazines. One for sending you supplies you might need from a pharmacy. Even one that lets you order your groceries online and then brings them to your house for you. An old-fashioned concept in some ways, a wonderful innovation in others. Once a week I select my supplies on their website. They have everything, this company—everything you could possibly think of. Prepared foods & raw ingredients. Desserts & breakfasts & wine & toilet paper. Cheese & deli meat & ice cream & cake & bagels & Pop'ems, little doughy confections that Entenmann's bakes & then sprinkles with holiday-themed colors. Now it is October & my Pop'ems are orange and black.

A man brings my food to my home on Tuesday nights. I made sure to choose the *after 5 p.m.* option when I joined, which pleases me:

I like to think the deliveryman might believe I work all day and am just getting home. I'm very silly in this way! On the phone with customer service representatives, I casually mention family or work. How are you today, Mr Opp? asks the lady representative from Bank of America, and I sigh and say, Swamped. A little joke. In the same way, I delight in answering the door for my grocery delivery with a tie loosened about my neck and an air of exhaustion and world-weary distractedness. You can leave it just inside the door, I always say, & then walk into the kitchen, calling back over my shoulder little mundanities about the weather or a sports team. Once the boxes are all accounted for, I tip the driver with cash that I keep hidden in a drawer on my nightstand, on the inside of a hollow book. I obtained the book as a child—it was my prized possession, a hollow book!—and it has proven useful to me since. All the food I order for delivery is paid for by credit card on the phone. Tipping is the only thing I need cash for, so for a long time I have relied on the large store of bills that years ago I procured from the bank. I have no plan for when they run out. I never thought I'd need one.

The very very last time I went out of my house was in September of 2001, when I grew so lonesome watching the news that I opened my door and walked to the bottom of my stoop and sat on it, my head in my hands, for an hour. & I wished I had someone to talk to. It felt as if the world could end. Some very bad memories came to me one after another in a row. I heard what I thought was a woman screaming but that turned out to be peacocks that occupy the courtyard of a church near my brownstone. Then I hauled myself up and I walked to the end of the block, and then I walked one block beyond that, & then another, & then another. Finally I reached the corner of Ninth Street and Eighth Avenue, where two groups of women were standing in tight little circles, visibly upset. One young lady, holding a bewildered two-year-old in her arms, was crying and being heartily consoled by a friend. When I walked by them they hushed and looked. Beyond them I had a view all the way down Ninth Street toward the water & the horizon, and if I squinted and looked to my right I thought I could see black smoke rising into the sky, though I could not see downtown. Now I used to go into Manhattan quite a bit when I was younger & Manhattan was of course where I used to teach & although I didn't like teaching I thought of my students and my former colleagues & prayed for their safety and well-being. I thought of you & felt glad your dreams of living in Manhattan had not come true. I was overwhelmed with sorrow and nostalgia—self-pity and pity for others, which, in me, are often the same emotion. I stood until my feet could no longer bear my own weight and then I lumbered back, pausing seven times to catch my breath. The women were gone now and the streets were empty. At the bottom of my stoop I looked up to the top of my own twelve steps and vowed that I would not leave again, because you see I had no one to call, and no one called me on that day, & so that's how I knew I did not need to go out of my house anymore.

Since that day I have been completely reclusive. Of course my natural tendency has been toward solitude from the time I was a boy, but for many years I had family & other people who kept me from shuttering myself in too tightly. I had you for a while, and people like you. But I am no longer in touch with any friends or relatives. My mother was dear to me but she died young. For several reasons that I will give you if you care to know, I do not speak to the rest of my family. Nevertheless, they have made me financially stable for the rest of my life & I do not need to earn money to be so. This too has helped me to get bigger and bigger & has allowed me to stay inside my cocoon of a house.

•••

Now I spend each day in much the same way. In the morning I furtively collect the newspaper from its place on my stoop. I paid the deliveryman once to make sure that he placed it at the very top. I read all of the articles. I read the obituaries, all of them, every day. I cook or assemble feasts for myself. I wake up and plan the day's meals and when I have something particularly good in the house I feel happy. I roam from room to room, a ghost, a large red-faced ghost, & sometimes I stop and look at a picture on the wall, & sometimes, in a particular corner or room, a memory comes to me of my past, and I pause until it has washed over me, until I feel once again alone. Sometimes I write to you. Sometimes a piece of my own furniture will make me stop and wonder where it came from. It's a feeling of disconnectedness: I don't know & I have no one to ask. Mostly, though, my house has grown so familiar to me that I don't see it.

The evening of what has come to be called, on the news, 9/11, I wrote you a letter to inquire about your whereabouts & within a week I had a letter back from you. You said you & your loved ones were fine. Whether or not you have known it you have been my anchor in the world. You & your letters & your very existence have provided me with more comfort than I can explain.

These are the things you must know about me & this is my apology for the many years I have misled you by intent or omission. The slow descent of my health & the ascent of my reclusiveness have occasionally made it difficult for me to come up with suitable material for correspondence, & the fact of the matter is that I couldn't bear the thought of an end to ours.

In spite of everything, at heart I am still the same

Arthur

When I had finished it I held the letter in my hands before me & imagined sending it. Imagined very clearly folding it into sharp thirds & taking with my right hand the envelope & inserting with my left the letter. & then sealing it. & then inscribing it with Charlene's address, which I know as well as my own. O you coward, you coward, I thought, if you were worth anything you'd do it. While writing it I had felt a sort of grand relief, to be unburdening myself after so long, to someone I cared for so deeply. It was the letter I had always imagined writing to her. But unsurprisingly I was too afraid to send it, & so I told myself that it was a selfish sort of honesty, the sort that Charlene didn't need to be encumbered with anyway.

The events that prompted me to write it are as follows.

First, three days ago, the phone rang. I had been doing absolutely nothing & it gave me a very great shock. I nearly jumped out of my skin. I waited a few rings to let my breathing settle before I answered.

A voice came through the wires. "Arthur?" someone said. "Arthur Opp?"

Now I do not get many personal calls & my heart leapt at who it might be.

"Yes," I said, I whispered.

It was Charlene Turner. I did not expect to hear her voice ever again in my life but O God I was very glad to. I nearly cried out but stopped myself. I clapped a hand over my mouth instead & bit the inner flesh of it.

It has been nearly two decades since I last saw her. The in-person relationship we had many years ago evolved naturally into a sort of steady and faithful written correspondence. But over these many years, our letters have become inexpressibly important to me. An outsider might call us only pen pals but over time I feel I have come to know Charlene Turner as well as I have ever known anyone, & have tentatively imagined that one day we would see each other again, we would resume our relationship, & all in all it would be very natural & easy.

Still: her call unnerved me.

We talked briefly & I tried to sound quite calm and relaxed but accidentally I told an extraordinary number of lies.

I wanted to say *Have you been receiving my letters*—it has been nearly a year since I have heard from her, and she used to write more often than that—but instead I said "How have you been."

She said, "All right." In such a way that it sounded as if she wanted me to understand the opposite.

We spoke for a while about nothing. I updated her on William, the brother whose closeness to me I exaggerated on a whim in one of my notes to her. I told her he was doing very well and was in fact retiring next year after a celebrated career as an architect. I told her that last month I had visited family in England and that yesterday I'd spent in Manhattan, visiting an old friend. Then I told her I'd taken up photography.

"Great," said Charlene, & I too said "Great."

"Are you still teaching?" said Charlene.

"No, I've stopped teaching," I said—I said without thinking.

And she said *O no* in such a way that she sounded utterly utterly disappointed & forlorn.

So I said "But I tutor now." Just so it would seem as if I had been doing a little something all these years.

At this she brightened & told me that this was in fact why she was calling.

"I'm going to send you a letter, Arthur," said Charlene. When I focused on her voice I realized she sounded very strange, faraway & remorseful, & slower than she was when I knew her, as if her tongue had gotten heavier. She very possibly sounded drunk. It was two in the afternoon.

"All right," I said.

"Look for it," she said. "You're still at the same address," she said.

"I am," I said.

"Look for it," she said again.

"All right," I said.

"What will be in it," I said, but she had already hung up the phone.

I sat on the couch for a while. Then I went into my bedroom & sat on my bed. Then I opened the drawer of my bedside table & from it pulled a stack of all the letters Charlene ever sent me. They are a slim volume altogether, perhaps forty pages in sum. Her handwriting in these letters is tight as a drum, small and overlapping. I read all of them in a row that evening—an indulgence I have rarely allowed myself over our two decades of correspondence—& I granted myself permission, just for a moment, to dream of Charlene, to remember our brief relationship with the same affection & passion that, for many years, has sustained me.

& then this morning, with nothing much else to do, I sat down and wrote the letter to her that I have composed over & over again in my head— the truth-telling letter, the healing admission of my darkest secrets—the letter I knew I would have to send her if we were ever to meet again. The letter I would, indeed, send her right this moment if I were not very cowardly indeed. As it turns out, however, I am.

Here is Charlene Turner: Walking into my classroom two decades ago, her cheeks as pink as a tulip, her face as round as a penny. Short and small, rabbitish, the youngest in the room by a decade. I too am young. The class is a seminar & we sit at a long oval table & as teacher I am at the head of it. Her lips do not gracefully close over her teeth. The frames of her glasses are too wide & they give her a look of being mildly cross-eyed. Her bangs are worked into an astounding arc at the top of her head. One can tell she has put thought into her outfit. Her shoulder pads threaten to eclipse her. She has turned up the cuffs of her blazer. She wears red and green and yellow. Accordingly she looks like a stoplight.

It is a night class. The other students are older, mothers and retirees. They are dressed in long black skirts and flowing blouses. Many are rich and idle, many are taking this class for pleasure. Not Charlene Turner. One by one we go round the table, identifying ourselves. I give my full name with Dr in front of it & then I tell my students to call me whatever they like. When Charlene's turn comes she opens her mouth and a very small noise comes out.

"Could you speak up, please?" I ask her.

"Charlene Turner," she says, & in her accent I detect something beautifully native, a New-Yorkness that none of the other students possess. She nearly drops the first *r* in her name. She comes very close to dropping it. When she speaks, she ducks her head like a boxer. "Welcome, Charlene," is what I say.

The university at which we met was an institution founded on progressive values & most of its students were similarly progressive. I taught in the extension program, in which nearly all of the students were also unusual in some way: commuters, adults who'd taken a few years to work after high school, people with fulltime jobs who were enrolled in a degree program in the evening. Nontrads, we called them. (That I ever casually used this jargon, that I ever even knew it, amazes me.) Charlene Turner did & did not fit this mold. She had taken one year off after graduating from high school. Whether she was "progressive" or not, according to the school's tacit definition of it, I cannot say—we never spoke of politics. She lived with her parents in Yonkers. She worked as a receptionist in a dental office. Twice a week she took the subway in to attend my class: an hour's commute each way. But all of this I discovered later. At first she was just a student in my class, & a very quiet one at that.

She said nothing in class. She gazed at me

steadily from halfway down our seminar table, blinking occasionally through her large glasses, observing her classmates respectfully. Only once during the entire semester did she ever speak, and it was to volunteer an answer that was incorrect. I didn't have the heart to correct her myself, so I turned to the class and allowed them to, and after that she returned to silence. But she came to visit me in my office several times. The first time she had the same wide-eyed look upon her face that she had in class, & she asked me a question that I can no longer remember about one of the texts that we'd read. She was very quiet still, & I did most of the talking. I shared an office in those days with another associate professor named Hans Hueber, whom I did not like, and upon her exit he turned to me & smiled & rolled his eyes as if he wanted me to be complicit in his ridicule of Charlene's lack of intellect, or poise, or whatever it was he thought of her. But I would not meet his gaze.

She came to see me several times after that & we talked. Hans Hueber stopped smirking & turned to sighing in annoyance upon her entrance. Charlene had no natural aptitude for the sort of literature we were reading. She ascribed emotions to the characters that, it was clear, she herself would feel in their place—or she judged them as people, rather than literature. When asked to critically analyze a text, she would list all the reasons that a character was good or bad, right or wrong. She wrote a whole paper on *Medea* in which she stated, over and over again, in several different ways, that Medea was selfish and evil. In my comments, I told her she had to think about the meaning of the text, to formulate an argument about the text. To think of Medea as a tool for unlocking the play's hidden code. She came to my office hours & told me she did not understand. She looked hurt & bewildered. She thought she had done well.

"Why do you think she's selfish?" I asked her.

"She shouldn't have killed her children," said Charlene. "She should have killed herself."

I remember it all. I remember her expression.

"But killing her children was her way of protecting them," I said. I was playing devil's advocate. "She didn't want them to suffer."

"They could have taken care of themselves," said Charlene. She looked at me fiercely. She was wearing a bright pink sweater with a ridiculous pattern on it. She wore this sweater quite a bit. Her bangs were especially high that day. She put one small & bony hand on my desk and left it there, a kind of appeal. She would not be swayed. I found myself not wanting to sway her. Her refusal or inability to think academically about the texts struck me as something noble. I now realize that I probably failed her as a teacher. But by then I was captivated by her & I lost my own ability to think critically. Maybe I did her a disservice. I think I did. I think I treated her differently than I would have treated any other student.

She continued to visit me in my office quite regularly. Once she brought me an apple from the fruit stand on the corner—Hans Hueber chuckled aloud—and I wondered briefly if she had read someplace that apples are the thing to give a teacher. She told me she wanted to major in English. I didn't think she would do well, but I didn't tell her so. Whenever Hans Hueber was not in the office, our conversations turned to other things: I asked her what high school had been like for her, & what brought her to this particular university. She was footing her tuition bill herself. I once asked her why she had not chosen to go someplace closer to her home, & she looked at me incredulously & said that she couldn't have imagined going anyplace else. It was in the city, she said. By the "city" she meant, exclusively, Manhattan, which she worshipped & fetishized as the physical manifestation of every fulfilled dream. Furthermore, she said, she couldn't possibly have gone anyplace with anyone she knew from high school. This I understood; I too had had a miserable experience in high school.

It was during these conversations that I came to believe she was similar to me in many ways, & also that I had something to offer her. That I could help her in some way. The semester ended & I watched her walk out of my classroom after our final class and I felt a deep and abiding fear come over me that I would never see her again.

But shortly after classes were over, in late December, I received my first letter from her. It was written out by hand—she had typed, on a typewriter, all her other papers for me; I'd never seen her handwriting before—and addressed to my office at the university. For the first time she called me "Arthur" instead of "Professor Opp." It seemed like a conscious and strenuous decision. She said to me, *Dear Arthur, This is Charlene Turner. Thank you for your class, the best class I've ever taken.* (She had not taken any other college classes and, as far as I know, never did again.) She told me about books she was reading & things she was thinking about. Movies she'd seen. She signed it, *Fondly, Charlene Turner.*

I read it twice. & then I read it three more times. I had never in all my life received such a letter. I tucked the letter into my shirt pocket. I carried it around with me all day like a good-luck charm. I brought it home with me on the subway & read it again when I got home. & before I went to bed I sat down at my dining room table to write a reply—the first of the hundreds of letters to Charlene that I would write in my lifetime.

After a few exchanges, I told Marty Stein, who was my dearest friend until her death in 1997.

Marty I met as a graduate student at Columbia. She was a year ahead of me, perpetually hunched over, scurrying from place to place like a mouse in glasses. It was Marty—expert on the work of Gertrude Stein, Djuna Barnes, Virginia Woolf; willfully and perhaps exaggeratedly ignorant about much of the rest of the canon—who got me a job at the college that became my home for nearly two decades. In return, it was I who convinced her to move to Brooklyn in the fall of 1979. I got her an apartment on the top floor of the brownstone next to mine, & together, platonically, we whiled away hours & hours at school & at home.

Partly I told her to make it feel real. I told Marty everything. She was drinking tea on my couch. I said, "One of my students is writing to me."

Marty looked at me. "A woman?" she said. Marty would never have used the word *girl,* though that's what Charlene was: a girl, O very girlish.

I said yes.

"What's she saying?" asked Marty.

"Anything she wants to," I said.

"Have you written back?"

"Yes."

"How many times?"

I paused. "Five times," I said.

"She's written to you five times, and you've written to her five times," said Marty.

"Approximately."

"Do you love her?"

"Probably," I said. I felt hopeless and desperate. Marty put her tea on the table so that she could throw her hands into the air and let them fall on either side of her.

She thought my friendship with Charlene was ridiculous. She thought it smacked of patriarchy. "How *old* is she?" she asked me, & I told her truthfully that I did not know. I thought at first that she was in her twenties. I was thirty-nine at the time. But I came to find out that she was even younger than I'd figured. Nineteen at the time of our meeting. Twenty the last time I saw her.

Eventually she suggested, again by letter, that we meet outside of school. It was February. She hadn't been my student for two months. Still, it was especially brave of her & I could sense the bravery in her penmanship, darker than usual, more deliberate & neat. I chose the place in my reply. It was a café near Gramercy Park. Far enough from the university, I thought, so that I didn't worry about being seen by a colleague; near enough so I could get there quickly after class.

I have to admit that it was an exploitative choice: it was a perfect little shop. Dimly glowing inside, little flowers on the tables, white lights where the wall met the ceiling. The reassuring smell of a fireplace. I arrived before she did & sat with a book that I looked at but did not read. The door, hung with bells, made a noise as it opened and there she was, Charlene Turner, wearing a purple down coat that came to her ankles. It was very cold outside.

Although in her letter she had used my first name, now she reverted to *Professor Opp,* and I made a lousy senseless joke. "Dr," I said, & she got very embarrassed and said, "Doctor, Doctor."

"I'm joking," I said, but it was too late, & even after I implored her to call me by my first name, she mainly avoided addressing me directly.

At first we had not much to say to one another. She looked around the shop jerkily, her head as quick as a sparrow's, her eyes moving in circles. But later she seemed calm enough to look around her at least a little bit, & I saw it having its effect on her: the charming cosmopolitan place, three Frenchwomen in a corner, two Russians at the bar.

She told me about her childhood, about her hopes for the future.

She told me several things about herself that I have never forgotten.

She wanted it all. The shop & the city & the Russians. She wanted no longer to be lonely.

In the end it was this feeling that drew us toward each other & that kept us there. I sensed her loneliness the moment she walked into my classroom, & I thought it likely that she could sense mine, although I tried to shield her from it. Neither of us had much in the way of family. She confessed to me that her parents didn't even know she had taken a class in the city; they would have thought it was a waste of money. She confessed to me that she was unable to continue her education at the university, for the time being, because she could no longer afford it. & again I had an urge, as I always do with people I like or love, to take care of her: to—simply—give her what she needed. Anything her heart desired. But I would have felt foolish & presumptuous offering her anything, so I didn't, & I have spent many years wondering if perhaps I should have.

We spent hours together talking. I took her to see things I believed she would find interesting: plays & concerts & cultural events of the sort that New York City is famous for. I took her to several of my favorite restaurants. One evening, toward the end of spring, we ventured over to the pier at Christopher Street & threw pieces of a soft pretzel to some ducks that had congregated nearby, & she bent forward toward the water, one hand on her knee, the other held out eagerly toward the birds. This image of Charlene Turner has become fixed in my mind forever: it is how I think of her even now, her hair pulled back, wearing a drab brown coat that was very unlike the bright clothes beneath it. When the birds swam toward her and accepted her gift, she raised a hand as if in victory, & turned to me smiling. I watched her. She was dear to me.

Nevertheless, that spring I felt slightly unnatural: this was not any Arthur Opp I knew, taking someone out on dates, planning & executing gallant little excursions here & there. Always I was waiting for the bottom to drop out of things, for Charlene Turner to stop returning my telephone calls & letters.

So when she did stop returning my telephone calls, I was almost relieved. & when she continued to return my letters, I was gratified & happy. In May I received a note from her that said she was having some family trouble & would not be able to see me for a while. She was very sorry, she said, & very sad, & she would miss me.

When I responded, saying I understood & I wished her well, I assumed it would be our last exchange. But she kept writing to me. For years & years she wrote to me.

What she could not have known, & what I decided, after some deliberation, not to tell her, was that our brief relationship had several serious consequences for me.

I never felt the need to be furtive about our friendship, & so once or twice we were seen by my colleagues when Charlene met me at the end of a school day, & I would smile at them obliviously, & say hello. Another time, while out with Charlene for a Saturday dinner in a nice midtown restaurant, I saw the dean of Arts & Sciences, & said hello to her, & introduced her to Charlene by name. Certainly the thought had crossed my mind that what we were doing might be—frowned upon, in some vague way, but in general my relationship with Charlene felt so innocent, so lovely, that it was hard to imagine that anyone would sanction me for it. Besides, I told myself, Charlene was no longer my student, nor even a student at the university itself.

Therefore I was very surprised to be rung up in my office one afternoon by the dean, who asked me if I could come by. This was at the very end of spring semester, after Charlene had already announced to me, by letter, that she would be unable to continue to see me. I thought perhaps I had forgotten to do something—it was my weakness as a professor. I was constantly forgetting meetings, forgetting paperwork, forgetting compliance with one initiative or another.

I rumbled into the dean's office & sat down across the desk from her, expecting to be asked for a favor, or to be scolded for some small item or other. But she did not engage in small talk.

"There has been some discussion," said the dean, "about you and a student."

She paused and looked at me for a moment as

if trying to determine my innocence or guilt by the look on my face.

Which must only have registered as surprise—truly, I was so surprised that I couldn't even speak. I opened my mouth and closed it again.

"Are you currently having a relationship with a student?" she asked me. She was attempting to be courteous, professional. She asked me the question as if she were a doctor.

"No, I am not," I said. It was the truth.

"Were you," said the dean, consulting some papers before her as if they pertained to our conversation, "with a young woman named Charlene Turner at Franco's when I saw you there earlier this spring? Was that Ms. Turner?"

"Yes," I said. "But Charlene Turner isn't a student here anymore."

"She is indeed," said the dean, and proffered to me the paper she had been holding in her hands, which, as it turned out—did pertain. It was Charlene Turner's transcript. On it was a course from that spring, Modern Literature, which I had recommended to her specifically at the end of fall semester, but which I thought she had dropped.

"She hasn't been attending," I said.

"I believe that's beside the point," said the dean. "As you're aware, it violates the university's code of ethics for a professor to be engaged in a romantic relationship with a student—

especially a student whom he or she has taught."

"Who made the complaint?" I asked her. I'm not sure why I did, knowing that she would not answer. It came out of me unstoppably. I had my suspicions. Hans Hueber's face popped into my head.

Of course she would not answer. She told me that it was her duty, since the situation had been brought to her attention, to report it to the university's ethics board. The ethics board, consisting of five of my colleagues, two administrators, and three elected students, would then determine whether a hearing was necessary.

Needless to say I was quite upset. My relationship with teaching was fraught, it is fair to say, but in general I loved it dearly. Nothing touched my heart so much as a student who seemed genuinely to have learned something from me, & nothing made me feel so connected to the world as being the vessel through which someone else's discoveries, or philosophy, or art, poured into another human being.

I went home that evening & had a good cry, a thing that in general I rarely allow myself to do. I called my friend Marty Stein over when it became too much to bear on my own. She came into my house & I began to tell her about the terrible injustice that had befallen me. But from the look on her face it seemed she already knew, which she confirmed upon my asking.

"Why didn't you tell me?" I asked her.

She was wearing a capelike garment and she clutched it tighter and tighter about herself.

"I didn't want to upset you unnecessarily," she said.

"But now I am very upset," I said.

"I know you are," said Marty. "I'm sorry."

She told me that she thought maybe nothing would come of it, but you know how gossip works, she said. She said she thought maybe the story had been blown out of proportion, or certain falsehoods had been added to it.

"The rumor is," said Marty, "that you began seeing her while she was still your student."

"Utterly untrue," I said, & Marty told me she believed me, of course, & that she had attempted to correct anyone who repeated it to her, without, of course, letting on that she knew anything at all. "We'll fix it," Marty said. "Don't worry." She made me feel much better that evening, & by its end even had me convinced that maybe there would be no hearing at all, & that over the summer everyone would forget about it, & so forth.

So when, the following week, I received a letter notifying me that I was to appear before the ethics board, I was quite thoroughly disheartened.

The semester was drawing to a close by then. I had a batch of final papers come in, forty in sum, and I brought them home and put them on my dining room table and looked at them every time I passed. I sat down with them several times but I could not concentrate. My mind would skip ahead to the hearing. The end-of-semester grading deadline came and went. I was certain that a pile of dunning letters was accumulating in my mailbox—from the registrar, from my department chair, perhaps from the dean—but I did not go into school to get them. One evening my phone began ringing and I let the message machine answer it. It was the dean, informing me that my grades were a week late, asking me to please call her as soon as possible.

I never did. On the morning of my hearing I pulled out my suit from my closet, the suit I very rarely had any occasion to wear, and laid it on my bed. I looked at it. I put it away.

I sat down in a chair, and looked at myself in the mirror that once sat atop my dresser, and knew in that moment that I would not return to the university, for I could not face them. O it was too humiliating.

I never told Charlene Turner any of this. I did not fault her for it—I faulted myself, only—and I wanted her to remember our time together as fondly as I did. Like me, Charlene Turner never returned to school. If she did, she never mentioned it to me in the letters she continued to send me for many years. She had one semester of college & has since worked as a receptionist at various places. In her letters, she wrote to me mainly of her aspirations—to return to college, to move to the city & get a better job, one that paid more money—to buy a nice apartment in a nice part of town, to have several dogs. She complained to me about her coworkers & her parents & then when her parents died, one after another, she told me & I sent her condolences & flowers. She told me about movies she had seen & television shows she liked & petty things that happened in her neighborhood. Stories from her childhood that, she said, she had never revealed to anyone. She began to ask me for recommendations for books to read. To me it seemed as if she was asking me to educate her—& so I tried to. I sent her books to read & asked her to report back to me. She told me she was Irish by descent & so I sent her the *Táin Bó Cúailnge*, Kinsella's translation, and I sent her *Dubliners*. I sent her a whole course in Irish literature. She read what I sent her—I'm fairly certain she did—& she told me what she thought, always as passionately as if the characters were friends or enemies of hers.

In person, our relationship lasted only a few months, but our written correspondence has lasted eighteen years. I now feel a kinship with Charlene Turner that I have rarely felt in my life —perhaps with Marty, perhaps with my mother.

It would be impossible to explain why I like her so much, why I liked her from the start. Partly, of course, it was that she liked me & I felt that I wanted to help her however I could. And partly it was that I recognized myself in her—in her awkwardness, her loneliness, her being very out of place, an outsider in a room full of compatriots. These feelings I recognized as my own. She spoke differently than her classmates. She had that accent, which I came to love, & that style of dress, & a sort of timid hopefulness that won me completely. One of the things I loved most about her, what I valued, was her lack of awareness. It was as if she did not see her surroundings, was not aware of elbowing the man next to her in her hurry to be seated, in her hurry to return to invisibility. She was like this, always. Walking down a street she would lag behind, looking in windows, or walk a full block ahead, unnoticing. Once I bent down to tie my shoe and when I looked up she was gone. I walked for five blocks before she found me, blinking, saying "I'm sorry! O I'm sorry!" and then laughing a little at herself, & then taking my arm.

I received, today, the letter she promised me during our phone call. It came in a square blue envelope that was meant for a card or an invitation. The envelope looked previously used. It was sealed with tape. I sat with it on my couch for quite some time before opening it. I touched every dull corner of it with the pad of my index finger. Holding it made me nostalgic for a time when I received letters from Charlene Turner regularly.

I held the little blue envelope in my hands &, before opening it, compared it to the older letters I had from her. Her handwriting had slowed & expanded. My address on the front of it was written in wider & lazier letters. Her return address was barely legible.

I stuck a finger into one corner of the taped-down flap & I ripped open the envelope all at once.

Inside there was no letter. There was only a small photograph.

I did not know what to make of it at first. It was a boy, fair-haired, sixteen or seventeen maybe, posed for the camera & holding a baseball bat. Wearing a uniform I did not recognize. Something about him looked familiar but he was nobody I knew.

Then I turned the photograph over and there on the back was written, in Charlene's fattened handwriting, *My Son Kel.*

I turned it over again to look. & then I turned it back. I did not know what to say to myself. If indeed this was her son it meant she had had one for a very long time without telling me. I did not know why she offered no elaboration. I felt maybe she was upset with me or was being spiteful. Or that maybe she was telling me to get on with my life or was saying to me, in a vicious way, *Stop writing to me. Look what I have that you do not have, Arthur.* I didn't know. I didn't know.

I considered calling her but I was blind to her motives & bewildered. My shyness overcame me. So for the rest of the afternoon I did nothing at all, but became very upset for reasons I can't fully explain, & very aware of my legacy and my place in the world, & ate a great deal, & then finally sat down at my table again, & then walked to the front door, & then to the couch, & then into the bathroom to confront myself in the mirror, & then back to my dining room table, & then to bed, to bed.

I spent all of Saturday stewing in my worries, speculating about Charlene's intentions in sending me the picture of her son. I ate a great deal. I wondered if I should call her on the telephone. I didn't.

I ruminated for a while on my size. There is a game I play in which I attempt to justify my weight. I'm six feet and three inches tall, so sometimes I tell myself that I'm *burly* or a *big guy.* Both conjure images of health and fun. A woodsman, a football player, a Newport News commercial, for heaven's sake. Some football players weigh close to four hundred pounds. But football players also have arms that are huge, huge, & legs that are like tree trunks.

But I carry most of my weight in my gut, & no part of me has ever been firm. Since the age of ten, I've been fleshy & great, with soft arms and legs, dimpled knees, fingers that look like sausages. At this point my gut has expanded to the point of grotesquerie. My gut hangs down between my legs when I sit down. I pull my pants above it & that is the other difference. Acceptably fat men wear their pants below their guts. I knew I was unacceptably fat the day I bought pants big enough to accommodate my girth someplace above my navel, pants manufactured for men like me. Obese men. I try to deny it, to catch myself looking normal at certain angles in my front window. But for the little one over my bathroom sink, I do not keep mirrors. I do not like walking past them & catching accidental glimpses of myself. When I need to see myself I use the three-paneled window, facing Fifth Street, that serves this purpose after the sun sets. Dark on the out-side, light on the inside: Arthur Opp at his window, turning and turning as if he is upright on some invisible rotisserie. (The neighbors probably think I am very strange!) I do this for a reason: it is so that I can keep track of my size, so that I don't wake up one day unable to walk.

After several hours of this sort of self-pitying reflection I had decided that, in the end, it would be very bad to see Charlene Turner again. I had thoroughly convinced myself that I should not be seen by anyone.

But then everything changed, for then my telephone rang again. & this time I knew it would be her.

"Arthur Opp," I said.

"Can you believe it," said Charlene.

I was wary of her. I said no I could not.

"He's in high school, can you believe it?"

Once more I said no.

"Isn't he something," said Charlene.

This went on for a while until finally I felt I could safely assume that she hadn't sent me a picture of her son out of a desire to silence me or because she wished for me to stop sending her letters. I was quite relieved.

But for the second time I heard something in her voice that was deeper & slower than it should have been, & this made me concerned. Then again I have spent so long recalling Charlene Turner at twenty that I suppose it was unfair of me to expect her to sound just the same.

Such a long silence ensued that finally I felt I had nothing to lose by asking her whatever I pleased. I felt I had permission to & a right to. So I asked her why she had never told me about him & she let out a very long sigh.

& then she told me a story. Many years ago, she said, but not too long after the last time we saw each other, she married a man named Keller with whom she was not in love. She had not wanted to tell me. (I became dizzy thinking up reasons why.) She continued to write to me as if nothing had happened. Soon she had a son, but—because of her prior omission—could not find a natural way to tell me about him. So she never did, and so on: she & her husband divorced. She didn't tell me. She was left with his name—she is Charlene Turner Keller now. She never told me. She raised

47

her son alone. She didn't tell me. "You'd love him," she said firmly, on the phone. & I believed I would. Kel Keller. An odd, endearing name.

Then she came to the meat of it, & the reason for her contacting me, & the reason that I am now quite alarmed.

She said he wasn't doing very well in school but would be getting ready to apply for college soon. She said he had lots of friends but maybe needed a little bit of guidance. She told me I was the smartest person she'd ever met which meant more to me than I can possibly convey. & she told me that I was the first person she'd thought of. "Reason I called you," she said, "is this. Do you think you could help him?"

"What does he especially need help with?" I asked her, & she said college applications. She said he was very unfocused. "He plays baseball," she said. "He's got baseball on the brain."

"I see," I said, & looked frantically about my house, & clutched the hem of my shirt in my right hand in dread.

"We could come to you," said Charlene. "Whenever it's best."

"I'll have to look at my schedule," I said.

At this point I was sweating. Several thoughts occurred to me simultaneously: among them, what I would tell Charlene when, inevitably, she asked me why I'd stopped teaching.

But all she said was, "All right. Look at your schedule," she said, "and then call me back.

"I've told him all about you," she said.

When we hung up I could not catch my breath & I could not imagine what I would do. There were a few things to immediately consider:

1. The pleasure that having Charlene & her son in my life would afford me
2. The fact that I have become very used to my little life, & that it is not after all a bad one
3. All the little exaggerations, all the omissions, all the outright lies I've told her in the many letters I've sent her over the years
4. But at least she too has been less than truthful
5. The appearance of my house, its disrepair
6. My own appearance
7. When I answered the phone it took me a moment but then her voice came through the wires like electricity & I knew who it was without asking
8. When she lost touch many years ago I thought it meant that she had forgotten me. But as it turns out she has not forgotten me & has been thinking about me. She said it to me. O just like that.

After mulling things over for several hours, I decided upon an initial course of action.

• • •

Writing the letter & confessing some version of the truth was the first step. For while the idea of doing it gave me a great deal of anxiety, the thought of simply having Charlene & her son appear on my doorstep—of throwing the door open & saying Look at me, look at my house— was infinitely worse.

The second involved readying both of us as much as I possibly could in case Charlene still decided to come. To prove to myself that I was serious, I did something very frightening. I opened the phone book and ran my finger down a list of cleaning services until I found one deplorably named *Home-Maid*. I called them & asked if they had somebody who could help me.

Yes, they said. Her name is Yolanda. She's coming tomorrow.

& no one has been in this house for seven years.

Dear Charlene, *I wrote,*

It would give me a great deal of pleasure to invite you both to my home & to meet Kel. I would be happy to provide him with any counsel I might be able to give. I agree with you that there are few things more important for a young man than a good education, & although certain aspects of the application process have changed since I taught, I believe I might still be able to offer some advice on schools or take a look at his essays. It would be lovely to see you too after all these years.

That said there are several things that you should know. I have changed quite a bit since you last knew me. By this I mean that I have gained quite a bit of weight. I say this so that you won't be shocked.

I have also—I am embarrassed to say this—I have also been untruthful in several ways over the years. I do not travel, really. I do not keep in touch with any of the other professors I once knew, nor any of the students. My friend Marty Stein, of whom I frequently have spoken, died in 1997. I do have a brother named William but we are estranged, & I am also estranged from my father. My mother is dead. I have no children, sisters, aunts, or uncles. At one time I had friends but now I rarely go out & I rarely have visitors. I am 58 yrs old now.

I do not know why I lied. Perhaps it was to have something interesting to tell you in my letters. Our correspondence has been very dear to me. I wish to make a fresh start now & to form a friendship with you based on truth. The one thing that gives me hope is knowing— I hope you will forgive me for saying it—that you, too, have had your secrets. I do not hold this against you. I hope you can forgive me as well.

Please consider this an invitation to come over anytime you like. I will wait for your call or your response.

Fondly,
Arthur

Then I opened my front door & put the letter in my mailbox & tipped the happy little red flag up.

Today marked the first visit of the girl from Home-Maid. Yolanda. I spent the morning thinking of what to wear. I couldn't bring myself to do the wash, the wash being located inside of a closet that is not very maneuverable. Instead I took each one of my seven shirts out from the closet and laid them on my bed & inspected them for lint, holes, food, stains, & odors. The winner was my blue shirt so I put it on, making sure to align the buttons properly, & wetted a comb & ran it through my hair, & washed my face and hands as I was taught to, scrubbing behind my ears, scrubbing my nails especially.

I arranged myself on my couch: a glass of ice water placed virtuously on the end table, my glasses at the tip of my nose. I was reading something I thought would be impressive, a fat book on politics.

Noon came and went. I waited fifteen minutes & then began having a dream of Chinese food: the greased and glowing kind, unnaturally orange chicken with sesame seeds nestled in its crevices; white rice in buttery clumps that come apart wonderfully in the mouth; potstickers, ridged and hard at the seam and soft at the belly; crab rangoons, a crunch followed by lush bland creaminess; chocolate cake—nothing Chinese about it, but the best dessert for a meal of this kind, the sweet bitterness an antidote & a complement to all that salt.

Suddenly I became afraid of opening the door. I said a prayer that she wouldn't come. I lifted my phone & had the idea of calling this agency, Home-Maid, & telling them that I had fallen ill and couldn't have company. Before I could do this the doorbell buzzed.

I froze. A thrill of adrenaline went from my nose to the tips of my fingers. For what felt like an absurd amount of time I sat on my couch and did not move; I held my book before my face and looked up at nothing. Upon her second buzz I rose from the couch, rocking in place once or twice for momentum. I shuffled toward the door, still carrying my book. I was breathing hard; a drop of sweat rolled down my back. *Coming,* I said, so quietly that she might not have heard me.

I opened one half of the great double door. In front of me stood a little girl: she looked so young that at first I took her to be a lost child, the wrong person entirely. But she was wearing a uniform, a stiff, light blue dress with a white collar and pockets at each hip, like what waitresses wear in country diners. She was so tiny that it was too big for her. The shoulder seams were too wide for her shoulders and the waist was low, like the waist of a flapper's dress. The hem too fell farther down her legs than seemed natural. A black purse hung off a long strap on her shoulder. On her feet were pink sneakers with little white stars on the tongue. She was looking at me wide-eyed, perhaps in terror.

"Yolanda?" I said.

She nodded.

"I'm Arthur Opp," I said.

She nodded again. She had no coat & she was clutching her arms to her sides and clasping her hands in front of her.

"Please come in," I said.

When she stepped inside my house a kind of spell was broken. My pulse increased; I felt a tumbling-down inside of me, & then shame. I looked at my surroundings frankly. The girl was still silent. She was standing on her tiptoes slightly, as if she were afraid of fully committing to the job.

"This is it," I said rather lamely.

She turned toward the piano. She approached it tentatively, placing her feet one in front of the other, heel to toe, a shy awkward walk. She held her arms out slightly from her sides like a gosling. When she reached it she touched the top of it with one finger and left a dark & dustless mark—a gesture that at first seemed rude to me and then simply inquisitive.

I wondered if the place smelled bad. I imagined that to an outsider it would smell like food &

dust & stuffiness, the hot oppressed smell of a house that gets no air. I should have opened all the windows, I thought, but it was too late.

I'd done my best to clear up all the food and the containers I had lying around, but I had missed several things that now sprang to my attention. Hiding in the floor-to-ceiling bookshelf was a take-out box with a metal handle. Above & below it were books in disorganized piles. Papers and mugs and little useless things like pennies and straws. Small piles of receipts had somehow found their way onto every available surface; I suppose I put them there whenever a delivery person hands me one. One end of the dining room table was drowning under papers and boxes. Scads of plastic bags hung off the backs of the chairs. Years ago I wrapped several towels around the newel at the base of my staircase for reasons I no longer recall; they have remained there ever since, stiffening with age. Worst of all: the piles of papers that have somehow accumulated at the perimeter of every room. Junk mail & magazines & books; newspapers & napkins & menus that had all somehow become invisible to me in the past decade. Part of the scenery.

So I felt very upset.

"Show me the kitchen," Yolanda said suddenly.

I pointed the way & I made sure she went first so I could walk behind her and not be seen.

This was a bad moment. I watched the tiny

back of her and looked down & realized exactly how I must look, always, to anyone who sees me.

The kitchen was worse. She went through it opening cabinets and drawers—within each of them was a nest of crockery and pots and dishrags and cutlery and bowls—and, though I had done the dishes in preparation for her visit, they were all sitting where I left them to dry by the sink.

"No dishwasher," said Yolanda.

I shook my head.

At that moment a mouse leapt out of one of the cabinets that Yolanda had left open and ran frantically in circles before darting out of the room. The girl shrieked & launched herself out of its path and then, once it was safely out of sight, clutched her heart and doubled over.

"Whoopsy!" I said, or something bright like that. "Well, there you go!"

"Mr Opp," said Yolanda, "do you have a mouse problem?"

"No, no, no, no, no," I said. "I haven't seen one in years, actually." (It was a lie.)

"I can't work with mice," said the girl.

I felt deeply embarrassed. "I assure you you won't have to," I said. This was with more coldness than I had intended, so I added: "Sorry."

I told her about the rest of the house.

"The top two floors are bedrooms," I said. (I

pictured them. I can always picture them. It has been years since I have seen them. Third floor, two blue bedrooms with chintz curtains. All of them matching. My mother loved the curtains. Second floor, my childhood bedroom, a wooden train set still assembled. Second floor, the good bedroom for guests who never came. O the dust that must be burying them. O the disuse.) "Downstairs we have an office and a library."

"A library in your house?" asked Yolanda.

"Well—no," I said. "I just mean that there's a desk down there, and that's where we keep all the books."

"Are you married?" she asked.

I realized then that I had said *we:* a habit I have never lost.

"No," I told her, "I'm not married."

An awkward pause ensued.

"You want me to start now?" she said.

"No," I said. "I just thought you could have a look around."

This was when my panic started: a pounding in my head & heart, a chill down my spine. *Out of my house,* I wanted to say. *Out, out, out.* Instead I sat down abruptly on my couch. The girl blinked.

"Can you come back another time?" I asked.

"You still have to pay for today," said the girl. "That's part of the deal."

"I paid Home-Maid over the phone already," I said. "It's all taken care of."

I wondered suddenly if I should tip her.

She shrugged and hoisted her purse up higher on her slight shoulder. "You'll call?" she asked.

"Yes," I said, but I intended to call Home-Maid before then and tell them not to send her anymore. Her or anybody.

When she was gone my house felt very empty as if it had noticed for the first time its own neglect.

I needed consolation so I made a feast for myself. Cookies made from coconut and macadamias and white chocolate. A bowl of peanut M&M's. A few bagels, coated obscenely with seeds and grains and tasty little granules of salt. Bagels, laden with heavy coats of butter *and* cream cheese, and topped with a lonesome tomato slice, red & bleeding with juice. A pitcher of whole milk with a tall glass next to it. An Oreo-crusted chocolate cake. Three hamburgers and potato salad and creamed spinach that I had delivered from the diner on Seventh Avenue. I warmed the spinach on my stove. I put a dollop of cream cheese in the center of it. White in a sea of pearly green.

I gave myself permission to eat all of this & felt the thrilling release that such permission delivers. A soft little munching sound escaped me and immediately I tensed; I hate hearing myself. I do not talk to myself. I do not have conversations with myself in my home, the way I imagine some people do. It's silly. My own voice repulses me.

Suddenly I remembered why I love very much to be alone, why I love to be utterly alone in my own quiet house, & love not to be looked at.

I had a very entertaining book to read. I turned on the radio & just by good luck it was Michelangeli's version of a prelude by Debussy called "La fille aux cheveux de lin" which always calls to mind a specific memory of summertime.

In this moment I was happy.

When, later, the phone rang, I leapt for it as best I could.

"Arthur Opp," I said, but no one was there.

"Hello? Hello?" I said. All I heard was breathing. Beyond that, the low hum of something like a refrigerator. Hearing it opened some old familiar chasm of need in me & allowed an unbearable loneliness to penetrate me just for a moment, just for the time it took me to appreciate the invisibility of the caller, the fact that it could have been anyone, anyone on the other end, but then the line went dead.

For several days I have been waiting for Charlene to reply to my confessional letter. To pass the time I have been watching television, reading, pacing, cooking, eating, writing, & examining the picture that Charlene sent me of her son.

Charlene herself I remember as shy, quiet, blithe, small, curious, & observant. Therefore these were the qualities I automatically attributed to her boy as well until I looked closely at his picture, which made me reconsider my first impression. He is a different sort of boy altogether.

It is very strange to look at him. He is a portrait of potential energy. He is holding a bat. He is a big fair boy very determined to succeed. His batting helmet is casting a shadow over his left eye. His torso is a loaded spring, his forearms flexed and ready, his wrists cocked precisely. A fine blond fur on his arms is catching the sun. He is wearing a green and gold uniform & on the front of it I can see the letters G-I-A. The background of the shot is blurry. He looks as if he might swing at the photographer. He looks like an athlete.

I can tell he's a dreamer. He fears things. The death of his mother, perhaps, or his own death.

Disobedience. Authority. He is trustworthy but he doesn't trust others. In his heart there is bravery & cowardice. He is a baby & a man. His face is a boy's face. His face is a crystal ball.

I am sure that other pictures of him show him smiling. I am sure that several girls have pictures of him smiling & that sort of thing. I am sure that several girls have pictures of him without his knowing it.

He is happy in school, I can sense it, and I want to say to him congratulations. On the baseball field he is thunderous and frightening to his opponents. In general he is probably not a favorite amongst his teachers but if he tried he would be.

His friends uphold him as their compass.

At lunch he never has to search to find a seat. Little things like that. He barely even notices.

He congratulates his teammates with a slap of the hand. He thumps them on their backs and they thump him on his. His coach collars him about the neck when he has done especially well.

His mother, when I knew her, wore clothing that was bright as peacock feathers. She wore red lipstick. She was impossibly young. She was shy. She did not speak very much. She wrote to me. I was in love with her.

If they decide to visit I must be prepared. I have been thinking of all the various ways I can make the house presentable. & myself presentable. I have been asking myself, What would a young boy like to eat? and telling myself, He would like to eat potato salad, hamburgers, hot dogs, and steak.

I'll have particular things for Charlene as well. I remember the things that she liked & I will make it a point to have them on hand.

After the debacle of the girl Yolanda's visit, I decided to try to clean my house myself. I got as far as pulling all of the books out of the shelves to dust them but by the time I did this I was quite tired & I had to sit down for a while. & then I sat for a while more, & now the books are still on the floor in a pile.

About a month ago a family just moved into the brownstone next door, the one formerly occupied by Marie Spencer &, in the upstairs apartment, Marty. This family is perfect: a young husband and wife, their three tiny sons. They seem perpetually to be going to or coming from the park. Yesterday it was very warm for the end of October and I caught them all walking down the street at noon. The baby was in a stroller pushed by his daddy. The two older ones were scampering ahead like two puppies or foals in a field. Who among you works? I thought—as if I am one to say anything at all.

As I was spying on them, my new neighbors, one of the boys caught me watching and held up a small brave hand in my direction. A salute. I lowered the curtain quickly & imagined becoming terrifying to him, some blown-up Boo Radley. I vowed in that moment to introduce myself to them, to go out on my stoop and say hello. Marty would have wanted me to. I felt a pang in my gut and had to sit down.

But then, a few seconds later, there came a knock at my door & I turned around and parted the curtain again, ever so slightly, & saw it was the young father who was standing on my stoop. The rest of his family was waiting for him silently on the sidewalk. My heart began to pound. O my goodness, I thought. I wonder if he wants to yell at me. I wonder what he wants at all. But I was not able to find out because I could not will myself to move. I was too afraid.

Then I was angry with myself for several hours after that & to make up for it I decided to reconsider this girl Yolanda. You know I thought I was not going to have her back but I told myself I had to give her another try. For one thing I think I am growing allergic to all of the dust in my house, for my own attempts to clean make me very short of breath. I called Home-Maid yesterday and asked if they would come again.

The operator said "What time, please?"

"Eleven in the morning would be excellent."

She paused. Then told me that I'd have Nancy this time.

"No," I said, "I had Yolanda."

"She's booked then," said the operator.

"When is she available, please?" I asked.

It's not that I liked her so much, it's just that she had already seen the worst & I couldn't go through it again with someone new. So Yolanda came at 1 p.m. today and I opened the door for her.

She began cleaning this time. I wasn't quite sure where to put myself so I wandered out of rooms that she was in & into rooms that she was not in. For example she started in the living room and so I hid in my bedroom reading. I heard her tiny footfall as she pattered around dusting. And then I heard her stacking things. And then I heard a little knock on my bedroom door. I was sitting on the edge of my bed, not wanting to lie down in case she should need anything.

"Yes? Come in," I said, and the door swung open and she popped her head in.

"Do you have a vacuum?" she asked.

I blanched a bit because I knew that I did have one but could not for the life of me remember where it was. I told her as much, feeling very embarrassed because now she knew that I didn't vacuum.

"I'll look for it," said Yolanda, and took off for parts unknown.

I heard her running up the stairs & she was up there for about ten minutes opening and shutting doors & again I felt pierced by something. To have a little someone up there after all these years. I pictured her opening each door in turn, first the doors on the third floor—my mother's chintz curtains fluttering, delighted to be set in motion after years of stagnancy—and then the doors on the second. I pictured my little train set and the collection of pictures I tacked on the wall as a child. O they were being seen by someone else. Next I heard her descending into the basement and a moment later she came up the stairs and shouted to me triumphantly that she had found it.

It sounded like a lawn mower starting. It had not been used in so long. She vacuumed the whole main floor and when she came into my room I shuffled out of it. Already the living room and dining room looked very different. Cleaner yes but also touched somehow. Different because someone else had touched them. I sat carefully down on my couch and put my hands next to me on either side. My couch felt different too. & the whole place had lost its regular smell and now smelled like lemon and pine.

Not knowing what to do I turned on the television but I wasn't really paying attention to what was on. I was paying attention to the noises Yolanda was making as she moved about my room. Unlike me she talks to herself. I could hear her little childish whispers, the *p*'s and *b*'s and the clicks and *tsk*s. I think she was speaking in Spanish and I wanted to know what she was saying & I was afraid to know what she was saying all at once. I was afraid she was speaking out in annoyance & saying all the things that I thought about myself like how horribly dirty I had let my very dear house become.

Every now and then she emerged from my room carrying some little bit of garbage that I had not even noticed. A napkin or a plastic bag or a shampoo bottle. She took books out and put them on the bookshelf. Every time she passed me she offered me a little smile & said nothing. I pretended to watch the television, which was showing *Cash Cab*.

By four o'clock she had cleaned the whole downstairs and five or six full garbage bags were sitting by my front door. I did not ask her what was in them. I presumed that I would not want to know.

"When does garbage go out?" asked Yolanda.

"I'll do it," I said. I felt hot in the face.

She shrugged and said "Red, blue, and yellow."

"I'm sorry?" I said.

"Primary colors," she said, & pushed her chin toward the television, where the host of *Cash Cab* was saying "*Ooooh,* close, the correct answer is red, blue, and yellow."

"I love this show," she said, and she came around the front of an armchair and sat down hard in it with a sigh.

She looked at her watch.

"You mind if I stay here for a little bit? I got a ride coming," she said.

The truth was that I did mind. It had been a trying day and I was ready to have my house to myself again, but I could not for a minute imagine telling her that.

"By all means," I said, and then we sat there in an uncomfortable silence for a commercial had come on and I didn't know whether to make a move to change the channel or just to let things be.

Neither of us said anything except the girl hummed under her breath, some song I did not know. I was sitting on my couch with my back to the picture window & she was in the armchair to my left. She looked out the window frequently to check for whomever was coming for her. I would have done the same but I could not turn around. Both of us were angled toward the television which had become the third person in the room.

When my show came back on I was able to relax a bit more & the girl impressed me by saying more answers than I thought she would know. She shouted them gladly when she knew them, pointing one finger at the television. I knew almost everything but I only muttered the answers very quietly for fear of seeming like a showoff, which is probably a leftover from my school days.

I could see her in my peripheral vision. She was so tiny that her feet stuck straight out in front of her and did not touch the floor. Her little pink sneakers pointed at the ceiling. Her toes tapped together. When she craned to look out the window she gripped the arms of the chair and pushed herself up & her mouth fell open.

I tried hard to think of something to say to her before the next commercial break arrived but before I could a little tinny horn sounded outside, and Yolanda said "Ooh! My ride."

She hopped up and once again hoisted her little purse up on her shoulder and said "You talked to the company?"

"Yes indeed," I said.

"When am I coming back?"

"Two days," I said, and held up my fingers in a V, idiotically.

"See you then!" she said, and skipped out the door, slamming it a bit too hard behind her.

I made myself count to five before hauling myself up so that I could look out the window behind me.

I put one knee on the couch and leaned forward to peer down Fifth Street. All I saw was her back as she clung to the driver of a powder-blue Vespa that was speeding loudly away. The driver I did not see.

This morning I woke up from a dream about my childhood & immediately the self-pity that I have been feeling set in like a disease. You see Charlene still has not called or responded. & at this point she has had my letter, my confession, for nearly two weeks.

But rather than wallowing I decided I would be in a good mood & congratulated myself on the progress I have recently made (I spent yesterday trying to organize my pots & pans, a process that required a great deal of bending over & reaching up) & decided that maybe I should not be sad that Charlene has not called. In fact, I decided, it is likely that I should be quite worried about her. There is the possibility of drug use or drunkenness. I keep hearing her voice in my head & no—it does not sound right. There is the matter of her ex-husband. Last name Keller. By my calculations she would have met him shortly after I knew her or even during the time that I knew her which is a painful thought. On the phone she told me he left her when their son was only four years old. I am horrified by this & think he should be very ashamed. I wondered if Charlene's calling me was in fact a cry for help. This is a possibility that, I am embarrassed to admit, thrills me.

• • •

Therefore I decided that rather than waiting indefinitely I would take some initiative & call her myself. To do this I would have to put aside my pride, but—as this is something I have been doing all my life—I have a talent for it.

I would call her, I decided, & I would invite her and her son to my house in two weeks. This would give me time to further the beautification of both my house & myself. I felt happy & alive; I was practically whistling as I rose from my bed.

I performed all of my morning ablutions very carefully for Yolanda was arriving at eleven.

At 10:30 I sat down on my sofa & placed the phone on my lap. I lifted the receiver & dialed Charlene's number, which I memorized the first time she gave it to me.

The phone rang seven times & I had nearly given up hope when suddenly I heard a sort of clatter on the other end.

"Hello," she said, after taking a little breath.

"This is Arthur," I said.

A second pause, this time longer.

"Charlene?" I said.

"This isn't Charlene," said Charlene.

"I'm sorry?" said I.

"Wrong number," said Charlene, & then she said it again, & then she hung up the phone.

I looked at the receiver in my hand for a long

time. The dial tone came out at me viciously. I considered looking up her number & trying her again, but there was no point—I knew it had been Charlene on the other end. I also knew certainly, this time, that she was drunk or drugged or something of the sort. It made me heartsick & I did not know what to do.

At eleven Yolanda came. I fear I was short with her. I had a group of thoughts whirling through my mind in turn, involving the emotions of shame (for in sending her such an honest letter, I had made Charlene my confessor, and it seemed to me that her refusal to talk to me was an act of rejection) and fear (for her safety; for her health; for her son). Then while Yolanda was vacuuming the living room I brushed up against her accidentally in the process of making my way to the bathroom. I certainly didn't mean to, & I was horrified when it happened—I always make very sure not to come anywhere near her. I shouted, "Sorry! O I'm sorry," and drew in my stomach immediately, though ineffectually, but she didn't respond.

I happened to be looking out the window today right at the time Yolanda arrived. And when she arrived she did so by Vespa again & this time I saw the driver. He got off and they kissed goodbye. He was young, about her age, and meat-headed. Large muscles & that sort of thing. He was small in stature but taller than her. He was tattooed; I could see one creeping up his neck from under the collar of his coat. A scrawling blue script. When he took his helmet off I saw he had a tight short haircut like a Marine.

They spoke for a moment while he sat on the seat of his bike & she stood before him. Then she leaned in to him and he put his arms around her and they stood like that for a while silently & I did not like the look on his face. Then she turned away from him & trotted up my stoop and he called after her & she waved him off playfully. He kept watching her.

She rang the bell and I went to the door & hesitated to open it because of the young man outside but when I opened it he was already driving away.

"Hi," she said, and came right in & tossed her purse on the floor by the door, already very much at home. "I guess I'll start upstairs today?"

"Well—" I said. "Well."

I felt the need to make lots of excuses for the state of the upstairs but I couldn't really think of any that would not call attention to my weight. Which does not need to be called attention to. So all I said was that I thought it was probably very dusty and I apologized.

Without waiting for me to say anything else, she went to the kitchen and got her bucket of cleaning supplies and then trotted gaily up the stairs & for the first time I noticed that she looked like someone in love.

I heard by her footsteps that she had gone all the way to the top floor & I wondered what she would find.

Meanwhile I sat up very properly on my couch. I cannot move myself around quickly so every time she has been here I've been careful with what I'm doing & watching & reading & eating. She could catch me at any time doing anything. So while she is in my house I generally don't have anything to eat, nothing at all. Today I tried to read at first but my eyes wouldn't focus on the words and I kept reading the same paragraph over and over again. So then I tried turning on the television and Dr Phil was on, who, I am reluctant to admit, is a special favorite of mine. Bald, ursine, mustachioed Dr Phil wears gray suits and pink shirts, invites fat ladies onto his show, and then tells them why they are fat. The ladies cry & agree with him mostly. Many of them have been molested or abused. Many of them have husbands who say terrible things to them about their weight. Dr Phil tells these husbands that they are no prizes either. I have a hopeless halfhearted fantasy of going on this show and receiving a benediction from Dr Phil, a hug, a promise of rescue and relief. *You don't deserve this,* he says to the ladies. *You deserve better than this.*

I watched him for an hour. The story was a very pretty young woman and an ugly young man on the verge of divorce and disaster. They could not get along you see, and Dr Phil was finding out why not by watching the footage from hidden cameras that he had put all over their house.

O shut up, shut up, the woman was saying. On camera. And at one point her terrible husband took her by the shoulders and squeezed her, sort of, & Dr Phil paused the tape there, which is where I also would have paused the tape, and said *What are you thinking.*

Suddenly I realized I was hungry. It was past noon and I had not eaten for a couple of hours. But I did not want to eat when Yolanda was in the house because I did not want her to be disgusted by me. I was contemplating going into the kitchen to get the healthiest thing I could find when Yolanda's phone rang. I heard it from inside her little black purse. It was some sort of high, high whine & a rumbling beat below. Rap music.

It was just out of my reach, on the floor between the couch and the front door. I scooted toward it. I waited to hear if she would come pounding down the stairs for it, but she didn't. For reasons I can't explain I rocked myself off the couch and timidly approached it, and then I reached down into her purse—the ringing had already stopped—and brought out the cell phone, which was pink and covered in rhinestones that looked as if they had been applied by Yolanda herself.

I flipped open her phone. There, in a bubble, it said *1 missed call: Junior Baby Love. 12:56 p.m.*

Then I heard the sprightly Yolanda's footfall on the stairs and I dropped the phone into her purse and hastened back to my place on the couch but I was breathing quite hard when I sat back down and I realized that I had forgotten to flip her phone shut.

She appeared very quickly, confirming my theory that I always have to be on my best behavior when Yolanda is in the house.

She looked at me suspiciously.

"My phone ring?" she asked.

"Is that what that noise was?" I asked. Innocently.

She went to her purse and took her phone out with two fingers, holding it up in its flipped-open state and looking at me.

"Is everything all right?" I asked, and she nodded.

"O Yolanda," I said, to change the subject. "O Yolanda, I have never said this before, but please feel free to make yourself at home while you're here. For example, would you like a glass of water?"

She considered my offer silently.

I looked at my watch. "I see it's twelve fifty-six now," I said. "Are you hungry?"

She nodded. And then she said, "Do you have any milk actually?"

"To drink?"

"Yeah."

"I certainly do," I said, & then I tried to get up off the couch as gracefully as I could but I failed & had to rock several times.

"I can get it," said Yolanda, & I said "Nonsense nonsense. As a matter of fact I was going to make lunch & would you like some." (At this point I had launched myself successfully and was standing on my own two feet.)

"What do you have?"

I paused. I wasn't quite sure what to offer a girl like Yolanda. She herself was delicate and therefore deserved delicacies. But ideas for delicacies escaped me.

"Do you like sandwiches?" I asked, and she nodded.

"What kind? I should have . . ."

& then I realized that I had everything, almost everything anyone could dream of in my house.

"You got PB&J?" asked the girl.

"I do." (That peanut butter is a peculiar favorite of mine, that I mix it with vanilla ice cream—I did not mention.)

"Can I have one?" she asked.

"Certainly," I said. "Sit right here & watch whatever you like."

I handed her the remote and walked into the kitchen & there I found whole milk & crusty white French bread & raspberry preserves & Skippy peanut butter. I poured her a tall glass of milk and spread the peanut butter & jelly thickly onto the bread and then I took a soup spoon out of the drawer and helped myself to a mouthful of Skippy from the jar. & then I went into the freezer and helped myself to a mouthful of ice cream. & then cold hot fudge from the refrigerator. & then my stomach started rumbling badly so I opened my pantry and got out a bag of potato chips and ate as many as I could very quickly just to quiet my gut.

From the other room I heard her murmuring & laughing & assumed she had returned Junior Baby Love's phone call.

When I was finished, I waited until I was certain she had finished her conversation. Then I walked back through the swinging kitchen door & through the dining room & into the living room where Yolanda was waiting expectantly & watching a soap that I don't watch.

"Thank you!" she said brightly. Her feet once again were sticking out ahead of her and she was bobbing them up and down.

I placed the sandwich and the milk on the table before her & she ate the sandwich very meticulously and left the hard crust on the plate. Her little tooth marks had crenellated the remains.

In silence we watched the soap opera. At one point Yolanda said "You know what's going on?"

"No I don't," I confessed.

"She's sleeping with his son," said Yolanda, pointing at a tight shot of a middle-aged female character and an older man. "But he don't know."

"Oooh," I said, but I still couldn't follow.

After a moment I asked, "What are you finding upstairs?"

She shrugged, her eyes glued to the television. "Not too bad," she said. "Lotta dust."

Yolanda saw the picture of Kel Keller today and asked who he was and for just a moment I was tempted to say he was my son but then I realized the preposterousness of that, how she would know in an instant that nobody who looked like him could have come from anyone who looked like me.

"My nephew," I said.

"Cute. How old?" she said, and I have to admit that I was proud, absurd as that is.

"Seventeen," I said, but really I was guessing because his mother did not tell me his age.

"Too young for me," said Yolanda. "I got two years on him."

I saw she had finished her glass of milk completely so I asked if she would like another.

"I'll get it," she said, & hopped off the couch to go into the kitchen. After that she went back upstairs. & that was the end of our conversation for the day, except that on her way out she came to me with a book she'd found upstairs and asked to borrow it.

I was delighted until I saw what it was: some awful romance novel from the 1960s that was not mine & that I had never seen in my life. & I felt as if Yolanda had found out a sad secret about my mother that I was not prepared to confront.

"You can keep it," I told her, wanting it out of my sight, & she put it into her little purse.

I did not see Junior Baby Love waiting for her outside this time. & I realized I don't even know where Yolanda lives, nor anything else about her.

I wrote out a transcript. It went, "Charlene, this is Arthur. I know it's you, Charlene, and I'm worried. I want to help you. Can I help you?" I waited a week & called Charlene again & there was no answer. Then I waited another week & called Charlene & there was no answer.

For a month Yolanda has been coming regularly & the two of us have gotten to be friends. One day she came trotting down the stairs with some photograph albums she had found in a particular room (I knew right where they were—in a book-shelf in a guest room on the third floor) & she was smiling, & she told me, "Look what I found!"

From the look on her face I could tell she had been through them already.

All my bones were frozen tight & I could not even speak to tell her I did not want to see them.

She sat down next to me and opened the first one contentedly.

"Is that you?" she asked me, pointing to a baby, & I nodded.

"Is that your mother & father?" she asked me. & again I nodded.

"Wowwwww," she said, as she turned the pages. "Look at you!"

When I couldn't bear it anymore I stood up as abruptly as I could and excused myself, & then I went into the bathroom & held myself up by the sink. In the other room I could picture her, little Yolanda, seeing my memories one after another. Laid out on the page.

When I came out again she had returned upstairs, and with her went the albums. She's very kind you see. She can read me.

I have begun to teach her things & to encourage her as if she were my child. She is a receptive learner, but she also teaches *me* things: she does every time she is here, whether or not she realizes it. She tells me what she is watching and reading. She loves to watch reruns of the late-night comedy program *Mad TV* & she often describes or reenacts sketches from that show with great vigor, laughing at her own recollection of it, ending each retelling with, *It was so funny.* I don't know what her ambitions in life are, though I have asked her. She dodges these questions with a shrug and a smile. I don't know if she finished high school but I have to assume she did not. This is a shame because she is very smart, with a knowledge of trivia that is well beyond her years. When we watch *Cash Cab* she shouts out many answers very loudly.

Over the past few weeks I have grown to look forward to her visits. Mainly she does not seem embarrassed by me, which allows me to relax. There is an easiness about her that I hold dear. She is not overly concerned with whether or not she is being polite. She asks and says what she wants & she does what she wants. & thrillingly she judges people who need judging—on television, in the stories she recounts from her life outside my home.

•••

All of this is to say that I have grown quite fond of her & so it was with great sadness that I watched the events of today unfold.

First of all Yolanda called me this morning. This alone was strange, for today is Sunday which is a day she does not work. On the telephone she asked if she could come today instead of tomorrow—for tomorrow she had some things to attend to. "All right with me," I said, because it did not matter in the least, & in fact mostly I cannot tell the days apart except by her visits.

But when she came in she was upset. She would not look at me, which was also strange because normally she smiles a lot and says *Hey Mr Arthur.* (She came in calling me *Mr Opp,* & tho I encouraged her to use my given name, she seems to have reached a compromise in her own mind by combining the two.)

So this morning she said nothing to me, just opened the door—I gave her a key last week—and walked past where I was sitting in the living room and headed directly into the kitchen. Then she returned to the living room and walked past me again on her way up the stairs, her bucket in hand.

When she was halfway up the stairs I said her name once very softly but I do not think she heard, or else she chose to ignore me.

I was confused because I thought we had been getting along so well this whole time, & I had been looking forward to showing her a couple of things I had found in the newspaper that I thought she might like (one was an article about a comedian she has told me about, & one was an article about fun things to do in the city for people who are not yet 21). I sat on the couch with both neatly clipped articles on the table before me & I wondered what to do.

Yolanda was banging around loudly upstairs. Normally when she's up there I cannot hear her but for a whisper or an occasional footstep or a song or the creak of my old old house. Today I heard clearly everything that she was picking up and putting down. Once she even slammed a door.

I was wondering if perhaps she was annoyed with me about something, & I racked my brain for what it could be. Perhaps the money I was giving to Home-Maid was not enough & I was supposed to pay her directly or tip her & this was etiquette that I did not know about. I could fix this.

I worked my way up off the couch and walked to the base of the stairs.

"Yolanda?" I said again, but she did not respond. To be fair I could not get myself to really shout to her, & I said her name in a fairly normal voice, so she probably didn't hear me.

Tentatively I put a foot onto the bottom step and then I heaved my other foot onto it, pulling myself up by the banister.

& then I did this again & again. Seven times I did this.

Now I was breathing quite heavily and I felt several trickles of sweat find their way down the back of my neck and under my collar.

"Yolanda?" I said again. Nothing. Just her banging away. It sounded as if she were moving furniture.

I looked back over my shoulder & realized that I had gotten myself into a precarious position. However far up I went, I had to get back down. I was halfway up the first flight & suddenly I had a vision of losing my balance and tumbling backward & I started to get very dizzy and nauseated. I wanted to sit down but the steps were too small to accommodate me.

& that is when there came a vigorous knocking at my front door. It was accompanied by the sound of my doorbell buzzing several times in a row.

The banging upstairs stopped. I heard Yolanda emerge from whatever room she was in & walk down the second-floor corridor, & then I saw her face pop over the railing up there.

She seemed unfazed by the sight of me on the stairs.

Look at me, I wanted to tell her—*I've climbed these for you.*

"Who is it?" she whispered.
"I don't know," I whispered back.
"Can you get it?" she asked.

It took me a couple of minutes to get to the door
& during this time the knocking got more and
more vigorous.

I opened an inner door just a very small crack.
There was a young man on the other side of the
glass outer door, standing with his feet planted
squarely on my stoop. I recognized him instantly:
it was Junior Baby Love. He was wearing a neat
blue bandanna tied around his forehead and on
top of that a spotless Yankees cap with a gold
sticker on it. He was wearing jeans that fitted
him tightly to his skinny ankles and a sort of large
aviator's jacket. He was a handsome boy but
looked rough & his tattoos were not well done in
my opinion. The one on his neck, I now saw, said
a lady's name, and it was not Yolanda.

His mouth fell open a little bit stupidly.

I opened the door wider to let him have a
really good look at me.

"May I help you?" I said finally, and he said he
was looking for Yolanda.

I looked back inside and saw that Yolanda was
still peering over the second-floor railing. She
shook her head no.

"I'm sorry," I said, "she's not here right
now."

But then JBL noticed her and said "I SEE YOU! COME OUT HERE! JUST LEMME TALK TO YOU!"

He was pointing at her and he moved as if he might pull open the glass door.

So at this point I positioned myself so that I blocked the entire doorway.

"Apparently Yolanda doesn't feel inclined to come outside," I said. "May I take a message?"

But Junior Baby Love would not be swayed. He was still shouting at Yolanda, & he was not saying nice things, so gently I shut the door on him, at which point he resumed his pounding, so hard that I was afraid for the glass.

After I shut the door I turned around and saw that Yolanda was sitting on the topmost step with her knees drawn up & her arms about them & her head lowered. & the poor thing was shaking with sobs.

I walked to the bottom of the stairs & I looked up at her. In this moment I wished more than I ever have to be mobile & to be able to take the stairs fleet as a deer.

Instead I stood at the bottom of them and said to her "O Yolanda! Don't cry . . ."

It had been a long time since I had seen any woman cry. Most recently it was probably Marty. & before that, Charlene. Before Charlene, my mother, constantly, unstoppably.

"O come down here," I said uselessly, and she shook her head against her knees.

"Can I get you anything?" I asked. "A glass of milk?"

The pounding stopped and outside we heard JBL start his Vespa and zoom away up Fifth Street.

Finally she hiccupped & lifted her head. "I'll take milk," she said.

"Well you have to come down here, then," I said coaxingly (tho I very much would have liked to bring it up to her, bring her a tray of milk and cookies as someone once did for me).

She didn't move.

"When I come back you'll be sitting on that couch," I said, more as a question than a command.

I went into the kitchen and tried to ask myself what would make a girl like Yolanda feel better. I decided that besides milk she would enjoy Pop'ems. To make them look nicer I put a few on a floral plate & then I put a few into my mouth as well.

What else, I thought.

I made her a PB&J & put it all onto a tray. & then, feeling the tray looked lackluster & perhaps that everything on it was too similar in consistency, I opened my refrigerator and put an apple onto the tray as well.

Then I backed out of the kitchen through the

swinging door, carrying the tray as carefully as I could, its contents rattling frighteningly as I lumbered along.

Surprisingly, Yolanda had followed my instructions and was sitting on the sofa in the living room. She looked very tiny. For a moment we were silent & it afforded me the opportunity to observe her openly as I never have. Her back is straight & her hair is neat, parted on the side and pulled back so tightly that on anyone else it would seem severe. But nothing is severe about Yolanda. She looks proper. Her face is square, her lips are full & almost completely lacking a dip in the topmost part of them. She wears little makeup. She has one small mole high on her right cheek-bone, which makes her look glamorous and starry eyed, as if it were a jewel she applied for dramatic effect. Her eyelashes are long & full. Her earrings are plain small silver hoops that cling to her tiny ears.

She lifted the glass of milk & drained it completely.

She looked at me plaintively & I did not know what to say to her to comfort her.

"Now," I said, "now—"

"You don't have to say anything," said Yolanda.

"Are you all right?" I asked.

"Yeah."

"Are you quite certain you're all right?"

This made her cry again, and she shook her

head and said "No, no, no." She wiped her nose on the sleeve of her cardigan & if I had not been so drained I would have certainly gotten her tissues.

I wanted to get up and sit next to her on the couch & put a gentle hand on her back as someone once did when I was young, but she seemed to me like a small frightened animal and I did not want to frighten her further. I stayed where I was.

"Now Yolanda," I said, "what is the matter."

"I have his baby," she said.

"I'm sorry? I don't understand," I said, and Yolanda made a *tsk* noise and threw her hands into the air.

"His baby," she said. "I'm pregnant."

"Junior's?" I asked, incredulously.

"How do you know his name?" she said.

To dodge this I asked her how far along she was.

"Almost five months," she said.

I do not know much about pregnancies but I would have thought the girl would be larger. It is true that her stiff oversized uniform hides her, for the most part, and her cardigans do as well, but even when I looked at her belly I could barely see anything at all.

"And you aren't happy about it, I suppose?"

At this she snapped her head up and looked at me with such vitriol that I twitched.

"Of course I am," she said.

Silence.

Finally I gathered enough courage to venture, "Then what . . . ?"

"I had to break up with him," she said.

"Why?"

"He's not really good enough," she said.

"What do you mean?"

"Like he doesn't work."

"Ever?"

"Sometimes," she acknowledged. "He works for his uncles at their garage. But no real work."

She lifted the sandwich from her plate & bit into it miserably.

"And is he a good person?" I asked.

She rolled her eyes. The girl does not hold back what she is feeling, you see.

"Plus he used to date this girl and she's still calling him. It's *complicated,*" she said.

Clearly it was.

We sat together silently & then she asked if she could turn on the television & I said of course she could.

We watched the news for a while.

"These are good," she said finally, & I noticed she had eaten all the Pop'ems.

"Yes, I like those too," I said. & I realized it was the first time I had ever referred to my eating in front of her.

She seemed considerably happier after a while, & she even asked if I would tell her a story, which I took to be her way of humoring me, so I said, "Did you know that in 1960 there was a huge plane crash right on Seventh Avenue and Sterling? & that as a young boy I saw it?"

"Not that kind of story," said Yolanda.

So instead I told her the story of Deirdre of the Sorrows & her valiance and strength.

After a couple of hours she said she had to go.

& I was worried about her because she did not have a ride but she said she could take the subway, no problem.

"I'll pay for a cab," I said. "Please let me."

"No, thank you," she said, very polite.

"Please be careful," I said, & then she was gone.

It was only one o'clock in the afternoon. I had a number of emotions rattling around inside of me and the whole day before me to mull them over. If I were a pacer I would have paced, but I am a sitter so I sat.

I am embarrassed to admit I was thinking of what it would be like to adopt Yolanda, sort of, to tell her that she could live with me & grow her child here. That I could really care for her & help her. That I could help her child. Wild crazed fantasies, all.

For one thing I rely on television shows for all of my ideas about being a parent. No, not the terrible sitcoms—but the *reality shows*. I some-times watch a program that shows real couples as they prepare for the birth of their child & then actually have it.

I can't watch them without crying, silly as they are. I have a favorite type of father: young working-class fathers, especially ones who wear baseball caps and trainers. I feel somehow that these will be the best fathers of them all. These will be the ones who toss balls with their children, whose children will use them as jungle gyms. These are the fathers who kneel by their wife's side & kiss her hands as she pushes & sweats & groans out the baby. Then when the baby is born these are the fathers who cry out in ecstasy, who lean over their wives & put their faces close to them & tell them *I love you, I love you.*

Of course I would be nothing like these fathers but they move me. When I was a younger man, only a bit older than Charlene's son, I thought I would certainly have children: it was just something that one did. Alas it has not happened.

But I still think about it. Holding a wet purple baby against your chest, knowing that it is yours, knowing that you will be in charge of it. This is what is waiting for Yolanda.

I was in a brown study. There was a trembling inside me. I felt that something in me had broken, like my ribs themselves had been cracked open and something wanted to get out. Since I have been bound to my home, I have often felt that it has become a physical manifestation of Plato's cave, and that I am the man in it. & that my mind is bouncing off all of the walls and ceilings even if my body cannot. I felt a bit claustrophobic & I longed to go outside so instead I opened the doors & then I inhaled deeply. It was cold out and I stood there in the doorframe and allowed myself to shiver for a while.

Then, without giving myself enough time to really mull things over, I walked back inside and lifted the phone and dialed Charlene's phone number, which I have memorized.

I made myself go numb. I did not even have my transcript in case she answered. The phone rang five times.

And then for the first time a message machine picked up, & for the first time I heard the boy's voice, higher than I expected, younger than his picture seemed.

You've reached the Kellers, his voice said. *We can't take your call right now. You know what to do.*

I waited for the beep and then I hung up.

Because I didn't.

I Want
to Tell Her

When she is very bad, usually I will tell her things to calm her down. I will tell her Mom, Mom. We have to be quiet because the neighbors will call. We have to be very quiet. Come up here with me on the couch. Come watch your show. Then I will wait for her to fall asleep, and then I will leave her on the couch and see her in the morning.

Or I will lie to her by saying things about Dr. Greene, her hero. Dr. Greene asked how you were and I had to tell him that you'd been misbehaving, I will say. You have to be better for Dr. Greene.

Or I will leave. I will leave her where she lies. I will leave her bouncing off the walls with drunkenness, or crying, or trying to cook. I will get in the car and leave, and in my guilty heart I will tell myself she deserves it.

Tonight, when I walk in the door, I do none of these things because she is passed out already. She is lying on the living room floor in a pile, facedown, her red bathrobe covering her like a blanket and hiked up on one leg disturbingly. She is holding a portable phone in her hands & her thumb is on one of the buttons. A piece of hair has fallen across her gray damp face like a mustache. My God she's dead is what I think. She's dead this time.

I drop onto my knees beside her and for reasons I don't understand I rip my baseball cap off and throw it across the room. I shake her very hard, one hand on each shoulder, then flip her over completely, which is maybe not smart. I cry immediately. There's no deciding not to. My mouth fills with water, my eyes, all the parts of my face and frame go numb, numb. WAKE up, I say. WAKE up.

It takes a second and then she opens her eyes, half smiling, someone coming out of a dream. She reaches up very slowly and pats my face, then tucks her hands under her head and sort of nestles into the carpet.

Night, she says.

I smell it on her. The bitter backtone of half-digested rum. The stink of never showering. When I am feeling gentle sometimes I cut her hair for her and her toenails.

After a very long moment she opens one eye again and says, Kel, Kelly, do you love me? Do you love me, honey?

No, I say, and she does a little pout.

I think, You don't love *me*. But it's a lie I tell myself because in fact I know she does. Love me.

What are you doing, why are you doing this, I say.

She closes her eyes again. She goes, *Aahh*. As if she were going to sleep in a comfortable bed.

I watch her for longer than normal, until my

back starts to hurt from crouching, until my knees throb.

Get up, I whisper. Get the fuck up the stairs. Go to bed.

When I was a baby she held me and kept me alive. This I tell myself at times to stop me from hitting her squarely in the jaw.

I try to lift her but she won't be moved. She has gotten steadily heavier in the last two years and now she might outweigh me even though I'm tall and strong. She eats crap mostly, Cheez Doodles and chocolate, except when I force-feed her microwaved frozen vegetables that I buy from the store. Sometimes when she's very bad I feed her like a baby.

She's balding. Her hair's falling out. It began when I was ten and was one of the first things that prevented me from bringing people around her. I remember being in the car with her and the sun hitting her scalp and thinking Oh my God, my God, she's actually bald. Small fuzzy tufts of hair stand up from the top of her head. The rest of it has gotten long and is stringy or frizzy depending on when she has washed it last. She dyes it red except when she forgets to, and then it's gray and red. She has bad skin and what looks like a rash on her face. Almost always she has this. She puts one black line on each eyelid that's meant to be at her eyelashes but it drifts upward at the edges.

Shakily. All of my life she's worn terrible clothes that no one has worn since the 80s and she has never let herself be helped in this department, believe me I have tried. And she has two tattoos on her, a honeybee on her arm and a fucking electric guitar, an electric guitar with a long and snakelike cord that goes down her back and comes over her shoulder. She wears a bathing suit—she used to wear a bathing suit—without a back to show it off. She loves her tattoos. She's proud of them.

I give her a nudge with my foot rougher than I should. Then I stomp up the stairs feeling every wooden thud completely. I go to my own room and toss myself onto my bed hoping it will break.

I hear her wailing at me from downstairs. Keeeeeeel, she is saying, *help* me, *help* me.

But I can't.

Monday morning I walk downstairs and she's up. She's sitting at the table. She's bleary eyed and baggy faced. She's wearing a giant T-shirt and that red bathrobe over it. The T-shirt says, IT'S FIVE O'CLOCK SOMEWHERE. The bathrobe is red plaid and smelly. She smells like rum and Coke and, deeper than that, underneath it someplace, she smells sour, like curdled milk, like something rotting. She's smiling at me because she wants to apologize or because she can't remember last night.

Game day? she says.

I'm wearing my regular clothes today and if she knew anything she would know that on game days we wear other shit to school, our uniforms, green and gold stripes on our faces.

Not talking? she says. She has a half smile on as if to tell me she's willing to be patient, that she'll be very very patient with me.

I think of saying, *What's in your mug?*

I don't say it but I should. Someday I should say it. We've been pretending for several years that I don't notice all the things that I notice.

Good news, she says, Jan Howard called.

Jan Howard is our social worker. It's never good news when she calls.

I got the disability extension, she says.

Cool, I say.

She pauses. She holds the mug up to her face.

Kelly, she says. I have a friend I want you to meet. I called him on the phone.

I think, She's crazy all the way now. She has no friends. She does not go out.

Cool, I say.

He can help you with colleges, she says. He's very smart. We talked on the phone.

Cool, I say again.

Kelly, she says, and for a moment I think she is going to tell me something important, it's the worry in her eyes. But all she says is Have a good day.

I leave without anything, no goodbye.

She thinks she's dying. She is, probably, but she's doing it to herself. One time I came home very late from Trevor's and she had passed out on the couch with a pad of paper on her lap.

Dear Kel.

Do not read this until I am dead. If I am dead there are a couple things you should know. One is that I love you so much honey. Your a good kid always have been. Sometimes I can't believe your mine. If

It was terrible. I was embarrassed for her and I flipped the whole thing over and knocked it roughly out of her hands and onto the floor. The yellow pad she dug up God knows where. She didn't budge.

She drops little things into our conversations. I'll say something about next summer and she'll say *We'll see . . .* very dramatically, as if to say *If I'm around . . .*

Another time she made me write down her will for her, which was a pathetic undertaking because everything she had went to me. And she had nothing. Her parents are dead. She has no siblings. My dad left when I was four. Since then, since forever and ever, it's been the two of us alone.

Every day I drive half an hour from Yonkers to Pells Landing. I went to school in Yonkers all the way through middle school. My mom was better then. She grew up in Yonkers too, back when our neighborhood was OK. When they got married, she and my dad bought the house together and always said they were going to fix it up and never did. Our neighborhood got worse and worse. My mother found a job as a secretary at an elementary school in Yonkers right out of high school. But she wasn't happy there, so when I was eight, she applied for a job at Pells Landing High School. When they gave it to her, she cried.

I thought I'd go to Yonkers High. It was where my mother and father went. It was where my friends were all going. But I got into some trouble in eighth grade and it was a big deal when it happened. And to make everything worse, my friend Dee Marshall was involved, and Dee is the only son of her only friend Rhonda, so there went that friendship. My mother petitioned the Pells school board to let me go to high school there. It was without me knowing it. She didn't like my friends in Yonkers, she never did, even though they're good guys. She wanted to separate me from them, to drive me to school with her every morning, to give me a new start, she said. This was when she was still awake enough to care what I did.

I hated her for it. I had been to Pells enough growing up to know that it was nothing like Yonkers, old friendly ugly Yonkers, with duplexes and projects and rundown libraries and police stations and pubs. Pells Landing is the opposite of Yonkers. It's twenty miles north but it feels like a different world. The windows are cleaner, the lawns are always green. All the yards and streets are rolling and new. The doors are painted bright colors. There is a sailing club on the Hudson in Pells where rich families go in summer. Where rich kids go together. There is a restaurant at the marina. Trevor's parents are members and I have been there several times and I have ordered steak there. There is a country club in Pells and it's so old that I don't even know anyone whose family belongs. One girl in my high school, her family belongs, and even though we are not friends I know it about her. It's the thing that is always said next after her name.

My mom has always been too impressed with Pells. When she was better she talked about it quietly, as if it were more important than any-place else. When I was about eleven *Newsweek* named Pells High one of the ten best public schools in the country. It's a large school with small classes. Two thousand kids and not a class over twenty. Good sports programs and teachers, labs with new technology, a huge impressive library. The day that article was published my mother came home and called her mother, who was still alive at the time and basically the only person she talked to besides me, and said: Did you hear the news about us?

It made me ill.

When she was still working her boss was Dr. Greene, the vice principal in charge of eleventh grade. To this day Dr. Greene sees me in the hall and asks me in a low concerned voice how my mother is, which makes me want to punch him in his mouth. She worked for him for a really long time. He has never once called her since she left two years ago.

I knew everything about him and his life before I even met him. My mother used to come home and tell me all about the Greenes: Dr. Greene's wife Marjorie, and their two sons, Brian and Brent, fraternal twins. I know he golfs on the weekends and plays poker on Wednesdays. I know he has a boat at the marina and that the boat probably comes from his family money or his wife's money because he does not make that much. I know he reads voraciously, my mother's phrase. For Christmas every year she used to give him something that she carefully picked out, related to one of his four hobbies, and he would give her something generic and edible, a fruit basket or a cheese-of-the-month club member-ship. I've met all the Greenes at one point or another, from being dragged to awards dinners or staff appreciation picnics when I was a kid. I always hated Brian and Brent, who are five years younger than me and truly horrible kids. They used to whine and try to make me play boring games with them like Go Fish. They're little kids, my mother would say, so be nice.

Dr. Greene drives a red convertible, which is a ridiculous car for a vice principal to have.

This past Christmas my mother made him a card and asked me to give it to him, I'm not kidding, a homemade card. In crayon. I didn't even read it. I threw it out as soon as I got to school. On my way home that day I stopped at a CVS and bought her a box of chocolates and a card and said they were from Dr. Greene.

I am a senior now and have acquired invaluable knowledge of how to do things over the years. But on my first day of freshman year I had no idea. I showed up wearing red glossy basketball shorts past my knees, a plain white T-shirt that hung off my shoulders, and Nikes.

As soon as we arrived I knew I'd gotten it wrong. I was slumped in my seat while my mother was driving. She kept saying *Are you excited? Are you nervous? Are you excited?* but I wasn't speaking to her that day. She drove through the student parking lot and the first thing I noticed was that every car in it was nicer than hers. The second thing I noticed was a boy who was standing with his elbows on the roof of his BMW, watching us go by. Holt! Holt! someone yelled, and it was his name, and he whirled around and yelled back. He was dressed differently than I was. His cap was blue and ratty on the brim, a farmboy's frayed hat with dark shaggy hair beneath. His shirt looked to me like a business-man's, a blue long-sleeved oxford shirt that I could imagine a banker wearing. His shorts were plaid and fitted him. He was wearing flip-flops. To school. In Yonkers only girls had done that.

What's wrong, Kelly? my mother said, and I said *Nothing,* God, but everything was wrong. Who I was meant something different here than it did at home. At home I was in charge of all the boys at my school. I am not exaggerating, it was true. I was in charge of them as surely as if I had been elected. I told them things to do and they did them. I was not in charge of the girls but I remember the moment when they became aware of me and several small battles broke out amongst them about me. I was certain that I would be in charge of nobody at Pells and that no one would fight for me. I felt very alone.

My mother left me outside the main entrance.

Can I help you find your homeroom? she asked. I shook my head violently. I had memorized a map of the school the night before, memorized it completely, the first and second and third floors, so I wouldn't have to take it out in front of anyone in the hallway. I am very good with maps.

Have a great day, said my mother, and then she was gone.

I looked up at the school. Pells High is built like a castle. It has stone walls and turrets that I think are fake or at least I know no way to get inside them, and I have explored every corner of this school. It's set up on a hill with a perfect lawn that stretches down to the parking lots below. There are tennis courts and playing fields in front of it and more in back. Two low stone walls run the length of a walkway from the main road to the entrance. A driveway snakes up the side. PELLS LANDING HIGH SCHOOL, says a sign by the front door. HOME OF THE GIANTS.

Two girls walked by me and didn't look at me.

It was still early. I sat on one of the stone walls and watched as the slow trickle of students picked up speed. Not one person glanced my way.

Off the wall, please, said an administrator, and I realized suddenly that it was Dr. Greene.

Dr.—I said, and then shut up. I hadn't been recognized and it was better that way.

I did not want to be too early for homeroom. I lingered outside until I had five minutes to spare and then I walked directly through the green front door, letting the surge of bodies around me swallow me and make me small. The hallways at PLHS are lettered and my homeroom was in D-Hall, which was on the third floor.

No one was sitting down yet when I walked into homeroom. They were standing in clumps like they were at a party. The girls were shrieking with laughter and the boys were slapping each other's hands sideways in greeting. I didn't want to be the only one sitting but I felt I had no choice. I chose a desk and sat at it, rifling through my empty bookbag to give myself something to do. I did not recognize myself in anyone. The girls wore cardigans and dangling silver bracelets.

All of my classes surprised me. My classmates spoke perfect drawling lazy English. They spoke like rich adults.

I think, said one, that what Reagan was forgetting was that people *give a damn* about other people.

It was astonishing.

I had signed up for the dumb classes, the level two and three classes. What this means in Pells is classes for very smart and nerdy kids who are so smart and nerdy that school is uninteresting to them and so they have behavior problems and get bad grades. A boy in my bio class was wearing a cape.

At lunch I did not even try to go into the cafeteria. I found an empty classroom and sat down and put my head on my desk. If anyone asked I was going to say I was feeling sick. I hiked the sleeves of my giant white T-shirt over my shoulders and folded the waistband of my basketball shorts over once and then twice.

That night I went home and begged my mother for new clothes. I begged her not to make me go back to school without good clothes. She was actually happy. She never liked the stuff I wore, the baggy stuff. It was a nice night with her. We went to the mall and I used money I had saved from mowing lawns. I took it out of my wallet and we went to Target, where I bought shorts like the ones I'd seen the other boys wearing. We bought one pair of cheap brown flip-flops (since then I have learned that these are a giveaway, that these are the things that need to be expensive and leather), and a few T-shirts with collars. I let the clothes fit me. I let the shirts be tight across my shoulders and I let the shorts come to just above my knees. On the way out I convinced my mother to stop at J.Crew and I walked to the back, to the sale rack, and spotted two oxfords: one white and one blue. I wanted them very badly but they were so expensive, even on sale, that I almost wouldn't let her buy them, but she insisted. She loved them. She said they made me look grown-up. The white one was missing a button at the bottom and the blue one had a tiny tear at the back. I didn't care.

The next day was better. I was not sure if anyone

would recognize me from the day before. I had slouched through every class my first day but walking in I stood up straighter. I had grown a lot over the summer and a girl smiled at me on my way in. I was wearing the blue shirt.

In my first-period class, Señorita Klein went around the room asking, *Juegas al deportes?*

Sí, I said. *Yo juego al béisbol, al basquetbol, y al fútbol americano.*

The last wasn't true. I hadn't played football since I was a little kid doing Pop Warner because my friends did. But the kid next to me looked at me and later in the class, when Señorita Klein was writing on the board, he leaned over to me and said Yo. You play football.

Yeah, I said.

How come you didn't try out, he said.

I didn't know when they were, I said, but my heart was sinking. This was something my mother should have told me. I felt like a dud.

Captains' started middle of August, said the kid.

Chiquitos, said Señorita Klein. *Por favor.*

This kid was Trevor Cohen who is now my best friend, along with Kurt Aspenwall. Trevor got me on the football team. In the winter I played basketball. In the spring I tried out for baseball and made varsity and I was the first freshman to do this in five years. That spring we won state, which we also did last year. Baseball is the best

114

and most important thing to me. Sports in general are the one thing I have ever been very good at, excellent at, even, which I don't feel shy about saying because I am good at nothing else. But I can boast about this without much fear of comeuppance. I can throw and catch balls. I can run faster than most people. I can swing bats and launch my body like a missile toward the bodies of other players and I can knock them down. I can jump. I can tense my muscles and swallow the blows that come in my direction from elbows and shoulders and hips. I can puke and keep going. This is my talent. It glows inside me like a secret jewel.

My mother began going downhill when I was a sophomore which was also around the time that I started to really love school.

She had had her ups and downs. Always. It was what we called them, together. Outside the house she was normal. She cared what people thought of her and she saved all her madness for me. I would come home and find her flat on her back with sadness, or up and acting like a maniac. Happier than happy. She would have cleaned the house and she would have baked. She would say Have some! Or she would clutch me in her arms—this was when I was very little, too little to know that nobody else's mother was doing this— and hold me so long that my joints got stiff. She would rest her chin on my head and sometimes she would cry. I was afraid to move or breathe.

When I was little she would date sometimes. Never anything that lasted. Always boys she grew up with in Yonkers who turned into men that had never left. I tried to imagine what they were like when they were my age and I came up with the worst boys I knew. The boys I hated when I was younger, the boys I brawled with. When her dates came by the house I would never even look at them.

Besides these men and her work she had few connections to the outside world. She had few friends and now she has none. She liked some of the checkout clerks at the grocery store and would make conversation with them when she saw them, asking after their families. She liked Frank at the corner store. And for years, for as long as I can remember, she has had a pen pal named *Arthur Opp,* which was a name that I loved and would say to myself in a singsongy way, and whenever a letter from Arthur Opp would arrive I would tease her about it and she would snatch the letter from my hands and go into her bedroom to read it. Who is it? I would say, and she would say it was her secret admirer. Or a prince, or a king. The king of England, she said once. He even sent her little gifts once or twice, candy, chocolate. He sent her flowers when my grandparents died. When I pressed her for the truth she

116

would say he was an old friend, but she never let me read what he had sent.

She didn't drink the way she does now until a few years ago. The drinking came very slowly and a little at a time until one day I realized that she never never stops drinking. She drinks from the time she wakes up until the time she passes out. Most days. Most of every day.

I stopped liking her.

When she worked at Pells—when she was still OK enough to work—my Pells friends knew that she was my mother but we never acknowledged it, never once. She was a secretary at the school and they saw her and said hello to her but there was never any talk about it, never once. I spent more and more time with them. On weekends I was rarely home. I slept in their warm comfortable houses and on weeknights I stayed out late at practice and then took the train home, feeling very adult, taking the train from Pells Landing to Yonkers and then the bus to my home.

One day I went into her office to tell her that my practice had been canceled and she wasn't there. I went into Dr. Greene's office instead.

Have you seen my mom? I asked.

He was shuffling his papers around and he paused.

She went home sick, he said. He took a breath.

I waited.

Kel, he said.

Yes, I said.

—Has she been—OK?

I was leaning in the doorway. Yeah, I said. Why?

—She's seemed different recently.

She's great, I said.

The truth, of course, was that she was nothing close to great and the drinking was getting worse. She was also complaining more about her health. She was diagnosed with lupus when I was a little kid but it had never ever affected her, not once. She was one of the lucky ones, she used to tell me. A mild case. But when I was a sophomore she began inventing symptoms. She began telling me that different parts of her body hurt and that she was tired all the time. She'd be asleep at five. She'd tell me she was running a fever and ask me to put a hand on her forehead but she never felt hot to me.

When I walked in that afternoon, mad because I'd had to take the train, I found her on the couch (she lives there now, it's her home) and she looked very bad, even I had to admit. She pulled up the sleeve of her shirt and showed me a rash that she'd never had before. I told her it was probably eczema. She told me her body hurt her all over.

You didn't ask if I needed a ride, I said.

I thought you had practice, she said.

—You should have asked. It was canceled. I took the train.

God, I feel like shit, she said. She sort of propped herself up on her elbows. Honey, she said. Can you make me a Cuba libre?

She's the last person on earth to call them that. Everyone else says rum and Coke.

This was when I still made drinks for her. Before she hid it from me.

The next day she didn't go to school.

The day after that either.

For two weeks she didn't go to school and that's when I realized she wouldn't be back.

We had to petition the town again to let me stay at PLHS because my mom didn't work at the school anymore. Coach Ramirez took me with him to a school board meeting and told them, Here is a straight-A student with a very sick mom, and I dressed up in khakis and tucked my stupid shirt in. And I am a straight-C student if I am anything.

All this young man wants, said Coach, is to finish school with his friends and keep learning from the teachers who love him.

I guess they all felt bad enough for me to give me permission to stay.

A pretty woman, someone's mother, came up to me afterward and said she just couldn't imagine what I was going through and then she handed me a five-dollar bill. Literally just gave me a five-dollar bill. I didn't know what to do so I put it in my pocket without even thanking her. I wish I'd given it back.

Lindsay Harper pulls into the spot next to mine as I'm getting out of my car. She drives a Lexus that her dad gave her for her sweet sixteen. She's tiny and built and wearing a field hockey uniform, the skirt of it rolled to show her hard tan legs.

Keeeeeel, she says. She always says it like that, sweetly, sweetly, her voice descending from high to low.

She comes around the car and stands in front of me, her arms wrapped around each other shyly, wearing knee socks and rubber soccer sandals. She is unsure whether she is going to touch me. We both are. Finally I settle on grabbing her by the shoulders and pulling her in toward me, giving her a hard rub on the head. Owwww, she goes. She tries to wriggle free but I'm stronger.

Where ya goin, I say. I wonder if I smell like my house, like my mother in her damn FIVE O'CLOCK SOMEWHERE T-shirt.

Lindsay pushes her little fingers into my side and I release her.

My hair's all fucked up now! she says, combing it with her fingers, looking at her reflection in my car window. My shitty car. My mother's shitty car that she hasn't driven in two years. My driver's ed instructor took me to get my license.

I start walking. I am unsure of myself around her in a way I have never been with any girl. Accidentally, sometimes, I am rude to her.

Hey! she says. You don't wanna walk with me? Her bookbag is down by her feet and she scoops it up athletically and jogs toward me in one motion. It is what I noticed first about her: her hard determined striving for the ball, on the lacrosse field, at field hockey, on any field or anyplace, Lindsay is graceful.

I don't get crushes on girls. It almost never happens. Mostly I am avoiding girls with crushes on me. When I was twelve it started happening: a girl would summon all of her courage and approach me or phone me or pass me a note as if she were throwing a message over a wall, and if she was one of the twenty—in middle school in Yonkers there were approximately twenty girls at any time considered popular or pretty or slutty enough to respectably pursue—I would say yeah, sure, let's go out, and then we would meet up someplace, in a park, behind the school, and kiss, and give each other hickeys, and then the next day I would break up with her.

In high school the rules are different but the same. Everyone knows who can go out, who can hook up with each other. Risks are very rarely taken. There is something psychic going on, something unspoken. But I feel too noticed. All the girls I've gotten with in high school have known I think that I don't have girlfriends. I have never had a girlfriend. By keeping it this way I can feel less guilty.

But now there is Lindsay Harper—Lindsay with long dark hair, Lindsay with dark eyebrows and very light eyes. Every part of her body is firm and round or straight and slim. Her hands are smooth and tan, her nails are crescent moons. Holt Caldwell had a famous crush on her when she was a freshman and he was a senior and she even more famously didn't like him back. We have never been friends until now. She was not part of my group until this year and then suddenly she was, and now we're very very good friends, better than friends you could say. For the last four weekends we have gotten together and hung out with nobody else there. I have not told anyone, not even Trevor, for fear of breaking it. Every Friday I call her after school and say Hey, what are you up to? And she says Nothing! very quickly, before I have finished speaking, and then there is a pause on her end—here I can tell she is waiting for me to gather my bravery and suggest that we meet—which usually takes me around five seconds, and usually comes out uncertainly, like Maybe we could meet up tomorrow night? or Maybe I'll pick you up at your house?

I don't know if I am imagining the little bit of disappointment that has started to make its way into her voice. I want to make her happy but I'm not sure what she wants. A date, a real date like adults go on? I have never done such a thing with any girl. It frightens me to think how expensive something like a date would be. Mostly all my friends just get together where we can drink or smoke in peace. Sometimes we see a movie. I guess there are some boys, boys like Preston Hutton and George Bristol, who do take girls on dates, who do the unthinkable thing of asking out girls from other grades who they otherwise do not know. Girls they meet in class. As if they were in college. Boys like them drive very nice cars and have picked up their strange style of dating from watching movies about rich kids in the 80s. There are a lot of boys who love movies like *Ferris Bueller's Day Off* and *Say Anything* and *Pretty in Pink*. George Bristol, who was voted *Best-Dressed* this fall, actually wears blazers with the sleeves pushed up to his elbows. Fortunately for him he is very good at football so his weirdness is thought of as cool rather than ridiculous.

But I don't know how to be like those boys. I like what Lindsay and I do: we get together and go to the mall or the movies, or else we just drive around. We drive around and talk about stuff, or we go to the McDonald's drive-through the next town over or anyplace, a parking lot, it doesn't matter.

We have not kissed or even held hands. She

has touched my arm three times that I can recall. I have a secret question about whether Lindsay has actually gone all the way. There are rumors about her just like there are rumors about every pretty girl at school about their sluttiness or the opposite. With Lindsay it's the opposite. But I don't want to know. Or I guess I should say I don't want to know from anyone but her. I want her to confess it to me. I have a vision of her confessing it to me as a private breakable thing. I want to be the only one who knows it. I am not jealous, never have been, but I feel a pang when I think of anyone knowing Lindsay the way I do. Which is not to say I know her well, but I do know her—differently. I know her secretly.

This past weekend, at a movie, she rested her heavy head on my shoulder. I looked at her out of the side of my eye. Her hair fell across her face. She was dreamy and tired and close to me as she could be. I could not move for I was frozen. She's the best girl I've ever known.

She's walking beside me now, past the tennis courts and the green perfect fields in front of Pells High. We are walking up the cobbled pathway to the school. It's the first time we've done this together. Lindsay waves happily to Cleary O'Connor who is also wearing a field hockey skirt and green knee socks.

GO GIANTS! says Cleary, a short frightening

girl with thighs like support beams. Then she looks at me curiously. Hi Cleary, I say. It's the first time I've ever called her by name and she softens immediately and smiles at me.

Hi! she says, and it seems as if she wants to go on—she opens and closes her mouth twice—but she can't think of anything to say.

Lindsay is friendlier than I am. She says hello to everyone and when she stops to talk to her friend Christy I tell her I'll see her later and slip into school, relieved in a way to be alone again.

Trevor's waiting for me at my locker. You and Lindsay Harper, he says.

I shrug.

You and Lindsay Harpeeeeer, he says. He punches me gently in the gut. Then walks away.

My earliest memory is of my father who is also called Kel. Our last name is Keller. He gave me his name and he gave me his baseball and then when I was four he left and moved to Arizona. And I am still Kel Keller.

In my memory he is throwing me the baseball and I am catching it cleanly in my little glove. In my memory he is huge, though in pictures I have seen of him he's smaller, not much bigger than my mother. There is one whole photo album that exists of us as a family before he left. There are thirty or fifty pictures in it and they are all of my father and mother and me. My mother has always been a picture-taker. We have albums of just the two of us, albums with ridiculous frilly covers or the word *Family* going across the front of it. Pictures of my birthday parties in Yonkers when I was little. Others filled with my school photos, my baseball photos, my friends. Grandma and Grandpa and me at the beach. Of all of them my favorite is the earliest, the only one with my dad in it.

I have looked through that first photo album so many times that I can see it without seeing it. I can tell you the order of the photos and who is doing what in each. On the first page my father is mustached, skinny, wearing ripped ridiculous jeans and a Black Sabbath T-shirt. Next to him is my mother who is extremely pregnant and wearing a long dress. They are standing outside a house I don't recognize. Now that I am older I can tell how young they were. There, in the next one, is my mother, unrecognizable, her bangs one long strand that covers an eye, lying back on a hospital bed with me in her arms. She is sweaty-headed and smiling. My own face is turned in toward her. I can see the outline of my cheek. My father is next to us: black hair to his shoulders and that faint mustache, which makes him look younger rather than older. To be honest with you he looks ridiculous in this picture. Not much better in the rest.

More hospital pictures. In one he is holding me in his arms, not smiling. My mother's parents are standing behind him, also looking stern. There are no pictures of his parents. There are pictures of me growing. My parents bathing me in the sink. This is the only picture in which my parents look happy together and I wonder who's taking it. My father has his hand on my belly. He has a young-buck look.

There are pictures of me at my grandparents' house. Me in a swing in someone's backyard. Me eating in a high chair, blueberry something all over my face. Me and my mother and father at a beach. There are several more in this album but they are all of me and my mother and grand-parents. In one I am turning five, judging by the number of candles on the cake. Three adults stand behind me as I blow them out. My mother has a hand over her mouth as if she is surprised or upset.

When I was a kid I kept this album under my bed and looked at it at night when I was feeling scared, imagined desperately that he would come back even though when he left he did so without a word. I have not heard from him since.

My mother does not speak of him. I used to muster up my courage several times a year to ask her a question about him. Where are Dad's parents. Where was he born. Does he have brothers. She would always answer them, but the look on her face was so full of hurt that after a while it wasn't worth it to me. I became a scavenger, looking for facts about my father in other places. I know they met in high school. I know they had me when they were married, but very young. My mother's still young: twenty years younger than some of my friends' parents. She was only twenty when she had me which makes me wonder if I was an accident. A thought I try to shut off quickly.

Things I have found in my house that I believe belong to my father: a box in the basement with baseball stuff in it, a Mets pennant and some cards, mostly Mets players. I discovered it when I was seven and it caused me to get into several fights with my friends, because of course I immediately declared myself a diehard Mets fan, and my friends liked the Yankees. I didn't care. I fought them. Also in the box were several trophies from Yonkers High, where he and my mother went. My mother made me go to a different high school than they did, and the worst part, at first, was that I had been looking forward to going to the school my father had gone to, perhaps seeing his name on a banner or meeting a teacher who'd had him. I imagined that if I could do very well there at sports he would hear about it somehow. I was stupid. I also found some men's razors in the back of a drawer in the bathroom when I was twelve, before I ever needed to shave, and I ran one over my chin and cut myself. They were rusty. The last thing I found is the most embarrassing: a stack of *Hustlers* under an old couch in our basement. I don't know whose idea it was, my mother's or my father's, but someone decided to put a rough-edged carpet in one corner of our cold unfinished basement. On this carpet is the couch in question, a footstool, and a little table and a TV that doesn't work but probably did once. And under this couch I found the *Hustlers*. It felt as if my father could be someplace else in the house. There were his things. Just lying around. Of course I took them for myself because I was thirteen or fourteen and they were the most amazing things I'd ever seen. Discoveries like these gave me false hope when I was a kid that my father would come back for me. He should have known when he was leaving that I would find them at a tender age and that they would hurt me. He should have known.

I have lied about my father to all of my friends at my high school. I have told them he is dead. My freshman year I wrote an essay for my English teacher. The assignment was to write about a personal hero. *My father died when I was four,* it began, *but I think I inherited many things from him. For one thing his height. For another thing his great love of sports.* The first was a lie and the last was the truth.

I first noticed that I was good at baseball when I was very small, when our coaches still pitched to us. I could pitch too, really pitch. When my coach discovered this he told my mother and she told my grandfather and then from time to time he would practice with me when he saw me but he died when I was ten.

Baseball is the loneliest sport to play for someone who does not have a father. Everyone's dad lines up behind the chain-link fence at games. Everyone's dad has a catch with them in the backyard. Everyone's dad tells them stories about great games and teams and players. Pounds them with phrases like *Keep your eye on the ball. Swing through, swing through. Get in front of the ball, get in front of the ball, get in front of the goddamn ball.* I was not given these by anyone but coaches. Still I made them my own. I would chant them all day. At night I would turn on the radio and listen to Charlie Rasco the sportscaster tell me about sports. This was how I fell asleep. He told me a lot of things I would not otherwise have known and I pretended it was my father telling me these things, I am embarrassed but it's true. After school I would practice in the tiny dirt yard behind our house. I propped an old mattress against the back wall. My mother drew a red circle on it and a red dot inside the circle. I threw the ball at the mattress over and over again. When my mother was up for it I had her bat ground balls to me and I scooped them. This was rare. I did not want to be a pitcher but as a younger boy I was.

When I was twelve I was on an all-star team that went to the Little League World Series in central Pennsylvania. My mother took off work as soon as she found out we were going, which was especially hard because it was right before school started. Her car at the time was a horrible old Nissan that broke down when we were only half an hour away, and we almost didn't make it. I remember her standing on the side of the road, going *I'm so sorry, baby, I'm so sorry, Kel.* I was very mean to her and would not talk.

An old man in a baseball cap pulled over in a pickup truck and asked were we all right, and my mother told him no. My son's on his way to the Little League World Series, she said. You better come with me, then, said the old man.

I could tell that my mother did not want to but she did it for me. She sat in the middle and I sat on the far side and the old man called a towing company and got my mother's car towed for her. He was a very nice man and nothing to fear. He told us jokes on the way. Did you hear the Cubs got a new pitching machine? Yeah, it beat them five to one.

He asked me who my favorite player of all time was and I told him Mike Schmidt.

Attaboy, he said, because we were in Pennsylvania.

We got a phone call later from the garage. He'd paid for our car to be towed and fixed. My mother cried.

That was the best week of my life. We stayed in a terrible motel ten minutes from the nice hotel that everyone else stayed in. But twice I slept over in a friend's room and my mother said it was fine and didn't even seem sad or lonely. The nights I stayed with her we watched TV, huddled in bed, and got Chinese food from a place down the street. My mother laughed and made jokes and told me several stories about when she was a kid which usually she did not. One game I made a triple play all on my own. I caught a fly ball, tagged third base, and tagged the player running from second. I have never done that since.

We made it to the state semifinal and lost. But I didn't mind. On the way home the whole team went out for McDonald's. My mother had no one to talk to because all the other adults were couples, and she's shy, but she sat there and smiled and my coach went up to her and sat with her for a while, telling her how much promise I had and how proud he was of me. I had two Big Macs and a vanilla shake and fries and an apple pie. My mother said I could have anything I wanted, I deserved it.

This same man, Ted Jaworski, coached a summer league team too. He invited me on and I said I could not pay for it. I knew this without asking my mother. He raised the money for me. From that point on I have played for town and school and club. My summer team now is the Cardinals who are the top team in the state of New York. For three years I have played with the Cardinals from the end of the school year through the summer. We take the bus and travel all over the place. The boys on this team are my friends but not my good friends because we are all competitive with each other.

The first article about me came out when I was fourteen. *For Kel Keller, Baseball Is Life.* Someone came to interview me about baseball and growing up in Yonkers and going to school where I do, in Pells Landing, which happens to be the richest town in the state of New York—a fact that my mother does not fail to point out regularly. It was just after Pells won state for the first time in three decades. In playoffs I hit .570 with 12 RBIs. And I was still a freshman. He took a picture of me tossing a baseball in front of my house. I spent the morning before he came trying to clean up all the leaves and the spare papers and pieces of trash that had found their way onto our little lawn. I even asked my mom if I could paint our door which was peeling like a joke and she said no because paint is expensive. So our house looked crappy in the picture which is probably what the reporter wanted anyway. If you Google my name it's the first thing that comes up. This has always embarrassed me.

The most recent article came out last month and it was about my prospects as a major league player. I'm not kidding. It was the most exciting thing that ever happened to me in my life and I even showed it to my mother who cried, from sadness or happiness I'm not sure. She wants me to go to college first. Last year, my junior year, a bunch of college recruiters called me up or contacted me through my coaches. But I have never been a good student and pro ball is where I want to be.

So it was very exciting when it started last spring: a few bird-dog scouts began coming to some of my PLHS games, and a couple of them talked to Coach Ramirez about me, and Coach told me what they said. Over the summer a few more came to my Cardinals games. At Pells it was clear who they were there for; I was the only one who had a shot, and everyone knew it. But my league team is different. A bunch of us probably have a hope of getting drafted. Then last July, in the middle of a tournament in New Jersey, one of my teammates said *Do you guys know who that is?* and pointed to a gray-mustached man in the bleachers. A general murmur started. *Mets scout,* said the boy, and nodded slowly. All of us avoided each other's eyes. It was the first time a supervising scout had come out—all the others had been young guys, hungry for money, but this one was patient and kind of looked like it didn't matter to him whether we were good or not— and the best part was he was from the Mets. My father's team. I played like a tornado and I knocked one out of the park. At the end I had a chance at a grand slam but the pitcher walked me and I've never been madder in my life. The whole time I was thinking All I've ever wanted is to play for the Mets. Please let him be here for me. Please.

Afterward the whole team sort of hung around longer than we usually do. The scout was talking to our coach. All of us pretended to talk to each other and looked at them peripherally. Then Coach Jaworski said *Keller!* and waved me over. I tried not to smile but I smiled very much. The rest of my team bore holes into my back.

His name was Gerard Kane. He was as tall as I was and red-faced and he had Popeye arms and he wore sunglasses on a rope around his neck and a Mets cap. He was like everyone's father. He talked to me for a while that day and he came to several more of my games. At the end of the summer season he told me he was going to call me to set up a private workout with a pitcher and me. I wasn't going to tell my mother but when I got home the news burst out of me before I could stop it. I had no one else to tell. She wasn't as happy as she should have been. All she talks about is college. She does not understand that she is part of the reason I don't want to go. She said, Well, I guess it doesn't hurt to go practice. You can always make up your mind later.

But I'd already made up my mind.

It took longer than I thought it would for Gerard Kane to call. He waited all fall, in fact. I didn't blame him—the Mets had a good season. He was probably busy.

Last week, finally, my phone rang. It was an unknown number. I answered quick as I could.

Hello, may I please speak to Kel Keller? asked a girl I didn't know.

This is Kel, I said.

Hi, Kel, My name is Sarah, she said. I'm Gerard Kane's assistant?

Oh, hi, I said. My heart began pounding.

—Do you remember Mr. Kane?

Yeah, I said.

He's very sorry it's taken him this long to get in touch with you, she said. But he'd love to set up a private practice with you whenever you're available.

Sarah sounded pretty. She said a Saturday would be best, and what do my Saturdays look like? December 10th is the date we came up with. Three weeks away.

Since then I've been dreaming. My news has been following me around like a happy balloon. There is one thing I haven't told my mother: that if I get drafted I'll sign. She will not be happy when I tell her this. She wants me to go to college even though going to college will mean leaving her far behind. Which I cannot do. As I have said. She is holding on to some idea of what our lives will be. The idea that she had when she was working still, when I was a good scared boy who did whatever she told me to do. She always told me she had dropped out of college after one semester because she couldn't afford it. It was, she said, her biggest regret in life. She tells me, Kel, you'll be a doctor. Or some days, Kel, you'll be a professor. As if being a doctor or a professor was the best thing she could think of to be. As if she didn't know me at all, who I was and am. And in my head I thought to her, I'll be a ballplayer if it kills me. I know that every boy wants to be a ballplayer but I wanted it, I want it, more than anybody. I always have. I dream about it. Drifting off to sleep it comes to me suddenly: a vision of crowds in stands.

So I have to tell her. She'll cry. I have to tell her anyway.

Sometimes I feel like I'm trading my mother's dream for my father's. When I was younger I thought somehow that being good at baseball would bring my father to me. That what he could resist in a son he could not resist in a famous son. A famous baseball player. In photographs, his orange shirts told me this. His pennants and trophies.

Does he have other sons. That is the largest most frightening question that I have. Does he have other sons that he is raising to be tanned and white-headed, out in the Arizona desert, that he is raising to be better at baseball than me.

First period is history. Mr. Potts, our teacher, is a young guy who sits on his desk during class. He always has a coffee in a tall Styrofoam Dunkin' Donuts cup. When I see him in the afternoon he's still drinking out of it, which probably means that it is cold. On Fridays he wears jeans which is technically against the rules of our school for teachers—Trevor once found a faculty manual and it said so—but Mr. Potts doesn't care. He calls me Keller because he heard some boys in the hall calling me that. My friends call me Keller. Or Yonkers, or Bonkers, or Keeeel, plain Keeeeel, low in their throats and congratulatory. When the football team loses, Mr. Potts says Keller, what happened yesterday? Keller, he says, lookin' good today, like the hat. It's a joke. He's making friends with us.

We call him Pottsy. He doesn't mind.

The best teachers are the ones who want to be liked by you. All teachers want to be liked by you but the best ones are the ones who know who to go after, which kids to befriend. I'm one of the ones to befriend. If I like you everyone does. It's happened in all my classes.

One time I saw Pottsy in Yonkers standing outside of Rory Dolan's Pub and smoking. I was driving and I didn't stop. My little-kid instinct took over and I ducked my head, even, I did not want to be seen. He had one foot pressed against the wall behind him and he was wearing his baseball cap sideways like a fool, for a joke. He had friends on either side of him. Everyone was laughing.

When I come into class today Pottsy says What's on your feet, Keller? Tomatoes?

I'm wearing red huge basketball shoes. As I have found my place in this school I have begun to dress like I used to and this means whatever I want.

Jealous? I say.

I sit down next to Kurt and across from Lindsay. Our desks are set up in a horseshoe. This is the first class I've ever had with her even though we have gone to school together for four years. She's smarter than me. This year I took A.P. U.S. History II just for the hell of it, because I liked my history class last year and my teacher made me feel like I could.

Happy Monday, says Pottsy, and then he dives right in before everyone's settled. The Beats, he says. Who knows what the Beats are? The Beat Generation. Beatniks.

No one says anything.

Well you all should, says Pottsy. Because it was part of your reading assignment over the week-end.

We look at him blankly and see that he is getting the face he gets when we are not performing up to his standards.

No one? says Pottsy. No one at all can tell me who the Beats were?

In that case, says Pottsy, I won't have a conversation with myself. You guys will lead the class on the Beats yourselves on Thursday.

He goes around the room and pairs us up and gives each pair some aspect of the Beats to cover. By some miracle he puts me and Lindsay together. It is the first time we have worked together all semester.

I look at her quickly across the room and I'm happy when she returns my glance.

Five-minute presentations each, says Pottsy. Visual aids required.

Then he walks up to the board and draws an exclamation point, his favorite thing to do when we have misbehaved.

After class Lindsay comes up to me and says, You're my partner!

I am, I say.

Lindsay says, So, should I come to your house, or should you come to mine, orrrrrr . . .

It is a question I have too. Since we have been hanging out, Lindsay and I have met at various places—the movies, the mall—and twice I have picked her up from her house, but both times she was waiting for me on her porch. I have never been inside. I imagine that the inside of Lindsay's house is cavernous and light. I imagine that if she saw my block she would be frightened. But maybe I'm wrong.

Your house is closer to school, I say. You don't wanna come to Yonkers, anyway.

These are the jokes I make in advance. When I first got to Pells I played up my difference because I felt that it earned me a strange kind of respect. Realizing that I could not beat anyone from Pells Landing at being someone from Pells Landing, I became someone from Yonkers— which is a perfectly nice place to live, actually. But it's not Pells. Now I am so closely tied to Yonkers that it is what I am called. My friends from home would laugh at me. They'd be disgusted by me.

My house, then, says Lindsay. Can you come after practice tonight?

The answer is yes. I walk out of the classroom feeling light with anticipation.

In the hallway, I see a dozen people I know in quick succession and they all shout some version of my name. I am going to an appointment with my guidance counselor, Ms. Warren. She is going to tell me about all the colleges I can't get into.

When I walk into Ms. Warren's office she is eating a sandwich and part of it falls out into her lap. It's only 9 in the morning. She scrambles to remove the clump of ham and mayonnaise-y lettuce from her blue skirt and then dabs at the spot with a napkin.

Oh my gosh, she says. You surprised me.

Sorry, I say.

Ms. Warren is young and plump and she always has very red cheeks. From being embarrassed or from being overheated I don't know. She has lots of curly blond hair that she wears long down her back. She touches it constantly, flipping it back and forth with her hand. I can tell that she wants to be both young and old. She wants to be our age and she wants us to be damn sure that she's older than us.

I think I am making her nervous so I ask if I can sit down.

Sure, she says, and sort of pulls the other chair forward halfheartedly. She is facing her desk which is facing the window. She sits on a swivel chair and she turns slowly toward me after I have sat down. She is checking her face with her fingers. She is running her tongue over her teeth. She was not popular.

What brings you here today, Kel? she asks.

I look at her for a moment. You asked me to come, I say.

Oh, right, she says, and laughs. I forgot! The reason I asked you, she says, ruffling through some papers on her desk. The reason I asked you is because we still don't have information from you on where you're applying.

This is what Pells is like. In Yonkers this would not happen. In Yonkers if you wanted to go to college you would seek out a guidance counselor who would not know your name. You would make an appointment and if your grades were good they would tell you you could get in anywhere and if your grades were bad they would tell you to apply to several local colleges, mostly community colleges, and then transfer after a year. In Pells they practically stalk you. I think everyone goes to college. I don't know anyone who's not going.

Which is why Ms. Warren is surprised when I say, I don't think I'm actually going to apply.

She looks at me. She is speechless. I have just noticed a bread crumb on her collar.

What would you do instead? she asks.

Play baseball, I say.

Isn't that—what college is for? she asks.

—You can play baseball outside of college.

—Where?

—The majors.

She does not know whether to be skeptical. She opens and closes her mouth. I could rescue her but I don't. I could tell her about the scouts, about my private practice with Gerard Kane, the reason I have reason to hope. But I don't. I want to watch her talk—I want to smile and nod.

Now Kel, she says. I know you're very good at baseball. But who actually.

She doesn't finish. I am still quiet.

—Aren't the odds of *anyone* making it slim? Not just you, but, like.

She seems young now.

Of course, I say.

So. If you played baseball in *college,* you could have the best of both worlds! she says. She looks relieved. As if she has come across the answer.

I shake my head. I'm not good at school, I say.

She pulls up something on her computer. It is my record. C's across the board which is almost impressive if only because it is consistent. I got one F in English my freshman year and my mother yelled at me because she was so embarrassed. Because she still worked there. I got A's in phys ed and in art. Besides that, C's.

Now look at this, she says. A's in art?

I nod.

What if, she says. What if we could find you a school with a great art program? And you could major in graphic design, or in art, and you could play baseball on the side.

It's the first suggestion anyone has made to me that sounds remotely appealing. But I only say, Maybe.

There are several reasons I do not want to go to college. One is that I am afraid that if I don't go running after something with my whole heart that it will disappear as a way of punishing me. Another is that I sincerely do not think I will be good at college. And last there is my mother. I hate her but I want to help her. I want to make money doing something I love and I want to make lots of it and I can't make money in college. I want to make money so that I can hold it over her head and order her to stop pretending to be so sick. Order her to stop drinking. I want to buy her a huge clean house like the Harpers' or the Cohens'. I want her to invite Dr. Greene to her huge clean house and tell him Look what I have. Look at the things I have and the son I have. I want to buy her puppies to take care of and I want her to maybe meet a new husband. And maybe meet friends. I want to not have to worry about her all of the time. I want to get her a very good doctor. And I want to be close to her. Geographically. I have to stay close to home. There is no way I could go to any of the colleges that have recruited me because the farthest away is in California and the closest is two hours away. Two hours away is too many. My mother would not survive. I know that she wouldn't. I know that if I weren't there to come in and take the bottle out of her hands and pat her head and cut her hair and soothe her and tell her No, don't do a handstand, No, don't build a fire in the fireplace, No, you drink too much to do any of these things—that she would, when she got lonely enough she would, when she knew there would be no one checking in on her she would. She would kill herself. Slowly or suddenly she would kill herself.

Now I know that if I played professionally I would also be away, but it would not be so permanent. I'd go down to Florida for training, but I would not be there for four years. Or even for one year. I'd be able to tell her I was checking on her. I'd be able to go back and forth. And I would make money for us, very soon if I was lucky. Most important of all: I could bring her with me. Wherever I was she could come.

I can't tell Ms. Warren this so I tell her instead that I'll think about what she's suggesting. I say, *Thank you, I'll consider it.* Using my best adult voice. She is handing me things, brochure after brochure. She has found an art school that would be perfect for me. In Rochester. What doesn't she understand.

Or, she says. There's always community college too. Could you go to community college while you're playing professional baseball?

I can tell by the way she says *professional*

baseball that she doesn't believe I can do it and furthermore she knows nothing about it.

I guess I could, I say.

I think her goal is to keep PLHS's statistics as pristine as they can be. I think her task is to make every single student go to college because then PLHS can say that every single student goes to college. On their goddamn website.

As I'm getting up to leave she says my name.

Yep? I say.

I want you to know that I care about your future, she says.

I know, I say.

—Everyone cares about your future.

Again I have a vision of her as a high school student. We wouldn't have been friends.

After school, inside the locker room, the boys are getting ready. The walls are painted green and gold: Giants colors. It is warmly damp and it smells like chlorine even though we have no pool. There is something like a church about it. Mostly it is quiet. I love it in here and I always have. In movies they show locker rooms as rowdy places but I think they are not: here we're quiet and slow-moving. We breathe more evenly. We speak lowly. If somebody looks worried we leave him alone or we clap him on the back one time.

I'm the quarterback. I'm very good but I'm not the best in the state or even in our conference. Funny enough, that title belongs to Dee Marshall who I was friends with growing up in Yonkers. Whose mother Rhonda was friends with my mother, once upon a time, before my mother stopped having friends. They grew up together. Dee was my bad best friend in middle school, the one who I got into trouble with. In some ways he is the reason I am here. My mother was very glad when we stopped talking much after I went to Pells. She used to say things like *Rhonda's a good person but not a good mother.* As if she should talk about good mothers. Or *Rhonda was nuts growing up. It's no wonder about that poor*

149

kid. Dee is half black and half Rhonda and is the best athlete I've ever seen. He was my best friend for fourteen years. When I think of my old friends from Yonkers I hope they aren't mad at me but I think they are. I see them sometimes—on weekends I see them or at the store. Mostly I keep my head down. When I do see them we say some words to each other. At first they called me all the time and I called them back half the time. Now they don't call me anymore. They live in another world from mine.

Yonkers is part of our conference. In football and basketball they are better than us and mostly they win. For some reason this makes me happy. But in baseball we are better than they are, and we win every time. When I play any game against Yonkers I avoid eye contact. I say hello to my old friends and then I avoid eye contact with them thereafter. Dee Marshall is the most frightening and the angriest. I play him in basketball too and that is the worst. Even when we were kids it was the only place he ever showed any emotion. It's scary. It's the sight of him barreling toward you, all six feet and four inches of him, all of his muscles and veins working hard and together to plow past you or, if you are especially brave, to bowl you over. When his team wins, which is usually, he cries out once in victory, slaps the backs of his useless teammates, jumps occasionally into the air, bringing his heels up to meet his thighs. When we were sophomores I was assigned to guard him. After they beat us he pointed right at me and it was the most hateful look I ever got in my life. Dee I'm sorry, I wanted to tell him. I miss you every one of you. My teammates who leave from games in cars that are nicer than anything your parents can afford don't matter to me as much as you do.

I am all padded and suited up early, for once, and I walk out to the lobby of the gym, where PTA mothers sell concessions to their children, not to me. I always bring my snack from home. Trevor and Kurt and Chuck and Peters and Kramer and Cossy and Brian Heller and Jonesy and Matt Barnaby are all out there already, sitting on some benches. As soon as I walk toward them Trevor goes, You! And! Lindsay! Harper! which is apparently the only thing he can say these days. I don't know what you're talking about, I say, but I am smiling very much.

What the fuck, says Kurt.

Matt Barnaby is silent because he used to go out with Lindsay. She dumped him at the start of the year. I am sure he still likes her, who wouldn't. This does not make her off-limits to me. Matt and I are not friends. He is a junior. I don't particularly like him.

When did this happen? says Kurt. Is that where you've been every weekend?

I shrug. Maybe, I say.

I don't know exactly why I haven't told any of my friends. Why I waited for them to find out. I knew they would eventually. I guess it was that I didn't want to fuck anything up. I didn't want to disturb what was good and important to me. It was the same feeling that kept me from telling Ms. Warren my news. Saying things aloud makes them dangerous.

Have you been to her house? asks Kurt. He is the most talkative of all my friends and the girliest. He is also the second-best ballplayer we have.

I'm going after practice tonight, I say, leaving out the part about our history project, feeling mildly guilty for the lie it implies.

Have you been to fourth base? says Kurt. He is trying to be funny.

Have you? I say.

Matt Barnaby gets up from the bench and stretches and tries to casually walk away, pretending to go talk to some friends of his, but I know it's really because he wants to call me out but is afraid.

I sit down next to the rest of them and take out the snack I have brought in my backpack: I have a pack of Slim Jims that I bought at the deli on my corner and I have a hard roll with butter from the same place. I have a cookie that one of the lunch ladies gave me for being cute. I have a giant bag of chips that I should not eat while I'm in training but I can't help it, I love chips. I have a G2 from the vending machine. And peanut butter crackers that I make for myself at home and bring in a big Ziploc bag. I'll eat a little of this now and save the rest for after practice.

Keller, what the hell is all that, asks Peters.

Jealous? I say, and realize suddenly that it is what I say to everyone who ever teases me. About anything. Peters is eating pita bread or some shit like that. His mother probably packed it up for him with her own hands.

Kind of, he says.

I'm quiet. Among my friends I am quiet except for when I am very loud and calling someone out. Or when I am mad or upset or drunk.

My cell phone rings. Normally I am very good about squirreling away my cell phone and making sure it is on silent (they're strict here, they'll take it from you if it rings or if they even see it) but suddenly I feel it vibrating in my backpack. There is only one person it could be because all my friends are here and a chill comes over me. What does she want. Is she all right. Sneakily I look at the phone inside my bag.

It's an unavailable number. I wait to see if they'll leave a message. I wait to see if it is a hospital or a police station, but after a minute it becomes clear that there's no voice mail. And then I wonder if it was another scout.

• • •

We get up from the benches, we trot outside. Coach is in a bad mood. Probably because of the Yonkers game which he knows we will lose but must pretend we will win. It must be a terrible thing to be a coach. Today he cuts us no slack and me in particular. Separately he makes me take my drops until my legs shake. We do passing plays for an hour. I am distracted and I can't tell anyone why. Coach has the JV defensive line go up against us while our real defense is doing drills down the other end of the field. JV is supposed to play like Yonkers' defense, which is made up of boys that are probably three times their collective weight. We are the first-string offense and we should crush them. But my head's not in it. I hold the ball too long. I get sacked on the first play.

Later, when I throw a pass to no one, Coach says, KELLER! WHAT! IS! YOUR! DEAL!

I say nothing. I shake my helmeted head.

After practice, I shower. After I shower I get into my car. After I get into my car I take several breaths and put on *Sports Talk* and listen to Charlie Rasco. Then I head for Lindsay Harper's house down back roads that I've learned well over the years I've been at PLHS. It's 4:45 in the afternoon. The sky is orange.

Some days, driving around Pells Landing, I become so aware of how pretty it is that I forget everything that I should be worrying about. This is one of those days: most of the leaves are off the trees, but it's warm for November, and so every little family in Pells is out in the front yard of their gigantic home, raking and laughing and being very happy. There is a smell of wood smoke in the air and, not for the first time, I feel like an intruder, like somebody staking something out.

Lindsay's house is near Trevor's in one of the nicest neighborhoods in Pells. In high school everyone knows a few facts about almost everyone else, even if you've never spoken to them. Sometimes these are stories that follow a person for years, from eighth grade, from fifth: the kid who peed himself in gym class, the girl who cried when she got a B+. About me people probably say, He's poor and his mom is sick and crazy. No one's ever seen his house which probably means it's a dump. He's the best baseball player in school or in the state. He's stupid. I don't know. Before Lindsay and I started hanging out, these were the things I knew about her: her family, like most families in Pells, comes from money; her father is the superintendent of schools; her mother is a lawyer in the city and has a job defending large corporations; she used to have an older brother but he died when Lindsay was in middle school, which lends her an extra air of mystery and desirability.

Her house, when I first saw it, was a shock: the size of it. It is tan with brown beams all over it like an old-fashioned English house, and old. Two huge trees frame it. It has a big porch and a porch swing on it. As I pull into her driveway I look up at all the windows on the top floor and wonder which one is Lindsay's. I get out of my car, but before I have a chance to walk to the house, the front door flies open and two little blond girls come running toward me. They are sock-footed and skinny.

Are you Lindsay's friend? says one of them. They look about five and seven.

Yes, I say.

Could you please park over there, says the other, very polite, and gestures to a little space off the side of the driveway.

There? I ask, dumbly, and turn to follow their orders.

Lindsay appears in the doorway then and says What are they telling you!

To park over there, I say.

You guys. He's fine where he is, says Lindsay, and her sisters begin to complain.

We want to play *soccer,* says the littler one. On the *driveway.*

Play on the grass, says Lindsay, and then tells me to come inside.

Sorry, she says.

Her house is even nicer inside than I'd imagined. It has this kind of lobby with a ceiling so high our voices echo.

I start to follow her across it and then she turns and says Um—I'm so sorry—could you take your shoes off? My mom . . .

I am wearing two different socks and I am so embarrassed I almost leave.

Instead I make a joke about it, a stupid one, and Lindsay laughs.

There are red patterned carpets on the hardwood floor. All of the furniture is delicate and breakable. She introduces me to her two big dogs, Angelo and Maxie. Through eight glass doors at the other end of the living room I can see the Harpers' backyard: there is a pool, covered for winter, landscaped to look like a mountain lake, with low bushes and trees all around it. In one hallway there are seven or eight photographs of their family from the time Lindsay was very small. I glance at them quickly as we walk past. I see Lindsay as a baby and Lindsay at five, pig-tails and pierced ears. In all of them but the last one there is a boy. By the second-to-last he is almost a man. And in the last one he is not there. In the photos I recognize her father, a short bald-headed man, from the school board meeting I went to. I say a prayer that he will not be here to remember me.

You want something? asks Lindsay, as we enter the kitchen, filled with sharp-looking silver appliances and an island in the middle the size of my car. Soda? Are you hungry?

Smoothies! says a voice off to the side, and Lindsay's mother emerges from a nook that I didn't notice, wearing a red sweatsuit with a zipper up the front of it. It is meant for someone younger than she is and it shows the top of her freckled breasts. Her hair is dyed yellow. Her eyelashes are spidery.

Who's this! she asks brightly, and Lindsay says, I told you my friend Kel was coming over to do a history project.

Kel, I'm Jeanie Harper, says her mother, and she holds her hand out to me very officially and suddenly I remember Kurt Aspenwall telling me she was a lawyer. Welcome to our home.

Lindsay looks pained.

Do you want a smoothie, Kel? asks Mrs. Harper. I was just about to make smoothies.

Um, I say, and glance at Lindsay. If . . .

Have one! says Mrs. Harper.

OK, I say. The truth is that I do want a smoothie. I'm hungry. I like them. Thank you, I say.

You guys go ahead and start working, says Mrs. Harper, I'll bring them to you.

I don't want one, says Lindsay.

Linds, says her mother, but then she says OK, fine, and kind of throws her hands up in the air and rolls her eyes at me like *What am I going to do with her!*

Lindsay leads me to the basement which is finished and huge and cold and floored with a rough white carpet. A giant curved couch faces a low table and beyond it a flat-screen TV. The whole thing smells like strawberries or the sick sweet plastic of a doll.

All of a sudden I realize that we are alone and for the first time in a long while I get very nervous and can't think of what to say. The other times we have hung out it has felt different, less frightening. She is wearing warm-up pants and a tight T-shirt. Her dark hair is down around her shoulders and she keeps brushing it back from her face with her pretty hands which I want to do also. I remember her head on my shoulder, last weekend at the movie.

We talk about nothing for a while and then Lindsay talks about the project while I listen. Then Mrs. Harper comes downstairs with smoothies and hands me one and then hands Lindsay one.

I made you one anyway, Linds, she said, and then she sits down on the leather couch next to us, crossing her legs, propping her chin up with her right fist. Lindsay takes the smoothie and puts it on the table in front of us, as far away from her as possible.

What's your project, guys? Mrs. Harper asks brightly. I take a sip of the smoothie. It is the most delicious thing I've ever had in my life. I think it is made of raspberries. There are seeds in it that I burst between my teeth.

It's on the Beat Generation, I say, because Lindsay isn't saying anything.

Oooooh, says Mrs. Harper. Bongos and berets and stuff? She drums on her lap for a minute.

Thanks, Mom, says Lindsay. Thanks for the smoothies.

Mrs. Harper snaps her fingers repeatedly. That's how they clapped, she says. After poetry.

Thanks, Mom, Lindsay says again, shortly.

After her mother leaves Lindsay looks at me, worried. Do you think I was rude? she says.

I do think so but I say no.

We work on the project for an hour, reading passages aloud to each other and writing stuff down that doesn't even make sense. I had kind of figured that she would just do everything and I would watch because she is so much smarter than me and so much better than me at this kind of stuff. But she seems like she wants me to help.

Hang on, says Lindsay, and she springs gracefully from the couch and trots toward a door across from it. When she opens it I see it is a closet with many perfectly organized shelves. From one she removes a large stack of posterboard in many colors. From another she removes Magic Markers.

Wow, I say, why do you have all that stuff?

You know, says Lindsay. School projects and stuff.

It astounds me that someone can have a closet full of art supplies just for school projects.

She brings out a piece of light blue posterboard and says You're good at art, right?

We have never talked about it, so apparently this is one of the things that people at school say about me, and for some reason this makes me really happy. I have taken art every year. I shrug.

She tells me what to write on the poster and at first I'm not thinking and I write *The Beet Generation*—beet, like a goddamn vegetable— but on my second try it looks very good. We talk more naturally. I find my words: we talk about other people in our grade, the most natural subject to talk about. Her best friends are Christy and Jill. We talk about them and their boyfriends.

She asks me for the first time about other girlfriends I have had, and I say, truthfully, none.

That's not what I've heard, says Lindsay, but she lets it go, she doesn't ask anything more of me.

Now there is silence again. Now we are alone in Lindsay Harper's basement and neither of us is saying anything. Lindsay glances at me and then away. She is very still but for her left hand, which is coloring in the words that I have sketched.

I've been here at this moment dozens and dozens of times, with other girls. I try to imagine it: how it started, those times. How it normally starts. Normally it involves being drunk, but there was a time before I regularly got drunk when I knew how to do this, when I could lean toward a girl slowly and feel very certain that she wouldn't move away, when I could put a hand on a girl's waist and feel her stomach tense with desire, feel her body bend and move beneath my hand. I imagine reaching behind Lindsay and putting one hand on her back, just leaving it there on her smooth back, under her shirt. I imagine it so clearly that I can almost feel it happening.

It is almost dark outside. Only a tiny bit of light is coming in from the small windows set high in the basement walls. I move closer to Lindsay as imperceptibly as possible. I inch my right foot over and then my right thigh and then my left foot and my left thigh. Our arms touch. She is left-handed and I am right-handed.

She seems very calm, beside me. She keeps pausing to admire her work.

It's getting dark in here, she says finally, and then she turns toward me and I can still make out her light large eyes and she pauses and then I do put one hand on her side. And leave it there.

What are you, she says, and I think she is going to say *doing,* but she doesn't.

When I kiss her I almost knock her over backward. We do bend backward, she is up against the couch, and I try to gently encourage her onto it, but she doesn't move. We stay there, kneeling, twisted toward each other.

I put my hands on her back under her shirt because I have imagined it so thoroughly already. There is her skin. There is her smooth muscled back.

She makes a little noise like a mew. It shivers me.

Just then we hear the basement door fly open and one of her baby sisters shrieks *LINDSAY!* Then we hear them come barreling down the stairs, which we cannot see from where we are.

WHAT! Lindsay yells, and springs to her feet athletically before they can see us.

What, she says more quietly, when they appear. I am not as quick as Lindsay and I have one knee on the floor and the other leg up as if I am proposing.

Margo broke something, says the older one, and Margo nods solemnly.

My left taillight is shattered.

Jesus Christ, you guys, says Lindsay. How did this happen?

The older one points to little Margo.

I was swinging a baseball bat, says Margo.

Into his car? asks Lindsay.

—No, behind it. I swinged it backwards.

She looks as if she might cry.

Hey, it's OK! I say. Don't worry about it!

Like a jerk.

But I am very worried about it. I have no idea what it might cost but whatever it is I can't afford it.

I am . . . so . . . sorry, says Lindsay. Let me get my mom.

Before she can I say I have to go. I do not want her mother out there writing a check to me.

Please, says Lindsay, she'll want to help you . . .

But I get into my car. I am already leaving.

Wait, she says. Just wait one second.

I roll down the window.

—We're, there's a thing we're having, that we have every year after Thanksgiving.

I wait for her to go on.

My family? she says.

OK, I say.

You'll come? she says, and then: It's a whole thing. Lots of people are coming. Christy is.

Sure, I say.

OK great, says Lindsay. That's good.

Then I'll see you then, I say. Or before then in class.

It is a silly thing to say and I squeeze my right fist shut in embarrassment.

I keep it squeezed shut as I back out of her driveway, as if opening it would break a spell.

Believe it or not I am very happy on the way home, despite the taillight. I see Lindsay's face before my face and I feel her body next to mine. How foreign she is to me, every part of her, and my foreignness. Recalling any aspect of her sets me off. The frayed cuffs of her pants, the legs beneath them, her hair and its overwhelming girl smell, her hair—slightly damp from the shower (Lindsay in the shower—oh—). I imagine her imagining me and this also excites me. I have never felt this way about any girl.

I decide to take a drive. I drive up the Hudson a little ways to a beach that I know, where I have taken several girls. I park the car there and kill the lights. A few boats are dry-docked on a small marina and they remind me of what I might have someday. Lindsay herself reminds me of what I might have someday. Normally I don't skip ahead in my life but this is what Pells Landing does to a person: makes him dream of the future, of a huge rambling house and dogs named Angelo and Maxie and of having a baby boy and naming him after yourself. Of having a real job. Of richness, unbearable richness. I sit there until I get too cold and then start the engine and drive home.

Something about Lindsay makes me feel both brave and lucky, and I decide, while driving, that tonight is a good night to tell my mother that I've made up my mind completely. I will tell her firmly that it is my plan, my intention, to sign with a major league team if one wants me. That I will not go to college—not yet. If she's sober enough, I'll tell her these things.

When I pull into the driveway I see that the door is ajar and it confirms something for me. It is always a good thing when the door is ajar. It means my mother has been outside, to the corner store, or for a walk. When she has a good day sometimes she sits on our front steps and smokes a cigarette and waves at people who walk by on the street. Who are probably all afraid of her. But still.

I'm going to tell her that I have good news: this is how I will introduce the topic. I'll tell her about my meeting with Ms. Warren. I'll lie, and say that Ms. Warren encouraged me to do what I have to do.

Inside the house smells better than normal. She has cleaned. It smells like Pine-Sol. All the dishes are put away and her magazines are stacked in one place on the table. She has lined up my shoes and hers in a little place by the door. I try not to get my hopes up. Since she first got bad I've always had this feeling that one day I'll come home and she'll just be better, she'll have baked me cookies or some shit like that, she'll be wearing an apron. She'll smell good.

I don't hear the television.

Mom? I ask. Not loudly. No answer.

I walk into the living room to confirm that the television is off. It is the first time in recent memory that I've come into the house without the TV being on. Once I forgot to pay the basic cable bill and I came home to find my mother crying about it.

Mom, I say again.

Upstairs it is dark and silent.

There is a note on her closed bedroom door.

Dear Kel,
Do not come in. Call police.
Love, Mom.

Time slows. I kick the door open before I am too scared to open it and see the shape of her in her bed. The room is freezing and dark. I flip the overhead light on and see that she has gotten herself dressed for the first time in months. She is wearing jeans and a sweater. She is curled into a ball on her side. Her back is to me. Her knees are up by her chest. She looks as if she is asleep.

I understand suddenly that every other night I've come home and found her like this was just practice.

That this is what it feels like. This, this. Now.

Let me think a minute, I say aloud. For no reason. In a flash I am leaning over her and I see that she is white-faced and motionless. Different than she is when she's passed out. Deader. Again I shake her thinking it won't work this time, it won't work.

I turn her on her back and press my head to her chest and I can't hear anything. Suddenly she gasps. Then once again goes quiet.

I shout at her. Nothing that makes sense. No words. Just shouting and shaking. She does not respond.

I bring my cell phone out of my pocket and try to dial but I am trembling too badly and crying and I can't see it well. I grab the portable house phone and try that instead. I tell the 911 people MY MOTHER HAS KILLED HERSELF. I drop to my knees and say it again.

OK, stay calm, please, sir. First tell me if she's breathing.

I DON'T THINK SO, I say.

You've got to tell me for certain whether she's breathing, says the operator.

I hold a hand up to her mouth and nose. I feel nothing.

SHE ISN'T, I say.

—Is she bleeding? How did she try to kill herself?

It is then that I see a bottle tipped over next to her. Two pills are out. I grab the bottle and it says Valium (Diazepam). I don't know how she got it and I am stunned to think of her doing anything secretly without my knowing it. A goddamn half-empty Cuba libre is on the table next to her. She has puked a little bit on the pillow beside her.

SHE TOOK PILLS, I say.

What's your address, please? says the operator, and I tell her.

An ambulance is on its way, says the operator. Now here's what I need you to do. Tell me what kind of pills she took, sir.

VALIUM DIAZEPAM. I can't stop shouting. I can't stop shouting. I'm still trying to wake her up.

I hear a wail. It is not my mother. It is the ambulance. The front door is still open and I hear them come in. EMS, they say, Hello, Hello, and it sounds faraway and underwater.

I whisper. I have stopped shouting so I whisper. *She's here.*

Our house is small. I hear boots on our terrible old staircase.

In here, I whisper again, and when they come in I'm on my knees beside the bed.

I get out of the way by falling over, sort of. There are two of them a man and a woman.

Is this the victim? asks the man, and I nod.

Is this your mother? What's her name? he says.

Charlene, I whisper.

CHARLENE, they say together. CHARLENE. The man knuckles her chest very hard. TIME TO WAKE UP, says the girl. I realize suddenly that I know her, that she possibly is an older girl from the neighborhood.

How long has she been like this? says the man, putting his hand in front of her face.

—I don't know. I just got home from school.

They are putting their hands all over her. Her limp body. The man puts his hand before her face where I had mine. They are lifting her eyelids. They are lifting her shirt. I look away and then back. Sticky things go on her very pale skin. A tube goes down her throat.

Chair, says the man, and the girl pounds down the stairs and while she is gone the man asks me things I can't process about medication. My mouth opens and closes like a fish and I breathe faster and faster and faster.

When the girl comes back she looks at me for a moment and I see from her gaze that she recognizes me too and pities me. She says nothing. They strap my mother to the chair and shuttle her down and out and I am not sure if I am invited until the man says Come here.

I try to stand up but all of my limbs are numb as if they have fallen asleep. I force myself.

On my way out I notice an envelope on the floor. And my name is written on it. My baby nickname. Kelly.

I fold it and put it in my back pocket. Then I run downstairs.

Blessed

After over a month of silence from Charlene, I had begun to lose hope of hearing from her ever again. & I had begun to feel quite foolish for the ways in which I preemptively turned my life upside down in preparation for some visit that, by this morning, I felt sure would never in fact take place.

I didn't regret them, the several changes I had made—I feel very glad for having met Yolanda, & of course it is better for me to have someone to converse with & all that—but it reminded me once again of the foolishness of always being hopeful throughout my life, & then always being let down, in one way or another.

I was in the midst of contemplating this, when the strangest & most magical thing happened. & it felt to me as if someone really was answering my prayers. & for the first time since I was a child I felt close to God & blessed by His presence.

Charlene Turner Keller called me. Finally. When she did I nearly cried—despite my best efforts to persuade myself to move along, I still care deeply for her—& I buckled. I am very glad that I was sitting down.

This was our conversation.

Me: Hello?

Charlene: This is Charlene.

Me: Charlene. [You see I couldn't believe that this was actually happening, for I had worried that she would never call again.]

Charlene: Miss you. How you doing. [Again it was clear that she was intoxicated. It was early afternoon.]

Me: Very well, Charlene. How are you?

Charlene: Not so great. [In fact she sounded teary & strange.]

Me: I'm so sorry to hear that. Is anything the matter?

Charlene: Just the usual. [A very long silence.] Have you been calling me?

Me: Yes, I have. Did you receive my letter.

Charlene: Yes.

Charlene: I'm sorry.

Me: That's all right.

Me: I'm sorry too. Were you shocked?

Charlene: Has my son called?

Me: No, he hasn't. Was he supposed to?

[Another long pause ensued, and I could hear her breathing, heavy and labored, & I could hear in it that she was upset but I did not know what to do. So I said nothing. Until finally she spoke.]

Charlene: I want you to call him.

Me: Me? [What I was thinking I cannot say.]

Charlene: Yes. On his cell phone. [Her voice: higher than it should have been.]

[She dictated his number in that same strange high voice, the wavering high voice she has recently used that sounds both like and unlike the Charlene I once knew. I wrote down each digit she gave me on the newspaper in front of me, taking a pen from my shirt pocket.]

Charlene: You'll call him?
Me: I will.
Charlene: He needs your help.
Me: I certainly would like to help him.
Me: When should I call him?
Charlene: Today.
Me: All right, then.

[And there was nothing. For a very long time there was nothing. I heard her breathing and she heard me breathing and I did not want to say anything for her breathing comforted me. I could not tell if she was crying. Finally she spoke.]

Charlene: You'll like him.
Me: That's very good. I'm looking forward to talking to him.
Charlene: You will.
[Finally I could not take it.]
Me: O Charlene . . .

[& then she hung up. Before I could figure out why she was so upset.]

I sat with the receiver in my hand for several minutes, until its drone became part of the air around me, & then I placed it gently in its cradle. I picked it up again after taking several deep breaths, & then dialed the number she'd given me for her son. Before I lost courage.

It rang several times & then I heard not his voice but a song I didn't recognize—like the one on Yolanda's phone. Intimidated, I hung up before any *beep* could sound. It was just after 2 in the afternoon. A boy his age would be at school, anyway. Maybe in some fluorescent hallway, maybe clutching his bookbag and maneuvering through a crowd. I vowed to try him again tomorrow, at a likelier time of day. A thing I am looking forward to. Yes: old Arthur Opp has his hopes up, once more. That foolishness again.

Still. I feel different somehow than every time before. I have Yolanda in my life, & Yolanda has a child on the way, & Charlene has called again, & has given me a concrete task related to her son. I have a cupboard full of good things to eat & several particular favorites to watch on television tonight. I have a cleaner house than I have had in years & a more organized house. In all I feel as if my luck is turning, & as if some benevolent force has caused my life to explode, suddenly, fruitfully, to blossom into some ecstatic dream.

A Week

It is six in the evening on Monday and they are putting my mother in the back of an ambulance, hooking her up to an IV. The girl paramedic runs to the front of the ambulance to drive it. I'm in the back. The man asks me questions that I cannot hear or reply to. *Just let me think a minute,* I want to tell him.

Eventually he stops trying.

It seems as if my mother is breathing now but I can't tell. And I can't ask. And I want to put my hand on her but I don't because she is no longer mine, she belongs to the paramedic.

When we get to the hospital they jump out and take my mother with them and I jump out after them in time to see them running her in through the open emergency room door. I run after them. I can run faster than they can. Then they take her through swinging doors and I try to follow them but another nurse stops me in my tracks. I see the top of my mother's head disappear as the doors close. The way the light is hitting it makes her scalp shine through her thinning hair.

Can't come back here yet, kiddo, says the nurse, and then she looks back over her shoulder and says something to someone and then says to hang on.

Have a seat in the waiting room for one minute, she says.

I haven't found my voice yet but I don't want to obey her. I want to go with my mother. The nurse is a tall lady and fat and she gives me this look that's a mix of pity and warning so I listen. I walk backwards to a seat and I put my head down on my knees. I do not want to be looked at.

Someone sits down next to me and asks me for my mother's name and her birth date and her Social Security number and her insurance. I only know the first two. I don't know if she has any, I say, about insurance. I never lift my head.

When a young doctor comes out and asks me to follow him I do so reluctantly. He takes me to a little room and picks up his clipboard and pen and the first thing he tells me is he's not a doctor, he's a med student. He's not that much older than me. He asks me things about my mother like what medicine she takes and what sicknesses she has.

—Lupus.

He pauses. When was she diagnosed?

—I don't know. I was little. Ten years ago maybe.

—Is she being treated?

—She was at first.

—With what?

—I forget. The name.

—Plaquenil?

Maybe, I say.

—She doesn't take anything anymore?

—No.

—When's the last time she saw a doctor?

I don't know the answer to this. Five years, probably, I say.

—Why so long?

We're poor. She's drunk. All the time. I don't say this. I shrug.

He is jigging his leg up and down. I think he is very new.

So, he says. Has she tried this before?

What, I say.

He's stumped. He lifts and lowers his pen.

—Has she ever intentionally hurt herself?

I hesitate. She drinks too much, I say. She passes out a lot.

Eventually he releases me into the waiting room. I put my head down on my knees again. I stay this way for a very long time. I would like to say that I pray but I don't, I can't. My mind is blank and I keep it blank. When at last I lift my head I see that I am alone in the room but for one old lady sitting next to me and a couple sitting on the other side. This is the strongest I have ever wanted a family. Other people to worry with. I am the only person worrying for her and it feels to me like this diminishes her odds of recovery. To have many people praying for you suddenly seems like a necessary thing, and I consider telling the woman next to me what is happening if only to have another person thinking about my mom. She looks nice, the woman next to me. She's a grandmother I think. She's wearing grandmother shoes. She's knitting. I wish I could knit. I wish I could do something with my hands.

I can't speak, though. I can't do anything.

It's eight at night. I see by a clock on the wall.

My mind goes toward places I don't want it to go. I feel superstitious about letting it go there. Skipping ahead toward scenes I don't want to imagine. When I was a boy I did this sometimes. In elementary school I imagined her dead and then pinched myself to prevent it from happening. Always the same way: I imagined being called out of gym class, called to the principal's office, where Mr. Carty would sit me down to give me the news. I would react stoically at first and then run from the school. These were mixed fantasies. There was some pleasure in them someplace. The pleasure of feeling sorry for myself. The pleasure of making a clean break into misery after always dangling above its canyon. Then the pinch: Stop it, I told myself. And this I also tell myself now.

The swinging doors open and everyone in the waiting room looks up. It is for none of us, it is a nurse walking out the front door. Everyone looks down.

She is what I have. I am what she has.

Just let me think a minute.

If she dies I will have to find my father. But I am eighteen and therefore don't need a father who does not need me. I am eighteen and will be alone in this world.

Just let me think a minute.

If she dies I will live in the house by myself.

If she dies I can go anyplace I want to play baseball. Pinch.

If she dies I will be alone in this world.

I should call Trevor. I should call Lindsay. All I really want to do is call Lindsay and then put my head against her and fit her in my arms but I have never told her about my mother. Never once. Furthermore I never told my mother about her which makes Lindsay seem less real.

The doors swing open. An ancient doctor with a white lab coat and enormous gray eyebrows.

Mrs. Keller's son? he says.

I sort of raise my hand.

—Follow me, please.

We walk through those doors. He stops just inside them and leans against the wall so I do the same. Facing him.

What's your name? he says.

—Kel.

He raises his eyebrows again.

I'm Dr. Moscot, he says. He puts his hands behind his back and then crosses them in front. Right hand over left hand over file folder.

Let's keep walking, he says, and we go back into the same room that the med student took me to.

Have a seat, he says.

Now Kel, he says. Do you have a father?

In Arizona, I say. We're not in touch.

How about aunties or uncles, he says. Grandparents?

Again I shake my head. Now I know it is very bad. I am waiting to fall into the canyon. I am waiting for the plunge, for the drop.

I'm going to be very up-front with you, says Dr. Moscot, because I can tell you're a strong young man. Things don't look good. Your mother isn't responding at the moment. We're not quite sure how long she wasn't breathing for, and I hear you're not sure either. Her initial bloodwork seems to indicate that she consumed a large amount of Valium, and when you mix Valium with alcohol it's very dangerous. Do you understand?

He pauses.

He says, I'm afraid it's unlikely that she'll wake up. She was a very sick lady.

He sort of shakes his head.

I am very very silent. I cannot breathe or move. It is not so much a drop as a slow descent.

—The neurologist will be here first thing in the morning. We'll do some tests on her to see if her brain is working at all. You understand?

He won't stop saying this. I do not acknowledge him. I do not move.

I noticed the rash on her face, he says.

I force myself to nod.

—I hear she has lupus.

Mild, I say. It was always mild.

Again the huge eyebrows head north.

I see, he says.

I'm not so sure, he starts to say, but then he takes pity on me and stops.

He leans toward me. I lean away. She must have been in a lot of pain, he says. As if that will make me feel better.

Tell me if she'll wake up, I say.

—I can't tell you that.

What are the odds, I say.

I like odds. I like statistics.

—I can't tell you that.

But the look on his face.

Not good, he says finally. Never good in situations like these. Grim.

I can't help it and I cry. I don't want to cry in front of this man but I do. I cry a lot for a long time. Not loudly, I don't let myself cry loudly, which is what I want to do. I want to wail. I put my hands on my face to try to cover it but it's very bright in this little room and I feel as if I have a spotlight on me. I turn my back to him. I swivel around in my chair.

Do you want to see her? he asks me after a minute.

—Is she going to die tonight.

Probably not, he says. But you never know. We have her stabilized. Her brain is mainly what we're worried about, but it seems like her other organs were probably affected as well. You understand?

OK, I say.

—OK?

—I'll see her.

Pinch.

Dr. Moscot leads me down a hallway and up a flight of stairs. Then he swipes his ID and walks through a set of fire doors and we walk down another hallway. I walk behind him. We don't speak.

We come to a booth with two nurses in it and they are laughing. About what I don't know.

We walk past them and Dr. Moscot pulls back a curtain and there is my mother asleep. She looks green. She looks yellow and green. My first thought is how strange it is to see her out of the house at all. It's been years. My next is to wake her: it is what I do when I see her asleep, when I see her drunk and asleep.

Slowly I walk toward her, heel before toe, and I put one hand on her arm, avoiding the needle and tape. She is blanketed. Her baldness is exposed. Her rash stands out on her face, very red and irritated. One bluish glint of eyeball appears beneath her lashes. There is the honey-bee on her arm. There, snaking over her shoulder, is the blue-inked cord of her electric guitar.

OK, I say. OK.

I'll leave you for a while, says Dr. Moscot.

Nope, I say. I have to go.

—Where?

I look at him. It's none of his business.

Do you have somebody to go home to? asks Dr. Moscot.

Yes, I say. I could tell him something more— I could make up a lie to make him feel better but I don't. I don't want him to feel better.

I start walking. I wipe my face on the sleeve of my jacket and leave a trail of snot on it.

Young man, says Dr. Moscot. We have—

But I'm gone before he can finish, I'm through the double doors.

Walking through the waiting room is hard. The grandmother looks up from her knitting and gives me a heartbroken look. I run. I'm out the door before anyone else can see me. It's dark and cold outside and I rode here in the ambulance and now I don't know how to get home so I start walking.

I'm not really sure what to do. Just let me think, I keep saying. I don't want to go back to my house. I cannot bear the thought of sleeping in my own house without my mother there. I could call Trevor but I don't want to because I suddenly hate him. I take out my phone and I go through all the numbers in it.

I stop when I get to Dee Marshall's name. I haven't talked to him since he started hating me after I left Yonkers. But he was my best friend for fourteen years. I call him without thinking. I don't know why but it feels right to do this.

Dee Marshall doesn't answer. I leave a silent message. Five seconds long. I say nothing and hang up.

It takes me half an hour to walk to my home which is no longer a home. I do not go inside. Instead I get into the car and back out of the driveway. All of this I do unseeingly and unthinkingly. I do not look both ways. But no one hits me. This I take as a sign of something.

When I am nervous before a game I have a trick that I do. It involves turning off my brain. It involves not letting myself be nervous by simply not thinking about what I'm nervous about. I do this now. I turn off the pain by not letting myself give in to it. I drive toward the Saw Mill. And go up it. As if I am going to school.

Just let me think a minute.

Do not come in. Call police.

The horrible wrongness. The wrongness of doing something like that to me.

I put on 1050 AM and listen to Charlie Rasco.

Lawrence Tynes kicked an overtime field goal to lift the Giants over the Falcons yesterday. After the clock ran out on the first quarter, the Knicks' Nate Robinson jokingly shot a three-pointer for the Nets which his coach was not happy about. And callers are not happy about.

When I get to school I pull into the parking lot. It is a comfort to me to see the building, which really looks like a castle at night. They light it with spotlights and the stone glows beneath them. At school I am generally happy and relaxed. At school I have friends and I am respected. I have friends.

Charlie Rasco says Eli Manning is maturing as a leader.

I take out my phone and call the radio station which I used to do at night when I was a boy but have not done in years. When I was a boy I loved Charlie Rasco.

Someone who isn't Charlie answers the phone and says ESPN Radio.

I'm calling to talk to Charlie, I say.

About what, says the operator, who's eating. I can hear him eating something.

—Well, I'd like to talk to him about Eli Manning.

What about, he says again.

I have to disagree with him, I say. About Eli. I think if his last name wasn't Manning he'd be a backup in San Diego right now.

—What's your name?

Kel, I say.

—Cal?

—Yeah.

OK, says the operator. Hold please.

The radio is still on. Charlie is still talking but I can't really understand him anymore. I'm having trouble paying attention. Then a voice in my ear and a voice on the radio says, Cal's on the line with us now. Cal, what's up?

But my voice is gone again.

Cal? says Charlie. Looks like we lost him.

It's only now that I remember that I still have my mother's letter folded into my back pocket. I take it out and look at it.

There is her handwriting. *Kelly,* she wrote.

A trembling inside me. A rush. I put it down on the seat next to me. I can't read it yet, because of what it will mean if I do.

I sit perfectly still for a long time. I do not turn the radio off. When I start to get very cold I think of the places I could go, ruling out my house because it's not my house anymore. It's no one's house.

I think of driving to Dee Marshall's. He probably saw my call. But he hasn't called me back.

I think of driving to Lindsay Harper's, but the embarrassment of that, of waking her family, her two baby sisters, is too much for me.

Finally I decide on Trevor's house, because his parents already know me very well, and I have always had this feeling that they pride themselves on Trevor's friendship with someone like me, and that they feel that having me in their house makes them well and truly part of the world.

On Tuesday morning I wake up in the Cohens'
house, in one of their dozen beds, in one of their
many rooms. I know where I am right away.
There is no moment of recalling: I know everything. I have been dreaming about it.

Last night I got to Trevor's house and I sat in the
car in their circular driveway for about ten
minutes. There was Mr. Cohen's Audi and there
was Mrs. Cohen's BMW. I got scared to go up to
their door. It was after midnight. I tried calling
Trevor's phone but he did not answer. Finally I
summoned all of my courage and walked up to
the door and before I could ring the bell the
motion detector light went on. I started shaking
actually shaking and I stood there for a minute
deciding whether I was going to leave.

Before I could the door flew open. Mr. Cohen
stood there in his bathrobe squinting at me. He is
a stocky man with a lot of gray hair and round
glasses. I could tell he didn't recognize me at first.
Then from behind him I heard his wife say *Kel!*

Hi, I said. I didn't know what to say so I said hi.

Are you OK, sweetheart? asked Mrs. Cohen.
She came forward into the light and I could see
she was wearing a fancy silk robe that looked like

it was from Japan or China. Pink with birds on it. She is very very thin and I could see all the bones in her chest and all the veins in her bare feet.

Fine! I said.

—Are you . . . here to see Trevor?

I heard in her voice the fear that Trevor had turned into a bad kid overnight. That I had turned him into a bad kid who got visitors at midnight.

Well, I said. OK. My mom's in the hospital.

Oh no, said Mrs. Cohen. Oh, no. Come in, darling.

Trevor came downstairs then and kind of looked at me blankly. We were all still standing in their hallway.

Hey Trev, I said.

What are you doing here? he asked.

—Honey, Kel's mom is in the hospital. What happened, Kel? Do you want something to eat?

I felt Trevor looking at me. I had never felt lower in my life. I felt him staring at me.

Well, I said, I've never told you this. But she has lupus. She took a bad turn.

Trevor's father made a low humming noise. His mother put both hands on her face and went *Ohhhh*. Like, *Ohhhh, I've always wondered why people said your mom was so fucked up*.

What's lupus, said Trevor, and his mother whirled around to frown at him. It's very serious, Trevor, she said. It's a very serious disease. I mean—she looked back at me—isn't it?

Um, I said. I guess it can be.

194

Honey, said Mrs. Cohen, do you have family? Was anyone with you at the hospital?

I could tell this was a question she had always wanted to ask me.

His dad's dead, said Trevor.

Yeah, I have a big family, actually, I said, but they're all from California. Most of them live in California.

Say no more, said Mr. Cohen. What this boy needs is a bed!

Walt, said Mrs. Cohen, don't you think he might want something to *eat?* And she looked at me and rolled her eyes. He's probably been in the hospital for *hours.*

I'm OK, I said, and she said Don't be silly.

We all went into the kitchen. The Cohens have two refrigerators. That's something. Two refrigerators in one kitchen.

Mrs. Cohen opened one of them and said Let's see what Maxine put in here. Is there anything in particular you want?

Trevor had pulled a stool up to the island in the center of the room at this point and he was still gazing at me, kind of like he was annoyed. He was wearing pajama pants with rockets on them. If I'd been in a better place I would have made fun of him. His father was sitting next to him. I was hovering behind Mrs. Cohen as she went through her own refrigerator as if she'd never looked in it before.

Ham, she said. Turkey. Cheese. Sandwich? Fruit. Here's a roast chicken, she said. Then she opened the freezer. Ooh, ice cream, she said, and I said yes to that because it seemed the simplest to me.

I'll have some too, she whispered, and held a finger to her lips as if she were doing something very naughty. Guys?

Trevor and Mr. Cohen both shook their heads.

Mr. Cohen asked me what she was in the hospital for, exactly, and I said she had passed out which was the truth.

They're just keeping her there to do tests on her for a while, I said, which was partially the truth and partially a lie.

Mrs. Cohen and I ate vanilla ice cream together and then we all went upstairs. Trevor's little sister April who is a freshman at Pells was sleeping in her room but Mr. Cohen said I could take any of the other rooms. There were five to choose from. I chose the one next to Trevor's. Blue walls with a bright white bed.

Trevor gave me clothes to sleep in and after I changed and got into bed Mrs. Cohen knocked softly on my door.

If you need anything, honey, she said, and pointed down the hall at their room.

You know you're welcome to stay here any-time, she said.

I nodded.

They're nice to me. The Cohens.

• • •

Today, waking up in the Cohens' bright white bed, I must make the decision of whether or not to go to school. It is not a hard one: I'm going. If I missed school I'd have to miss practice and if I missed practice I'd have to miss the Thanksgiving Day game on Thursday and these are the only things right now that make me glad to be alive.

I get out of bed and take a shower in the bright white bathroom and put on the same clothes I wore yesterday except for a shirt I have borrowed from Trevor. I pick up my cell phone and call the number that Dr. Moscot gave me, as he instructed me to do, but the woman who answers my call tells me that he is not in yet. It is 6:50 a.m. Why would he be.

At midday I get a phone call from a Westchester number and the caller leaves a message. I sneak into the bathroom to listen to it: Dr. Moscot, asking me to please call him. I do, from the bathroom stall I am in.

Dr. Moscot says she had made a noise and that she has opened and closed her eyes. But please know, Kel, he says, that this doesn't necessarily mean she's recovering. It could mean she's entering a permanent vegetative state.

On top of this: her organs, many of them, are failing her.

The outlook is still not good, says the doctor.

I say nothing.

But there's still a chance, the doctor says. A little chance of anything.

He says, Do you want to come see her again?

And I say I do, I will.

During practice I miss a phone call from an unavailable number. Again. Again the caller does not leave a message.

At five I drive to the hospital and when I walk into her room she looks better than she did last night. She looks asleep and alive. She looks cleaner than she has in years. Somebody has washed her. And she moves a couple of times on her own and it seems so natural that I get kind of hopeful. I tell myself not to but I do. She looks peaceful.

On the way back to Trevor's I go into our house just to get some of my things and it feels like a ghost house. I run from it fast as I can.

Tonight, as I am waiting for sleep to come, I try to imagine my mother asleep as well, resting and happy. Then the next second I imagine her having terrible nightmares from which she cannot wake up.

Wednesday is the worst day so far. At school, in computer class, I Google *lupus*. It is a mistake. Believe it or not I have never done this before, which is something I'm now ashamed of. And as it turns out I've been a bad son, because the things I hated her for were not her fault. Not entirely.

I'm sorry for leaving her all alone every day. I should have found her friends. I should have come home after school. What did she do all day? What did she do in the house all day?

My mother. There were times when I loved her so thoroughly. I can remember things about her. The smell of her skin, the humanness of her skin, the secret that only babies know about their mothers. The smell of it especially in summer. The mother smell. Beneath everything else I could smell it on her still when I found her in her bed.

Trevor's house is so beautiful and so full of delicate things that I have to stop myself from breaking them one by one every night before bed. The antiques and the clocks and the little statues. The little paintings on the wall. The wallpaper itself is asking for ripping. The sheets for tearing. The vases full of enormous flowers for spilling.

I have gotten used to my very white bed. It's high off the ground and it feels like there are pillows underneath me when I sleep. My mother would love it and it would be good for her back and her joints. I would like to buy her a bed like this someday. Trevor's family maid Maxine makes it up for me while I am at school. I have a feeling she washes the sheets every day. Every day. I did not realize she would do this. That Trevor is used to this frightens me and makes me doubt him as a friend. Before school, I have started making my bed up very carefully the way she makes it up. With the comforter turned down one-third of its length. With the pillows plumped and organized in rows of blue and white and purple.

I have not spoken to Lindsay Harper since Monday. I don't know if I can go to her house after Thanksgiving dinner. I'm having dinner with the Cohens. How will I leave.

I don't know what to say to her. I'm sure she has heard something because Trevor has a humongous mouth and has probably told everyone what happened. She's probably heard. She called me once and did not leave a message. In history class today I did not meet her eye and at the end of it I left without stopping.

Recently a thousand questions have occurred to me that I would like to ask my mother. What were you like when you married Dad? Did you laugh more? Did you drink less? Did he think you were pretty? Did he treat you well at first?

I used to have this fantasy. I used to dream about going back in time to when she was a kid and being her friend and protector. I think I know what she was like when she was little and I think other kids wouldn't have been nice to her. When I too was little this used to upset me, the idea of this. I wanted to go back in time to be there whenever any little boy was too rough with her in sports, whenever any little girl whispered a mean word behind her back. I wanted to be there to guide her into acceptance and popularity which are gifts I have been given without knowing why or from where.

I still haven't read her note. In the hopes that she will come back.

Come back.

Thursday morning is Thanksgiving. When I wake up I start to plan what I will get for my mother to eat before I even open my eyes and then I remember. There is a bathroom between my room and Trevor's room and I can hear him in the shower. He sings when he's happy which he is on game days.

I'm nervous. Playing Yonkers always makes me nervous but today especially. Seeing Dee Marshall will make me remember lots of things about my younger life. About my mother.

I hear a creaking noise outside the window at the head of my bed and I flop onto my stomach and look into the backyard. Maxine is out there. It's seven in the morning and Maxine is out there turning a huge turkey on a spit. She's wearing jeans and a sweater instead of her uniform. I imagine the Cohens have encouraged her to do this as a way of making her feel casual and included. She's listening to her iPod and yawning.

Trevor and I have to get ready for the game. He pounds on the door between the bathroom and my room and says GET UP!

Up, I say.

While I'm getting ready Mrs. Cohen knocks on our doors and tells us we should eat breakfast before we leave. When I open my bedroom door I can't believe the smells that come drifting upstairs. I've slept at their house a lot of other times but this is amazing. It smells the way a beautiful magazine looks. Trevor's little sister April is sitting at the island in their kitchen when I come in and she swallows her juice very quickly and does not say hi to me. I don't think she has said one word to me since I've been here which I think is nerves rather than ill will.

Hey April, I say.

She waves at me without turning. She's nothing like Trevor. She's very smart and has long hair all the way down to her butt and she wears glasses every day and reads all the time and is even reading now at the island. She's very fat which I think Trevor and his entire family are embarrassed of. She's more than plump. Her body swallows the stool she's sitting on. Mrs. Cohen looks at her daughter from head to foot sometimes, I've noticed it, as if she is wishing to be able to do something about her, about her fatness. To do something about it the way you would do some-thing about a leaky faucet. It is something I don't like about Mrs. Cohen.

Oh Maxine, she says suddenly, looking out one of the huge windows that face the backyard. She has to turn that more slowly or it'll never brown.

She heads outside, apparently to coach Maxine on turkey turning.

April and I are the only ones in the kitchen and I want to say something, anything.

Who do you have this year? I ask.

For what? asks April, peering at me over the top of her glasses.

Um. I don't know, English, I say.

Ms. Langley, she says.

Oh, I say.

Fortunately Trevor comes in then all dressed and ready and he pounds his fist into his hand and says GIA! NTS!

Giants, I say.

Every year we play our Thanksgiving game at the same field that is neither in Yonkers nor Pells. When my mother was better and working at PLHS she used to go to them every year and bring me with her from the time I was a kid. It was the only time she ever rooted against Pells for anything: secretly we would cheer when Yonkers won; secretly we would huddle under a blanket on cold days and chant *Yon*kers, *Yon*kers, *Yon*kers under our breath and she would buy me a cider from the stands which I would wrap my little hands around for warmth.

She never saw me play on Thanksgiving because by the time I made varsity she was bad-off. On the way there I pretend that the Cohens are my parents and that Trevor and I are brothers but it feels wrong.

We ride in the back of the Cohens' SUV and Mrs. Cohen is swiveled around toward us for the whole ride. She is dark-haired and her skinny legs are crossed and wrapping around each other too many times.

Gonna win? she asks us brightly.

Doubt it, says Trevor, but I know he's being a wiseass because boys like Trevor always think they will win at everything they do no matter what history has shown them. Sometimes I feel this way and sometimes I don't. Right now I don't. I'm more nervous than I've ever been for any game. I'm nervous to see Dee Marshall. I'm worried that I will cry. I'm worried that my emotions will come gushing forth into a puddle on the field. I try my trick of turning off the faucet of my nerves but it does not work.

One thing I didn't even think of to worry about happens as soon as I get out of the car.

There is Lindsay.

Lindsay and her whole family. Her two blond baby sisters who broke my car. Her superintendent father. Her lawyer mother. The Cohens and the Harpers know each other of course and they come toward us.

Last night at 10 p.m. Lindsay texted me: *are u ok.*

I didn't write back.

Jeanie! says Mrs. Cohen, and Sharon! says Mrs.

Harper. They throw their arms around each other like old pals. Then Mrs. Harper sees me.

—Hi, Kel! How are you, sweetie?

I'm great, I say.

Will we see you later today? asks Mrs. Harper, and Mrs. Cohen turns and looks at me curiously.

Mom, says Lindsay, very very softly.

Well, I say. I'm actually kind of—staying with the Cohens right now. I don't.

Suddenly I cannot speak.

OK, says Mrs. Harper, looking confused.

Have a good game, says Lindsay, and she leads her whole family away by walking briskly toward the field.

The locker rooms aren't much here. They do not feel holy. They feel bright and unused. After his speech, right before we go out on the field, Coach gathers us in a huddle and says Now listen. Yonkers is tough. Those kids are tough and they're looking for blood. The only thing that means is we gotta be tougher. We gotta show them who's boss. Defense. Defense. Defense.

All together we go *GIA! NTS! GIANTS!* And break.

Before I can go out on the field Coach puts a hand on my shoulder and keeps me there. Everyone files past us. When the locker room is empty he looks at me and says Mr. Keller. Are you all right?

He is a quiet man who does not like to shout. He is well spoken except for when he is giving us our speeches and then he uses the same language that every coach has used throughout history out of some fear of breaking tradition.

I'm fine, I say.

I, he says, but then changes his mind. You're the key, he says. I have faith in you.

I want you to take a minute in here, he says, and gather yourself together, OK? Just take a minute.

He walks out. I sit down hard on the bench and put my head in my hands and realize that I do not want to be alone with my thoughts so I stay until I know Coach is gone and then leave.

When I walk out Dee Marshall is walking out of the locker room next door.

He comes right up to me. He's wearing his helmet already and I see his eyes above the bars of it.

You called me, he says, and I freeze up.

I say nothing.

Finally he says, I heard. About your mom.

I shrug. Yeah, well, I say.

How'd you hear? I ask. I can't help it.

That girl Tracy Diaz, he says, and suddenly the name of the girl EMT comes to me. I think of the sympathy on her face—she and the other guy shuttling my mother down the stairs, a thunder of footsteps—and tighten my fists.

I look around. He has the real version. I do not want any of my Pells friends to be near me right now.

How is she, he says.

Not good, I say, she's out. She might not wake up, ever wake up I mean.

My shoulders sink suddenly and I realize I have had them lifted to my ears for three days and I realize it is the first time I have uttered the truth aloud to anyone. My breathing steadies.

Man, he says, and shakes his head, and I miss seeing him every day. I miss him period.

You know, anytime you wanna come by, he says.

Really? I say.

Always, he says. You know. Anytime.

I don't know if it is this exchange or what but we lose spectacularly. 31 to 7. Dee is astoundingly good and I'm proud of him. Of his whole team. I have never played worse in my life. When I'm on the sideline no one talks to me. No one looks at me, not even Trevor. Coach sounds puzzled when he comes up to me. Are you *sure* you're OK? he asks, and I say I'm real sure.

After the game we pile into the Cohens' SUV. Parents up front. April in the back, one arm draped over the seat next to her, tapping out some rhythm on the upholstery. Me and Trev in the way back.

Trevor is furious. He cries when we lose, the baby. I know not to talk to him but I can tell that the Cohens are trying to figure out what to say.

Trev, says Mrs. Cohen, and Trevor says Do. Not. Speak to me.

Mrs. Cohen puts her hands up in the air like *Whoa, whoa,* and she turns fully around to smile at me. I smile back briefly. I like her.

Then Mr. Cohen glances at his wife, and then glances at me in the rearview mirror.

Hey Kel, he says. We were thinking. Would you—maybe it'd be nice to stop at the hospital today? After the meal? Say Happy Thanksgiving to your mom?

Maybe, I say.

There is a pause.

OK, says Mrs. Cohen. Well, would you like a ride there?

No thank you, I say.

Are you sure? says Mr. Cohen. Because we're not—

Guys, he said no, says April, from the back.

We're not far from it, says Mr. Cohen.

You *guys,* says April, and I love her suddenly.

When we get home there are tons of people in their house. The grandmother arrived while we were out and let herself in according to plan and she is running their kitchen like the captain of a ship. Trevor's aunts and uncles and cousins are all there.

Mrs. Cohen brings me around introducing me to everyone. It is clear by the overeager looks on their faces that they have already been told about me. About my mother.

Trevor goes directly to his room and does not say hi to anyone. He slams his door loudly enough for all of us to hear it.

Don't mind him, says Mr. Cohen.

I guess we don't have to ask if you won, says a man I assume is Trevor's uncle, and I smile weakly.

Do you want to go shower, honey? asks Mrs. Cohen. I realize I am standing in my full football gear and I still have my helmet tucked under my arm.

Sure, I say, and I walk away mechanically.

Well, I hear Mrs. Cohen say, thank God for you, Mom! We'd be eating at midnight if you hadn't—

And the grandmother says That poor *boy.*

I get dressed carefully. I noticed that everyone downstairs was wearing very nice clothes. The men were wearing jackets. Trevor's grandmother was wearing a dress and pearls. On my brief visit home I stuffed a ton of clothes into a laundry bag without really choosing, and then I brought the whole thing up to my room and left it in a corner. When I got home from school the next day most of the clothes were clean and folded and put into drawers in the white wicker dresser and the nice pants and shirts were ironed and hanging in the closet. I pick out Dockers and the blue shirt my mother bought for me freshman year, which still fits but barely. I shake them out briskly and then put them on. The shirt will barely button across my chest. I rummage in the bottom of the bag for my dress shoes and then I spit on them and lift up an edge of the bedspread and polish them.

I sit on my bed until I hear Trevor go downstairs, and then I follow him.

When I see him I'm ashamed. He's wearing a hooded sweatshirt and track pants and he's sockfooted. April's wearing jeans. Trevor's cousin Mark, who is his age and sort of a hippie and who I've met maybe twice, is wearing a T-shirt that says GONE PHISHIN' and his jeans have great gaping holes in them. Sometimes I still get things like this wrong. Quickly I kick off my shoes but it's too late. They've seen me and are staring. And the dress socks I'm wearing have holes in the heels.

At least *someone* around here looks nice! says Mrs. Cohen, swooping into the living room with a plate of cheese and meat. She kisses me on the cheek as she goes by, as if I have just arrived.

Toward the end of the meal Mrs. Cohen says You know what we used to do when I was a kid?

and no one hears her, so she clinks her glass with her knife and then drops it with a great clatter and suddenly I realize she is very drunk. I'm fascinated.

Excuse me, excuse me! says Mrs. Cohen.

Mom, Trevor says.

No, Trevor, listen, I'm serious, says Mrs. Cohen. This is what we used to do when *I* was a kid.

The table quiets.

We used to say what we were thankful for, says Mrs. Cohen. Is what we used to do.

For a moment she looks sad, or like she has forgotten where she is and what she's doing. Then she says, I'll go first. I'm thankful for my beautiful family—she looks around at each person at the table meaningfully, and because there are fifteen of us this takes a while—and for this house, and for Kel, who's—who's going through a hard time right now, and so we should all be very thankful for what we have. To Kel's mother, she says, and raises her glass.

I freeze.

Everyone freezes. Half of them raise their glasses an inch from the table and half of them do nothing.

Trevor props his head up on his fists.

April says, Um, I'll go. I'm thankful for—my friends, and I'm thankful for the food that we're eating. And for Grandma for cooking it.

You're welcome, April, sweetie, says the Grandma, almost as if she might cry.

Mr. Cohen says he's thankful for Barack Obama and everyone laughs and I can't tell why.

One after another they go around. When it is my turn I tell them I'm thankful for their hospitality and Mrs. Cohen says vehemently that I shouldn't be silly and that they love having me.

When it's Trevor's turn he says he's thankful this is over, and he stuffs a piece of turkey into his mouth, and the edge of it hangs out.

It's quiet after dinner. Everyone leaves. Trevor and April go to their rooms. Mr. Cohen goes into the basement which is where his huge impressive television is. The house becomes larger than ever, and every noise amplifies: the dripping of the sink, a car driving down the street faster than it should be. I offer to do the remaining dishes and Mrs. Cohen tells me not to be silly, but she's still drunk so after a minute she gets distracted and sits down at the island in the kitchen and I gently take over. The water feels nice. I run it as hot as I can stand it and the window before me steams up until my reflection disappears.

Mrs. Cohen pours herself another glass of wine but this time she offers me one too. I look at her. I can't tell what the right answer is.

No thank you, I say, and she looks disappointed. She reaches up and puts her brown straight hair into a pile on her head and holds it there, then lets it drop around her shoulders.

I turn back to the sink and the dishes.

You're a good kid, she says. Trevor's lucky to have a good friend like you.

Thank you, I say.

April's a good kid too. I worry—says Mrs. Cohen, but then changes her mind and stops.

She hums to herself and I can't tell what she's humming. I close my eyes for a moment because she can't see my face and imagine that she is my mother. That my mother is drinking behind me, yes she's drinking but she can take it—she can be loving and kind and she can do normal things from day to day. She can handle it. I miss her. I never even tried to help her.

When I'm done I go to leave and Mrs. Cohen says to me Handsome boy. She's not looking at me. She's looking into her glass.

A moment passes. Then another. I walk to the refrigerator and open and shut it.

Well, I say. I guess I.

And then, right then, my phone buzzes. I take it out of my pocket gratefully. It's a text from Dee Marshall. *Party at jims,* it says. *Come.*

I am quiet as I walk upstairs. Suddenly there is nothing I want more than to leave this house, to walk outside into the fall night and breathe in deeply and sharply, to change out of the clothes I am wearing and into something sloppy and old.

In the bedroom I sit on the bed and think that if I were a good son I would drive to the hospital and sit instead on my mother's bed, at her side, and put a cool hand on her forehead, as she used to do for me when I was a boy, and I would sing her a song of my choosing. And even if she couldn't hear me this would be the right thing to do. I also think that if I were a good boyfriend, or whatever I am, a good person, I would call Lindsay Harper and tell her I'm sorry for not coming to her house today, which I really am. Sorry. I'm sorry for letting her believe I had it in me to be good to her and normal. For letting her think I'd do right by her.

Anyway I'm not a good son or a good boy-friend or a good person so instead of doing these things I take off my too-small shirt and my cheap Dockers and I leave them rumpled on the floor out of this same badness. Then I quietly pull open every drawer in the dresser, looking for the worst and most terrible outfit I brought with me, and finally I find a pair of huge jeans I haven't put on since before I got to Pells. Now that I am bigger they fit me a little better but they are still baggier than what is fashionable and therefore they are right. I find a huge gray sweatshirt with a hood and I put the hood up. Then I find my tomato sneakers, the ones Pottsy made fun of, and I stick my feet into them with no socks. I look at myself in the mirror above the dresser and I see with satisfaction that I look awful, like the Grim Reaper under my gray hood: green under the eyes, a few days' worth of weak stubble on my chin and cheeks. Skinnier than I should be because I have not eaten right. I'm too tall for the mirror and I have to duck to see myself.

I walk quietly as I can into the hallway and try to sneak past Trevor's room but Trevor's door is open so I have to stop. He looks at me calmly from his bed.

What are you doing, he says.

He's caught me off-guard.

—Going to Yonkers.

He looks at me. Dude, he says, as if he can't believe my stupidity and traitorousness. Kel. We just fucking *lost* to Yonkers.

Yeah, well, I say, scratching the back of my hooded head. Friend's having a party.

I don't tell him who invited me.

Trevor shrugs. Whatever, he says.

—You wanna come?

—Nope.

OK, I say, and walk down the hall relieved.

But then Trevor emerges from his room and I know it's because he can't stand to be left out of anything. He has nothing to do tonight. I turn around.

I am aching to leave. I am standing there on the tips of my toes.

Trevor says fine he'll go. But only if we can roll in there with, like, a crew of four big guys, he says.

I want to laugh at him loudly. I want to tell him he's the most ridiculous person I've ever met and I can't believe I never realized it before this week. I want to tell him he deserves to lose at everything he ever does. Instead I tell him to invite whoever he wants.

Trevor drives. He puts on something boring and guitarish. He's on his phone calling his boys. I have realized that I cannot call them mine. Cossy can't come, his family says. Kurt says he'll meet us there and asks for the address. Peters is coming and Kramer is coming and Matt Barnaby, who I don't particularly want to see but Trevor likes him, so. We pick them up one after another at their homes, which are lit up inside and lined with little white lights outside and in general look like institutions more than houses. Museums.

Some of the driveways are still filled with cars. To get to Matt's house we drive right past Lindsay's and I strain to look without moving my head so Trevor does not make fun of me. Someone's standing in the driveway but I can't make out who it is.

When Matt Barnaby gets into the car he says We're going to Yonkers why?

And I'm happy when no one laughs or even replies to him.

When Kramer gets into the car he pulls out a liter-sized bottle of Coke that he has filled so it's mostly rum. He swigs from it and passes it around and when it gets to me I take several gulps in a row and wince and relax as the burn lowers into me.

When Peters gets into the car he asks me how my mother is and I tell him she's great, she's getting better and they think she'll be out by next week. It is the loneliest lie I ever told.

By the time we get off the Saw Mill I am glowing with rum warmth. I am smiling. When Matt Barnaby says something stupid I start calling him Junior and for some reason everyone thinks this is very funny, so I keep doing it. *What's that, Junior?*

I can tell he's getting mad but I don't care, I don't care, I don't care.

My cell phone goes off in the middle of one of

his stories and I say Hang on, Junior, just gotta take this real quick.

It's Dee Marshall.

Where you at? he says.

Five minutes, I say.

Who you with? he says.

Just some of my boys from school, I say.

Dee laughs in his low voice. Long as they're not jealous, he says, and I realize suddenly that it was Dee, five years ago, who first went around going *Jealous? Jealous?* That it's Dee I stole this from.

Who was that, asks Trevor, when I've hung up the phone.

This kid Jim having the party, I lie.

I'm not sure what will happen when we walk in and there is Dee Marshall and there are several other boys from the Yonkers football team, but I don't care. In some ways I am glad.

We're driving down McLean, which was a street that I spent a lot of time running up and down when I was a kid. My mother's favorite store is here: an Irish imports store. She had an Irish grandmother she used to tell me about. Tonight it looks sad and run-down. Empty because every-thing's closed for Thanksgiving.

Where . . . are . . . we . . . ? whispers Peters in a jokey spooky voice.

Turn here, I tell Trevor, and Trevor makes a careening right down Jim's street, which isn't the nicest street in Yonkers but I don't care, and neither is mine.

There are cars lining both sides of the road. So many that we have to drive to the end and then turn onto a different street to park.

I haven't been to Jim's since I was twelve or thirteen and because he doesn't play sports I haven't really seen him much since then either. Maybe once or twice. He grew up in a house full of brothers with a single father who was never around. I smoked my first cigarette with Jim and his older brother Pat when we were ten. I kissed Kelly Haslow in his junky backyard. Jim's was the house we went to when we wished to be bad.

Suddenly I wish that I could leave my Pells friends behind. Run up the stairs and fall into the warm embrace of Yonkers, of my real true friends from Yonkers. Instead, as we get out of Trevor's Audi, I turn around and say, Kramer, you still got that Coke bottle? and I take a very deep swig of it so that when I walk up the stairs at the front of the pack it is still blistering in my throat.

The outside of Jim's house looks as if it hasn't been painted in fifty years. There are rusted cans in front of the garage door, which is hanging askew on its hinges. Sad dead shrubs run in a line around the side of the house.

I try the door but it's locked so I ring the doorbell. I can hear the party inside, already going loud. Nobody answers for a while. A girl's loud voice makes its way out the window saying *No YOU no YOU no YOU!*

What's going on? Peters asks.

I turn to answer—my voice is stopped by the sight of them, my four friends, all earnest and tense, all dressed alike in bright bold-colored shirts and jeans that fit them very well. Boat shoes. All with the rich perfect haircuts their mothers buy them.

Before I can say anything the door flies open.

Jim is standing on the other side of it. He looks older than I thought he would. He's gotten fatter and he has the start of a beard. Kel Keller, he says, and he throws an arm over my shoulders and I am grateful to him and at the same time I wonder if Dee Marshall has told him about my mother.

Jim rotates me toward the crowded room and says my name again, louder, to the crowd. There is no hush but there are scattered glances my way, and then I hear my name repeated lowly around the room.

Jim's house on the inside is exactly as I remember it. Messy and empty of furniture and bare of carpet. A man's house but for the wall art of the floral or religious variety. When I came here as a little kid I used to wonder who had put it up.

Everyone's standing. In the hallway and living

221

room it is so dark that I have to wait for my eyes to adjust before I can move forward. Jim and I walk down the hall to the kitchen and my friends from Pells follow in a tight little line. When we walk past the people I used to know they do one of two things: if they're drunk they hug me or clutch my hand, and if they're not they frown at me.

When I went to school here these were all my friends. These are all people like me. Toughish boys who grew up poor or with one parent. Girls I dated or sisterly girls. I fit in here. I can feel my accent changing to greet theirs. We walk to the kitchen which is entirely linoleum with a sticky green floor and fluorescent lights. I see him first: Dee Marshall, massive and relaxed, leaning against a counter on the far side of the room. He's high off his ass, thank God, I can see it. There is no moment of tension, no face-off. He stands with two girls on each side of him. I only recognize one. All of them are different than Pells girls: harder, tanner, older-seeming. Dark makeup circling their eyes. Tight clothes and bodies and faces. Less smiling.

Dee points to me. I feel the trail of boys behind me shift and tense.

Then Dee's face lights up into a smile. Kel! he says, genuinely happy.

I walk over to him and we clasp hands and touch our shoulders together and then he asks the girls if they know me and all four of them nod. I was wrong I guess.

I turn and beckon to the boys from Pells and they sort of shuffle over, except Trevor, who stays back sullenly.

Peters, Kramer, Matt, I say, pointing them out. And that's Trevor back there.

Every single one of them knows Dee's name so I don't say it. Every single one of them got his ass handed to him by Dee Marshall eight hours ago.

They all nod to him coolly, and then Dee snaps four Buds from a six-pack on the counter behind him and tosses one to each of them. Underhand, not overhand, which is how I know there won't be any trouble.

Dee tells the girls to hang on a minute and walks me back into the other room. I glance over my shoulder and see my friends from Pells huddle together uncertainly, but suddenly I don't care. Suddenly I could care less. Let them get drunk and talk about me and then let them leave me here. Let them leave.

In the living room Dee and I sit in two chairs in the middle of everything and talk.

How's Rhonda? I ask him.

She found Jesus, he says, and kind of laughs and shrugs, because his mother was crazy when we were growing up, and he knows that I know that this is true.

She's better, he says, and then furrows his brow as if he isn't sure why he told me this.

After a while people come over to us and say hello to me and some of them tell me they're sorry to hear about my mother. It feels like family saying it and I nod slowly and gratefully each time. I'm drinking too fast. When Dee rolls a blunt I know I should decline but I want it in my system. Dee was the first person who ever got me high. And the first to sell me weed. I take a long slow hit and cough uncontrollably and embarrassingly. It's the tobacco. I am out of practice with blunts. Pells kids put little nubs of pot in cheap glass bowls that they buy from head shops in Times Square. I cough until I'm red in the face and tears are pooling in my eyes, but no one cares, no one notices. The mood in the room is slowing down and speeding up at once. In one corner Dan Ligiano is falling asleep with a beer in his hand and in another corner two people I don't know are making out.

A bunch of girls come over and sit on the floor in front of us. Most of them I recognize. Some of them I hooked up with in middle school or at the start of high school, when I still used to hang out in Yonkers on the weekends. Girls from Yonkers let you get away with more. The girls I hooked up with in Pells before Lindsay came along were more sure of themselves, more confident in their own goodness and worth. I could feel it the first time I kissed a girl from Pells. That she thought of herself as special. I look around now at the girls in this room and have sudden visions of some of them unclothed. I've lain on the grass in a park with some of them. I've been in a bed with some of them. I've put my hands all over them, all over their rib cages and breasts and legs and necks and, rarely, when I was feeling tender, their faces. I've taken off their clothing and they've taken off mine and we've acted out whatever rage or anxiety or lust we felt toward each other and then we got up off the bed— laughing sometimes, ashamed sometimes—and rejoined the party, subtly or unsubtly, depending. The weed is sinking into me and the rum and the beer and it's bringing out something in me that I thought might have been lost. I feel powerful and bold. I'm trying to catch their eyes, now, the girls I've known in this way. I'm trying to will them toward me.

Kel, says Dee, you remember when we played at that court on Warburton all the time?

He's talking about basketball. When we were twelve we played there after school every day. I nod. I am filled with happy certainty that I fit in here, that I am the king or the prince of something here.

A little blond girl comes up to Dee drunkenly and sits on his lap and I know her, I went to school with her once upon a time.

Sit on *his* lap, says Dee, who is trying to roll another blunt, and the girl obliges. She is light as a feather and swaying back and forth.

You remember me, she says, not asking.

Of course, I say.

I put my hand on her back, on the small of her back, unswervingly.

Peters comes into the room then wagging his phone. He looks happier or drunker.

Yo Kel! he says. Kurt's on the phone. How the hell do you get to this place?

Toss it, I say, and Peters chucks it across the room dangerously.

Kel? Kel? Kurt's saying on the phone.

I'm here, I say.

I'm so lost, says Kurt.

While I give him directions, the girl on my lap leans her head against my shoulder sweetly and casually and sort of pats my face. Her friends, three girls on the floor in front of us, fall over laughing.

Fuck *you!* she tells them, springing up, but it's a joke, and then she tells them she's sorry and she loves them too.

One by one the boys from Pells make their way into the living room and I see that they've found girls to talk to. The girls don't know what to make of them. They are halfway between humoring them and liking them. One of them is Steph Callahan who was always the most popular girl when I went to school here. She's strong and pretty and Matt Barnaby is trying to talk to her and she's trying to talk to Stacey Cavalieri.

Park behind Trevor's car, I tell Kurt. Drive till you see Trev's car and park behind it. There's a spot.

I hang up the phone. The girl on my lap kisses my cheek. A little murmur goes up from her friends.

I turn toward the girl on my lap and take her head and kiss it. I kiss her mouth. She takes my hand and I stand and we walk as if we are going toward the kitchen. Dee, behind me, says something I can't understand. I don't stop. We walk past my friends from Pells, who look at me and say nothing. We walk up the stairs, which are sticky with beer and maybe puke, and the girl leads me to a room that I know as Jim's from having been in there countless times when I was younger.

Jim's room, I say, and laugh because I think this is suddenly funny.

The girl doesn't know what she's doing. She opens the door and sees no one's inside and turns on the light. I see it is the same as the last time I was in here: basketball posters everywhere, clothes on the floor, a slanted ceiling, an unmade and sheetless bed. A ratty comforter slinking toward the floor on one side. Flat naked pillows. The girl turns the light off again and shuts the door and leads me toward the bed. I hit my head so hard on the slanted ceiling that I see stars and *Oh my God!* the girl says, but I'm OK, I'm fine.

Sit down, she says, and I sit on the mattress, shoving the comforter off entirely.

In the dark I imagine she is Lindsay Harper. I think of Lindsay's face and touch this girl on the cheek and ear.

We kiss. For a long time we kiss. I lie down and then she lies down and we kiss some more. I take her clothes off. She is smaller than Lindsay and thinner. She has none of Lindsay's firmness. She feels breakable, her bones are showing. I take my clothes off. She has gotten sleepy or afraid. She stops moving. I keep moving. I cover her. I hover over her.

Do you know my name, she says quietly.

And I know it, it's Jenny, but for some reason I say No, no, what is it?

And she says, Jennifer! and tries to make it sound like a joke, like a playful thing, but in her voice I hear that she is filled with self-doubt and regret.

I do it anyway. We do it. She is still and quiet as a stone. I don't finish. I stop before I finish.

The two of us lie on our backs next to each other. My head is pounding. The dark ceiling is moving slowly. I can see all the walls of Jim's room in the dark now because my eyes have adjusted. Most of the posters are basketball stars from the '70s to the present. Walt Frazier. Shaq, huge arms outstretched, mouth open. LeBron. Michael Jordan in his heyday, flying winglessly toward the basket for a slam dunk. Once Jim and Dee and I made a vow in this room to make it to the NBA together. We were eight or nine. Already I cared more about baseball but I wanted to fit in. Afterward I walked home to my mother's house.

I think maybe Jenny is crying. I don't want to find out. I want to cry too but I don't allow it. I want to put my hand on her hand and I want to cry. We lie on Jim O'Leary's bed silent and still. Until it becomes impossible to move, until I feel I am a statue, heavy and concrete.

There's a loud pounding on the door and Jenny clutches the comforter to herself and I try to do the same before the door flies open and lets in the light from the hallway.

Peters is there with Matt Barnaby.

What the *hell,* says Peters.

Get out! I say, but he says You gotta come downstairs, dude. Trevor's plowed and starting shit.

Shut the door! I say. Jenny has covered herself completely with the comforter and is pretending she does not exist, but her little feet are sticking out below it.

Who is that, says Matt Barnaby, laughing, just before Peters pulls the door shut.

Who was that, I hear him say again from the hallway.

We put our clothes back on and still we haven't spoken. She pulls the elastic out of her hair and piles it on top of her head again and ties it up tightly. Then she goes out ahead of me without a word.

When I walk out the boys are looking at me with raised eyebrows.

Where's Trevor, I say. I'm still drunk and I clutch the banister as we go down the stairs.

Trevor's out front, five inches from the face of someone much bigger than he is, and swaying.

This your boy? somebody says, and I nod sorrowfully because I wish he weren't.

Better get him under control, says the somebody. But suddenly I don't care. I stand back with the rest of the crowd. Kurt, who has found the place, apparently, and Peters step forward cautiously and go to pull him away but I say, Let him. Let him.

The kid Trevor's challenging is practically cracking his knuckles now, ready to go, when by some miracle, some fluke, the blue lights of a cop car come flashing up the street.

Bloop *bloop,* goes the car, and the crowd scatters like mice, into backyards and houses and down a little alley between Jim's house and his neighbor's. And we scatter too, grabbing Trevor on our way, dragging him. We each put a hand on the waistband of his jeans and his toes are rasping miserably along the pavement. He is saying things we can't understand.

Matt Barnaby takes out his iPhone and, giggling like an idiot, snaps a picture of him. Oh *man,* he says, blackmail.

Before Trevor gets in the car he says *Guys, guys, I can* handle *it,* stands on his own feet, sways like a leaf, and collapses.

Silently Kramer fishes in Trevor's pockets for his keys and then gets in the driver's seat.

I go with Kurt.

For the first five minutes of the ride we're silent.

I've sobered up a little but I'm still unpleasantly high and I'm starving.

Well, Kurt says finally, that was Yonkers.

No it wasn't, I say.

Kurt looks at me but I don't feel like explaining. Tomorrow, I know, and next week at school, my friends will tell stories about their *crazy* night in Yonkers, and how Trevor almost got into a fight, and how drunk Trevor was, and how there were all these people at this party, how the girls looked trashy, how the boys looked tough or poor or stupid.

Trevor's an asshole, says Kurt. It's unexpected.

Why? I ask.

Kurt shrugs. I dunno, he says, he just is. He

always has been. When we were little he used to hit me with his trucks.

I think his mom is nice, I say.

Me too, says Kurt.

Both his parents are, I say.

Kurt nods. He turns the radio to a station that plays old-school rap after 9 p.m. He is doing it for me, to be nice.

We pull into the Cohens' driveway and Kramer pulls Trevor's car in behind us. Immediately I know we're in trouble. It's one in the morning and all the downstairs lights are on. The front door flies open and Mr. Cohen comes out onto his steps.

Friday morning I wake up at 5:30 a.m. to the sound of my cell phone's alarm clock and feel as if I have been dried out completely, as if I have no water left in my body. I tiptoe to the bathroom and guzzle water straight from the sink and then I put on my clothes from last night without showering. I stink of processed alcohol and smoke and filth. I smell in some ways like my mother.

The hood on my sweatshirt goes up again.

I throw as much of my stuff as I can fit into a duffel bag and sling the strap across my body.

I find the unopened envelope with my mother's letter in it, the word *Kelly* smudged now from wear, and stick it into the back pocket of my jeans.

I poke my head out into the hallway and listen for a moment. I don't hear anyone which is good. I tiptoe down the stairs.

Last night, after Mr. Cohen came outside, Kramer and Peters dragged Trevor out of the car and up the driveway toward the house. He could walk a little better on his own by then but he was still swaying.

Oh my God, said Mrs. Cohen, joining her husband. She had apparently sobered up herself while waiting for her son to return. She was wearing her bird-covered robe and had her arms crossed around her middle so tightly that her hands could have touched in the back.

Oh my God, Walt, look at him, she said, and Mr. Cohen said I see him.

Heeeeey, said Trevor, waving a lazy hand above his head.

The other boys did not know what to do and hung back. I knew just what to do and I walked up to Trevor and slung an arm around him, very responsible, and I said to them, I think we better get him some water.

The Cohens cleared a path for us and I brought their son inside and flung him on the first couch I saw and went into the kitchen and got him some water which he immediately spilled down his shirt. Then he lay back on the couch like a rag doll.

Oh *Trevor,* said Mrs. Cohen.

She went and tried to lift his head up with her hands and dropped it again.

Geddoud, said Trevor. Grronabed.

Walt, said Mrs. Cohen, and Mr. Cohen tried uselessly to do what his wife could not. Mrs. Cohen meanwhile went across the room and sat on the edge of a chair. Her knees stuck out of her bird-covered robe. The top of it fell open just a bit and I saw the inside of her right breast. Her bone-ridged chest. I looked away.

When Mr. Cohen had Trevor sitting up, he looked at his wife and then he looked at me.

Well, said Mr. Cohen. You know, I'm not quite

sure how to handle this. He laughed a little angrily and squeezed the back of his neck.

I don't want to put you on the spot, he said. Trevor needs to hear this too. Maybe we should wait until morning to have a talk. Don't you think, Sharon?

Mrs. Cohen nodded, her head in her hands.

OK, then, said Mr. Cohen. Why don't you get some sleep.

I looked at them both.

I'm sorry, I said. I'm just really sorry about this.

No one said anything.

I walked up the stairs.

I set my cell phone alarm and lay awake until I could not keep my eyes open anymore.

This morning I leave the house as quietly as I can. I get in my car which takes three tries to start. By the time the engine turns over I am certain I have woken the whole house.

Pells Landing is silent. My car is making a noise like a tin can dragging. After a moment it begins to snow.

It's still dark out and some of the houses have Christmas lights on for the first time this year. My mind turns to Lindsay Harper and the things I sometimes dream of giving to her and for a moment I'm happy. It's not too late for us, I think. If I apologize to her. If I crack myself open to her and tell her all the things that so far I have

235

kept hidden from every friend I have. I imagine doing this: sitting before her cross-legged in her strawberry-scented basement, taking her hands in mine, letting words spill out of me like water, confessing to Lindsay Harper every sin I have, every fear I have, every hope. Then resting my head in her lap—my head, unburdened, light. I could do this. Suddenly I can see myself doing this and it seems to me the simple and lovely solution to every problem I've ever had.

The snow has picked up by the time I park in the hospital's parking lot and the cars on either side of me are white with it.

I'm underdressed in my sweatshirt and jeans and I run slipping across the lot, swerving to avoid an ambulance that roars in from the street.

The woman at the front desk looks at me lazily. Help you? she asks.

I'm here to visit Charlene Keller, I say.

Visiting's at eight, says this woman, fat and yellowheaded and unhappy.

But I'm her son, I say.

She looks at me. What unit, she asks.

I don't know, I say. She's—Dr. Moscot's patient.

Name again, says the woman.

Charlene Keller, I say, and this time I spell it.

Aright, says the woman. Fourth floor. Elevator down that hall. Tell the nurse up there what you want.

● ● ●

It's funny to think that this is only my mother's fifth day in the hospital. It feels like months. She's still in the last place I saw her, a curtained room, one of many centered around a nurses' station in the middle. This way, says the nurse on duty, and I follow her. She's wearing pink scrubs with teddy bears on them.

She leads me to my mother's bed. When I approach her, I see she looks just like she did last time. Her lips are slightly parted. She looks clean and restful. The tubes coming out of her don't look quite as frightening.

Hi, Charlene! the nurse says brightly. Hi, honey!

I say nothing.

She's been doin' good, says the nurse, but I don't know exactly what she means, and I don't ask.

I put down my hood. I don't touch her. I don't know what to do. I look at the nurse.

You can talk to her, says the nurse. Sometimes that helps.

Or sing to her, she says over her shoulder on her way out. Sing her her favorite songs.

The nurse shuts the curtain behind her. It's the two of us now.

I can't bring myself to sing. Instead I sit in the chair next to her bed and look at her, my mother, my still-living mother. My breathing mother.

Her chest and stomach going up and down slowly.

Mom, I whisper. It's Kel.

I think I see something flicker across her face.

It's Kel, I say again. Your son Kel.

A wave of guilt hits me hard. That I have not been here with her. That I have been in Pells Landing, her favorite favorite place on earth, without her. That I ate turkey in someone else's house.

I pull the chair closer. I put my elbows on my knees, and my chin on my hands. I pull the chair close enough so my shins touch the bed. For a while I sit and say nothing. The drone of the hospital gets louder. The drone of the fluorescent light above my mother's head.

All weekend I stay. It is a relief to be here. It is a long time. I pretend it is my home now. I go down and get myself lunch and dinner from the cafeteria each day. I sleep in the chair next to her bed, curled up into a tight little ball. My neck hurts. My back. The nurses come and go. One of them likes me better than all the other nurses do. Without asking she brings me ten issues of *ESPN* magazine and two issues of *Sports Illustrated*.

All day Friday I talk to my mother about my life. I tell her things I never dreamed of telling her. She lies there on her back and I think she looks peaceful. I tell her about Lindsay Harper. I tell her I think she would like Lindsay Harper, and that when she wakes up I'll introduce them. I tell her about Trevor's parents' house, the entire floor plan, and how they have a maid who makes their beds for them every day. And two refrigerators. I tell her about going to the party in Yonkers, missing my Yonkers friends. I tell her I've realized several things about my life. I tell her what I want to do in the future. I tell her that I have a private workout with a Mets scout in two weeks, which I already told her, but I tell her again. I know you want me to go to college, I tell her, but it's not right for me, it's not right. I tell her the things I thought about when I was little that I never had a reason to tell her. I ask her things about Dad and about herself. I tell her I'm sorry I've been so mean to her.

My cell phone rings at some point in the evening and wakes me from a nap. The unavailable number again. For the first time I am able to answer, and I do so as quick as I can, but there's no one on the other end.

Hello? Hello? Hello? I say. No one is there at all.

On Saturday afternoon I run out of things to talk to her about and on one of my trips downstairs I buy two of the magazines she likes, *Redbook* and *Cosmopolitan*, and I read aloud to her from them. I skip the embarrassing parts. I read advice on fashion and men and imagine it being useful to her someday. When I'm done with this I read the sports magazines. And drift in and out of sleep.

Different nurses come by a lot to check on her. Twelve times I see her hands move. Five times I see her open her eyes. Four times her head moves.

On Sunday morning the neurologist comes by to run another test on her. They wheel her out and leave me there. I don't try to be nice, I don't have it in me. When he comes back he tells me things do not look different.

He bites the inside of his cheek.

He opens and closes his mouth.

He wants to see if I understand the importance of what he's just said.

But I won't meet his eyes.

I nod slowly and I tell him OK.

The Cohens leave seven messages asking where I am which I feel bad not returning but I can't face them. Trevor texts me. Kurt and Peters and Kramer text me. Even Cossy.

Because I don't want them to worry about me, I text Trevor: *with mom in hosp. tell everyone for me. sorry.*

Trevor texts back, *i cant believe u just left.*

Then: *i'm in so much trouble.*

Monday morning I wake up and kiss my mother on the forehead and say goodbye. I go into the men's room and wash at the sink. Under my armpits, my hands, my face. I have almost a beard. My hair is getting too long for me. I open the duffel bag I brought with me from the Cohens' house and I rummage in it for something not too wrinkled and not too smelly and I come out with a polo. The only jeans I have are the ones I've been wearing all weekend. I pull my old sweatshirt on over the polo.

I walk outside. It's raining, freezing. The snow has melted but ice covers parts of the parking lot. A car has parked too close to mine and I have to climb in through the passenger's door of my car to get inside. On the drive to school it occurs to me that I have none of my books and that I have done none of my homework. But I can't miss a practice and I can't miss a game. They're the only things I feel like doing, so I go to school, I walk in through the front doors and walk into my homeroom and say hi to people, I talk to them. I feel empty as a balloon. I feel like my words are echoing off of something.

When I pass Trevor in the hallway he doesn't stop.

When I see Kurt in physics second period he says Oh my God, Kel, what's wrong with you, which is a strong thing for him to say. You look like shit, he says.

Is Trevor really mad? I ask.

What do you think, says Kurt.

Are his parents?

He shrugs.

My mom, I say, but I stop.

Ms. Dietrich begins class by giving us an exercise to do while she walks around and checks our notebooks to make sure we've done our homework.

Kel? she whispers, when she gets to me. I don't have paper and I don't have my textbook and I don't even have a pencil.

I forgot it, I say.

Forgot what? she whispers. Your homework? Your bookbag?

Everything, I say.

She sighs and moves on to Kurt, making a little red mark in her grade book.

While everyone else works on the problem she's given us, I reach into my back pocket for my mother's letter and take it out. I keep it below the desk and feel every corner and every edge of it. I stick a finger into a little pocket where the glue is coming loose a bit, but I don't pull. I think again of Lindsay, and of how nice it would be to see her. I want to find her after class. I know where she'll be.

· · ·

When the bell rings I stand and walk out quickly, and Ms. Dietrich goes, Kel, hang on a sec. Kel!

I don't stop. I walk faster.

I walk to A-Hall, where Lindsay Harper will just be getting out of French class. My lower lip goes numb when I see her and I pinch it.

She's with her friend Christy. They're walking toward me. The sight of Lindsay Harper releases something in me and I feel my muscles go loose in relief, I feel that everything will be OK if I can just tell her the things I've been wanting to tell her. I want to tell her. I want to tell her.

She sees me when there's still half the hall between us and stops, and her face twists as if in pain, and she grabs Christy's wrist.

Oh my God, I see Christy say, and she puts an arm in front of Lindsay protectively, and I don't know what's happening.

I don't pause. I keep walking faster and faster toward them. People are watching me now, I can see their heads swivel from me to Lindsay to me to Lindsay.

Lindsay's whole body is tense, her jaw is tense as if it's braced for impact. She puts both hands halfway toward me, palms out, as if to say stop.

When I reach her I try to take them and she pulls them away. I must look insane, I think—dirty sweatshirt, dirty jeans—unshaven, unshowered, insane.

What, I say, and Lindsay says, Don't talk to me, and Christy says, She doesn't want to talk to you.

Why—I say, and Lindsay says, Get away from me, and Christy says, Get away from her.

I don't understand, I say.

I'm sorry, I say.

Please, I say. Please let me just talk to you.

Christy grabs her hand and starts to walk down the hallway but Lindsay jerks free and stays facing me.

Then she pulls me by the elbow into an empty classroom and shuts the door behind us.

I am facing her. I should tell her everything. I imagine it.

I think you're an asshole, Lindsay Harper says.

I stare at her.

I know what you did with that girl Thanksgiving night, says Lindsay Harper, and I think you're an asshole.

I stare.

What are you talking about, I say.

Kel. Kel, says Lindsay Harper. Kel. Stop it. I knew what your reputation was before we started . . . whatever. It's just. I just never wanted to feel stupid.

Her face is red, red. Her ears are red. She is pointing at me, one tight finger extending from a bright little fist.

Where are you getting your information, I ask. My voice is so quiet I can barely hear it myself.

It doesn't *matter,* says Lindsay, and then she starts crying, two tears followed by several. She puts her hands over her face completely.

Tell me, I say. Tell me. Matt Barnaby?

The bell rings which means next period has started. Neither one of us moves.

She is still standing in front of me, fully upright, her back straight, her hands covering her face.

Tell me, Lindsay, I say. Please.

I move toward her and put one hand on each of her shoulders and she doesn't move.

I say, I want to tell you something. I want to tell you something.

I say it twice.

I pull her head to my chest and for a minute she is still and calm. I feel her breathing slow down. Then she slips out from under my arms and goes out of the classroom, shutting the door behind her quietly. I sit on the floor right where I am because I'm afraid my legs won't hold me. If I could cry I would but I can't right now.

I sit in the classroom for the whole of third period. I'm missing Pottsy's class but I couldn't go to it anyway. Lindsay's in it. It's not important. I crawl under several desks to get to the wall and lean my head against it and reel with aloneness.

I try telling myself things like *There's always Arizona,* but the idea of going and finding my absent father makes me hate myself. Why should I do that, I think. Why, when he's had fourteen years to come find me.

When the bell rings I walk slowly to the cafeteria, knowing I will have no one to sit with, knowing Trevor Cohen will not let me sit at his table. I sit at a different table, throwing the entire system off. Two junior girls glare at me. I have nothing to keep busy with. Nothing to read or look at. I stare at the dirt under my fingernails.

The next time I lift my head I'm facing two boys: Cossy Van Konig. And the bastard Matt Barnaby.

I don't even think I don't even talk.

I get out of my chair and walk toward them. I stop when I'm three inches from Matt Barnaby. I tower over him. I breathe in deeply so my chest expands. I lower my chin at him.

I'm gonna kill you, I say, and I mean it, and it isn't me talking, or maybe this was me all along and maybe I didn't know it.

You're fucking dead, I say.

What are you . . . says Matt Barnaby, and he puts a hand on my chest to stop me and I shove it off.

Don't touch me, I say. You're fucking dirt.

I'm throwing my chin out at him. I'm swaying side to side.

Look, man, says Matt, and he looks so scared

and dismayed that I feel bad for him for half of one second. And then I feel nothing.

Cossy goes, Kel, Jesus. Calm down.

I ignore him.

You told her, I say to Matt Barnaby. You fucking told her, you little bitch. You couldn't get with her so you told her instead.

His face changes and in it I see an admission of guilt.

Without hesitating I reel back and punch him as hard as I can. Straight across his face. I don't aim. I think I get his jaw and nose both. I haven't punched anyone since I was thirteen or fourteen and it feels good, it feels real.

The bastard Matt Barnaby is lifted off the floor. His hands go straight out to his right and left. He is thrown backward then he is on his ass on the floor. His hands come down last. He takes a chair down with him on his way. His nose is broken. It bleeds. He does not move for three or four seconds, and then it seems as if he can't breathe. He lies perfectly still but his eyes are open. Looking at me. Finally he takes a deep ragged breath and wails once.

Cossy is standing there shocked. One hand on his cheek. Oh my God, he says, oh my *God*. He crouches down next to Matt. I think, Maybe Matt Barnaby's jaw is broken too. Maybe his whole face.

I'm breathing hard. My hand is throbbing. I

can't open my fist. My throwing hand. Peripherally I see a little crowd forming and I see two teachers running toward me. I don't look at them. I look at Matt Barnaby on the floor before me.

Before anyone can put their hands on me I'm gone. I run very fast out of the cafeteria and then out of the closest set of doors to the outside. I'm halfway around the building from where my car is but no one gets in my way. I run faster.

My car starts reluctantly and then I leave the school, not slowing down for speed bumps, not slowing down for the guard that comes out of the front entrance and tries to wave me down.

KEL KELLER, he says. I hear him through my car window but I don't even look back.

I drive without really knowing where I'm going. I get on the Saw Mill and then get off the Saw Mill and drive north again on local roads. Back into Pells. It's been raining on and off all day and it's raining now and I put my wipers on and then my headlights. It's dark as night. Now I've really done it, I think, with something like satisfaction.

I think of dropping out. I think of Gerard Kane, if he'd still want me if I did.

Then I think of Matt Barnaby going to Lindsay's house this past weekend. Or calling her up. Saying, Lindsay, I have to tell you something that you might not want to hear.

And Lindsay going, Oh, what is it?

And Matt going, Well, it's about Kel.

And Lindsay going, Oh no, is he OK?

And Matt going, Well, yeah, he's OK. But listen, he did something really fucked up. I thought you'd want to be the first to hear about it. Because I care about you as a friend.

The bastard the bastard.

My knuckles are swollen. The knuckles of my right hand. My throwing hand. The upper hand on the bat.

I want to tell Lindsay something important.

I'm on a long stretch of empty road. The gas pedal beneath my right foot is pleasantly resistant. I step on it harder. The old engine of my old car roars in complaint.

And then I see the lights behind me, fifty yards back, then twenty five, then ten. Flashing blue lights.

The cop is young. Twenty-five maybe. He has orange eyebrows and at the base of his cap I can see short orange hair.

In a hurry, he says, when he comes to my window. Rain is coming down on his blue hat and his blue coat.

I shrug.

Do you know why I pulled you over? he asks.

For speeding, I say.

Sixty-five in a thirty-five, says the cop, and raises and lowers his eyebrows slowly.

And your left taillight is broken too, he says.

And! he says, looking at the sticker on my windshield: It looks like this car was due for an inspection in *August?*

He shakes his head back and forth slowly.

He asks for my license and registration and I give both to him after some rummaging around.

He looks at the registration. Who's Charlene Keller, he asks.

My mother, I say.

Does she know you have her car?

I nod. I can't speak.

OK, says the cop, stay put while I run these.

The street he's pulled me over on is a pretty one. There's a horse farm to my right and I watch a woman open and close a fence behind her and call to one of them. The blanketed horse comes to her and she clips a leash-thing onto his face-thing and then the two of them walk toward the barn.

While the cop is gone I think about doing crazy things. Starting the car up and peeling out. Trying to lose him on some backstreets. Driving to my mother's house and parking behind it and going inside it and never coming out again. Like her. Or: Jumping out of the car. Hiding in the woods. Hiding in the hayloft of the horse farm. Begging for shelter from the woman leading the horse.

He comes back before I can do anything and

asks me to step out of the car, then asks me to face it, and then asks me to put my hands behind my back, and then puts handcuffs on my wrists, and tells me—I swear he's nervous when he says it, it's probably his first time doing this—that he has to take me in. That there's a call out for me. That I'm wanted for assault. He tells me my rights.

I swear I don't even care. I sort of relax. I sort of feel relieved.

What about my car, I say.

We'll take care of it, he says. We'll tow it.

The redheaded Pells cop is making conversation with me.

So you go to the high school here, says the cop.

I don't respond.

I went to Pells too, says the cop.

He looks at me in the rearview.

—Who do you have for English?

I don't respond.

The car is warm inside and my nose starts running. I sniff once, twice. But I can't get at my nose and a quick string of snot runs down my mouth and chin. My throat tightens. I feel like I have finally been found out: like all of the years I have spent in Pells Landing have been leading up to this one moment. I want to cry but I don't.

When we arrive at the station he can no longer avoid looking at me.

He takes my elbow gently and we walk through the pretty front door of the Pells Landing Police Station, which is made of red brick and looks new and unused.

The woman at the front desk looks horrified.

Hi, Wendy, he says, as we walk past her. I think in his voice there is a hint of pride that he has captured somebody.

Through swinging doors. They take my cell phone from me. I am to be photographed by a man with a mustache.

Can I please wipe my damn nose, I say quietly, and the redheaded cop finally undoes my cuffs and walks me into the bathroom and watches as I put rough brown paper towels up to my face.

When I'm done in the bathroom the man takes my picture. My name is on a clipboard in front of me. Not Kel. My real name that no one calls me.

I am the only person in the station who doesn't work there. No one says anything to me.

The cop finally leads me to a room that looks like a break room. A hard and heavy wooden table with three chairs around it. He sits me down in one.

You're gonna have to hang out here for a while, he says.

On his way out he points to the mirrored wall that is certainly a window on the other side, as if to say: *We're watching you.*

Then he locks the door behind him.

I look at myself in the two-way mirror. The bags under my eyes are green indentations. My cheeks are empty. My beard is a man's beard, almost, for the first time. I put up my hood again and then lower it slowly.

The clock on the wall says that it is two o'clock, which means that practice will start soon and that I will miss it. If he has not heard already Coach will say Where's Kel? and Trevor and Cossy and Kramer and Peters and all of my friends will look at each other with false concern and then one of them will step forward and solemnly tell Coach what I did to Matt Barnaby. *And then he just took off running.*

A half hour goes by.

An hour.

At a quarter to three I remember the envelope in my back pocket and I take it out. I put it on the table before me. I smooth it with my fists.

Kelly. My mother's bubbly handwriting. As if she were a girl.

I imagine her writing it. Drunk as she ever was. The paper coming in and out of focus. Her hand shaking and slipping. I wonder if she took the pills before or after. I remember her writing letters with a dictionary on the table next to her when I was little. For when she had to look up spellings.

I'm not letting myself read it while she's alive. It is not right to. I was not meant to. It is a superstition that I cannot shake.

At three-thirty the door opens again and in walks a man, older than the cop who nabbed me, more sure of himself.

His badge says that he is Officer Connor. He looks tired and he looks like he feels bad for me. He has a gray mustache like Gerard Kane. I like him. I wonder if he has sons of his own, if he takes them to their baseball games.

Son, he says, pulling out a chair from the table. He grunts with the effort of sitting down. I'm Officer Connor.

I'm Kel, I say.

Now what exactly did you do, he says.

In the back of my mind I wonder if I should have a lawyer. It's what they do on TV shows, get lawyers. But I know I have no money so I don't think I can have one.

I have no reason to hide anything and in fact feel like maybe I want to go to jail, because everything bad has happened to me in the past week and nothing good. Baseball is the only thing I care about and now I have no one to tell about it.

I punched Matt Barnaby in his face, I say.

Who's Matt Barnaby? asks the officer.

The kid I punched, I say.

Hmmm, says Officer Connor. OK.

He scratches his head. And then you left school?

Yup, I say.

And you were going thirty miles over the speed limit when Officer Talifaris apprehended you, he says.

Yup, I say.

And your right taillight was broken and your inspection sticker was from August, he says.

Left, I say.

Left what?

Left taillight, I say.

He pauses and looks at me.

Where are you from, son? he asks.

Yonkers, I say.

Oh, yeah? Whereabouts?

Southwest, I say.

He raises his eyebrows. Southeast, he says, pointing to himself. Right off McLean.

He looks at me without saying anything for a long time. He looks like all of my friends' fathers, the ones from Yonkers. I want him to like me and respect me, to think that I am a good kid.

How come you go to school in Pells? he asks gently.

My mom—I start, but it's too much. I shake my head and then shake it some more.

He nods at my mother's letter which I am clutching with both hands.

What do you have there? he asks.

Nothing, I say, but my voice cracks and suddenly I can tell what's coming. Nothing, I say again, steadier. Don't cry, I think, you just can't cry.

Look, he says. Where are your parents?

Nowhere, I say.

They'll find out eventually, he says. Might as well get it over with.

Nowhere, nowhere, I say.

I won't cry. I stop it in my throat and hold it there like a fist. *Nowhere,* I say one more time.

And after that I don't talk.

Kel, says Officer Connor. Kel.

I want him to like me. I say nothing.

OK, he says, showing me his palms.

As he's leaving, he says, Did you get a chance to call anyone?

I shake my head.

Hang on, he says, and he comes back a moment later with a portable phone.

It's always a pay phone in the movies. A quarter for the pay phone.

Make it quick, he says on his way out.

I look at the phone. I have no one to call. I don't want to call anyone. I call Dr. Moscot's office. I've memorized the number.

Hello? says the woman who answers the phone.

Hi, I say. It's Charlene Keller's son. Is Dr. Moscot there?

Oh, hi, says the woman. I'm so sorry about your mother.

I pause. I pause.

When Dr. Moscot comes on the phone I already know in my heart what has happened. But I do not want him to say it.

We've been trying to get ahold of you, he says.

Well I haven't had my phone, I say.

Kel, says Dr. Moscot, and I say, Wait.

Kel, says Dr. Moscot.

Hang on a second, I say.

I'm very sorry to tell you this, says Dr. Moscot.

This is what it feels like, I keep thinking. *For so many years I've been wondering.*

When he hangs up I feel frozen and I keep the phone to my ear until I hear the dial tone. Then I lower it gently to the table.

There is nothing left to do but open her letter. There is nothing left to do but take one finger and poke it into the top right corner of the envelope and drag it downward slowly as I can.

Dear Kel

I'm so sorry honey. I don't ever want to hurt you or anything. I love you with all my heart and soul.

Kelly you might be mad at me but I am real sick and I think you know that's true, have been for a long time now. Its

There's others things to

When gramma and gramps died you were little and I was all by my self. Had no one in the world to help me. Now I don't' want you blaming yourself for any of this now or ever down your life, this is me doing this and always have been . . . this is a coward thing to do I know but listen

I truely think you will be better off. Listen you can do whatever it is that you like in your life with no worry for your mom, is she sick, is she drunk, etc etc

You can do great things, you're a baseball star aready, but Kel please go to college, I didn't

And look at me

Now Kel I have to tell you something hard that I should tell you a long time ago. Your dad isn't' who you think he is. Kel Keller just a boy who married me when I was scared and pregnant and too young to know right from right. Told me he wd raise you as his own son if I never told you otherwise. Or our families. Call you by his own name. Then let us go when you were little. And I couldn't tell dad and mom.

And I was always scared to tell you this but now I have something good to tell you: your dad is man named Arthur Opp. The one who sent me letters you remember. There you go, you always asked me were you named after him and I used to say no. But this was lie. He's a good man, very smart and got a lot of class. He'll tell you our story. He's very smart and got a lot of class. If I was smarter as a kid I would have done everything I could to keep him around. He is living in Brooklyn and I spoken to him

But you call him when you're ready. He s expecting a call from you. He'll take care of you I know it.

Kelly I love you, I'm sorry, I'll see you someday, we'll all be together

Mom.

Other Arthur

The first time I ever sat down to eat without the intention of stopping, I was nine years old. It was just after Easter. I was far too old for an Easter-egg hunt, especially a solo one, but that was the spring my father left, & that, therefore, was the spring my mother was very set on pretending everything was normal, & so after church on Easter Sunday she had walked into the house with me & said "Look, Arthur, the Easter Bunny has left presents all over the house for you!" Dutifully I roamed from room to room, looking behind drapes & under cushions, & dutifully my mother took several photographs on a camera that my father had left behind. Those pictures made their way into one of the photo albums that now live upstairs. I was already pudgy, & in them I look absurd: an overgrown boy wearing short pants & knee socks, holding a beribboned basket meant for a girl.

A few days after the Easter-egg hunt I came home after having a miserable time at school. My mother was out but I did not know when she would be back. Normally I was a good boy & did my homework straightaway, but I could not concentrate—several boys had cornered me on my walk home & had called me by several nick-names they had for me—& so I wandered around the house for a while before stopping in the kitchen. There, on top of our refrigerator, was the Easter basket, full to the brim with foil-clad chocolate eggs, what seemed to me to be hundreds of them but was probably less.

The taste of them was precise: chocolaty, waxen, made from cream and cocoa. At first I was casual about eating them. After dinner I would stroll toward the basket and grab a few, eating them one at a time while I read with my mother. But that afternoon I snatched the basket from atop the refrigerator & brought it up to my room. I was in a very stormy mood & I sat on the edge of my bed and looked down at my plumpness & felt very disgusted with myself for not being the sort of athletic boy that brutalized me on the playground. I began to eat.

I became an efficient machine. Each foil wrapper came off more smoothly than the next. The chocolates lost their taste but kept their texture. The smooth fattiness of them, the smooth brown glossiness. I thought of nothing but the eating. For twenty minutes I felt I was no longer inside of my body.

& this was the first time I discovered all the joys & possibilities of food.

I finished nearly half in my first sitting & felt very ill & I put the basket under my bed. To accomplish this I bent the high wicker handle until it broke. I vowed that I would never do such a thing again. But the next afternoon, my mother once again out of the house, I came home from school & finished the rest, & then went down into the kitchen to get more food, anything I could think of. Sugar sandwiches were a favorite of mine. Butter and sugar on soft white bread. I knew my mother could return at any time & I listened tensely for her key in the door, stuffing things into my mouth, swallowing dryly & painfully. I hid how much I was eating from her without wondering why.

Eventually she asked me what happened to my Easter basket & I told her that I took it to school to share with my friends.

How many times in my life have I reenacted that first episode? Thousands? Tens of thousands? For a time, when Yolanda was coming regularly, when I felt that the possibility of seeing Charlene again was real, I rarely ate at all except for mealtimes— & then it was only a reasonable amount, for me.

But these days I am up to my old tricks again, for I have been unable to reach Charlene's son, & I have been unable to find the bravery it would take to leave a message. Three times now I have failed. Twice I dialed the number & faltered & hung up. A third time he answered—I heard him answer—and my voice gave out. I physically could not speak. So although there was a moment when I actually thought I might reconnect with

Charlene or might meet her boy, that moment has passed. Hearing his voice took mine from me. And I have not heard again from Charlene Turner. I do not believe her boy needs a mentor or a tutor. I do not think he needs my help. I don't know why she contacted me to begin with. I told myself that if she wanted me in her life she would call me again, and then every day I woke up expecting a call until finally I told myself, Arthur, you must stop getting your hopes up, it is probably doing very bad things to your health. For example I got a cold after my third day of hopefulness. So now I am not at all hopeful but this means that I'm very very glum, & therefore have resumed certain eating habits that for a time I had successfully eliminated.

On top of this Yolanda has disappeared. I have called and called her little pink cell phone. Since leaving my house over a week ago, she has not returned. I called her phone five days in a row. Then I tried calling the agency, tho I was hesitant to do this for fear of getting her in trouble. I phrased it very casually: "I was wondering if you still employed a certain Yolanda who used to clean for me," but they said "O we haven't heard from her in a long time." So I then asked them if it might be possible for them to contact her and let her know I was interested in having her work for me again, "Because she was so thorough," I said.

And they said they had none of her information on file, which I presume was a lie. In any case it was a dead end.

I became very worried for her welfare, for the last time I saw her, her rabid lunatic boyfriend was practically pounding down my door to harm her. So I searched for her name online, to see if I could contact her parents or find a home address for her, or a landline. But nothing came up.

Once, when we were talking about the name of an actor we both liked, she mentioned that her full name was very long and elaborate.

"What is it?" I asked her.

"It's stupid," she said, embarrassed.

"Go on," I said, and she told me her full name was Yolanda Maria José Veracruz de la Vega, which became a phrase that I repeated in my head over & over again, a kind of a song. I liked the way she pronounced it: a soft little "Sh—" at the start of it all.

I searched for every possible combination of these names with no success.

So I have been feeling very low. It gets very dark very early now & some bad days I sit on my couch from sunup to sundown without moving, and on even worse days I lie in my bed. Except to eat.

Each night I tell myself that tomorrow it will be different and new—tomorrow it will be less bad, ever so slightly less bad. Tomorrow perhaps I will go for a walk, or jog in place, or pull out from under my bed the damned & dusty step-device that I once ordered from a catalogue, & step along to whatever Spandexed fitness expert happens to come on my television.

I never do.

Each night in bed I repeat the promise. I press my hands together up by my chest because they do not fit over my stomach—a stomach that flattens & expands when I lie down, nearly reaching the edges of my queen-sized bed—and pray to the same God I have prayed to since I was a very small Arthur. My God looks something like Santa Claus, white-bearded & starry & merry. Every night my prayer is the same. *Our Father, Who Art in Heaven,* it goes—I learned as a boy in Confirmation class that this was the way to start all prayers—*Please let me eat well tomorrow. Please let me be healthy and good. Please let me lose weight.* For it is still my intention someday to go out of the house. So I cross myself for good measure, & breathe deeply through my nose, & let my mind drift to places I have been or have always wanted to go to.

All in all I feel I am right back where I started in October, before Charlene Turner Keller called me, before I ever met Yolanda. I am one of the world's lonely.

Arizona's average annual temperature is 72 in the desert and 50 in the mountains. It leads the nation in copper mining. Its flower is the saguaro cactus blossom and its bird is the cactus wren. Phoenix is its capital. It is the 48th state. Celebrities with ties to Arizona include Curt Schilling, Danica Patrick, David Spade, Jordin Sparks, Kerri Strug, Phil Mickelson, and Meadowlark Lemon, the Clown Prince of the Harlem Globetrotters. Arizona has many ranches on it and many horses and cows.

As a younger boy I thought over and over again of running away to Arizona and when I found the Internet I used to look up images of Arizona and imagine my father the ranch hand. Whenever I was at a computer I would search for *Kel Keller,* hoping something about him would come up, but the only thing returned to me was me. Baseball stuff. And an artist, and an engineer, and a consultant, none of whom looked anything like the pictures of my father that I have seen. So then I would look up other things about Arizona.

There are homes on mountains in Arizona. There are deserts and flowering things. There are 2,210 miles between Yonkers and Arizona's northeastern corner, according to MapQuest, and it would take 35 hours to get there. I used to think about that when I was very low. I could be in Arizona in less than two days. There is something very calm and beautiful about that state the way I imagine it. I have never been anywhere outside of New York, Pennsylvania, Connecticut, and Massachusetts—all of these for baseball—but I feel I know what Arizona is like. I used to have dreams about it. There was a class trip to the Grand Canyon when I was in eighth grade and I wanted to go so badly that I tried to raise the money myself when my mother said it was too much. But I couldn't. I came close but I couldn't.

My first thought upon reading my mother's letter was Liar. You're lying, I thought. Or crazy, or so drugged and so drunk that you didn't know what you were saying.

I sat in the police station and felt like my legs were asleep. They felt numb suddenly and I thought maybe I was having a heart attack and dying. I waited and waited for somebody to come back and talk to me, to pick the phone up off the table, to take the letter out of my hands. I thought of ripping the letter up.

My mother was gone.

I did not want to lose my father.

I did not want to believe her.

I wanted to find Kel Keller and tell him—Dad,

Mom is dead. To say those words. *Dad.* Is what I always called him in my mind. He was *Daddy* to me when I was small. I remember it. I know I do.

I'll find him and ask him, I thought.

I had never met Arthur Opp and all I could think of was that I didn't want to. Arthur Opp to me was a secret that my mother and I had between us, a joke nearly, something we shared happily whenever a letter from him came. Her secret admirer. He was magical. He existed in my mind like Santa Claus. He was not supposed to be real and he certainly was not supposed to be my father.

I felt a slowing down of my body and a coldening of my veins. I read the letter again and tried to think of everything I ever knew about Kel Keller, my mother's ex-husband, and tried to see in my mind's eye the pictures that I saw of him growing up. I couldn't imagine him as anyone but my father.

The worst part was having to tell Officer Connor what had happened, when he came back into the room.

My mother died, I said to him, and it was puzzling to me to say those words aloud.

Just . . . now? asked Officer Connor.

I nodded, and then I put my head down on the table so he could not see, but he came around the table and put one hand on my shoulder and I wanted for him to leave it there forever, to feel the protection of his hand on my shoulder for the rest of my life.

They brought in a man to set bail and then took me outside. They drove me to three ATMs and I had just enough. But there's nothing left for me now, barely anything at all.

There are decisions I have to make, said the hospital. What to do with her body.
Her body. Her body.

When I left it was early evening and I had nowhere to go. They let me out on my own because I'm eighteen. They had towed my car to the station's parking lot and I owed them money for that and it would all be on some big huge bill that they'd hit me with later.
Where are you gonna go, baby? asked the woman at the desk when they signed me out. She was nice and older.
Home, I said, but the word sounded wrong.
I stood out on the front steps of the police station. It was cold but the rain had stopped. On the street, expensive cars went by slowly, and their drivers stared.

I pull up outside my mother's house. I think of her on the steps outside, as she was on good days.

Once she pulled me in between her knees and sat me down and leaned her elbows on my shoulders. This was when I was small enough not to protest.

You're getting so grown-up, said my mother. I was maybe ten.

No I'm not, I said, because I did not want to be. I always had a feeling that things would start to go wrong when I got older.

There was a drink she used to make: lemonade and iced tea mixed together. I have heard this called an Arnold Palmer, but she always called it iced lemon.

She put rum in it when I was older but when I was younger she drank it plain, we both did, and we sometimes sat out on the steps, and in these moments I felt happy.

At the top of the steps I put my key in the lock and turn it.

Inside it is freezing and strange. The sun has set. I flip the switch to my left and nothing happens. The electricity has probably been shut off. This happened whenever she forgot to pay the bill while I was growing up. Until finally I took responsibility for it when I was older. But the first time it happened, when I was little, we made a game of it, my mother and I: we put a blanket on the floor and used two little flashlights to light our way. The only kind of candles she had were birthday candles, the little ones, so she stuck plenty of these into a pot full of dirt that used to be a plant and then lit them. And put it into our fireplace, which has never worked, and called it our fire in the fireplace over and over again.

I stand still until my eyes adjust. I look for the outline of my mother on the couch. Horrible visions come to me of her ghost, and what it would look like—I imagine that if I wanted to see it, I could. I don't want to see you, I tell her. I don't want to see you yet.

I think of her body, her empty body inside of a drawer in the hospital. Filed away like information. Cold.

From the streetlights, from the fading light outside, I can faintly make out the contents of the room. I walk toward the kitchen with my arms outstretched. And there is the flashlight, plugged into the wall. It makes one bright spot on the walls and the floor and I swing it around and around looking for things I can't name.

I open the refrigerator. There is no cold inside. The smell of rotting things comes toward me and I shut it tight. In the pantry there are chips and things, my mother's junk—the stuff I bought for her and brought to her and which helped to kill her. I open one of the bags and stuff something roughly in my mouth. I chew without tasting.

I try adjusting the thermostat on the wall but there is no rush of noise from the basement, no click that tells me the heat's gone on.

Blankets.

I walk upstairs, still holding the bag of chips. At the top of them I know what I will see and I don't shine the flashlight on it. I feel around for it with my hands—the note that my mother taped to her bedroom door. It's burned into my brain. *Do not come in. Call police.*

She said: *Love, Mom.* That's what she wrote.

I tear the note off the door. I crumple it into a ball and throw it down the stairs.

I don't go into her bedroom. I can't yet. I pull her door shut.

When I go into my room I shine the flashlight around it and it's just as I left it, and I feel that it should have changed somehow, from a boy's room into a man's. The best memories I have of her are in here: when she would rescue me from whatever I'd imagined, when she'd come running for me in the night when I cried out. I woke up in this room once, six years old, running a fever, seeing or hallucinating frightening things in the dark. She came running for me in her red plaid robe, saying What is it, what is it, Kelly?

It was nuns. Black and diamond-shaped nuns, who floated by me one after another, faster and faster until they became a blur that I could not separate from the general dark of the room. I couldn't speak from fear. When my mother came in she was my hero and she sat on my bed. I feared for her ankles. I tried to tell her about the ankle-biter that lived under the bed and I couldn't.

Be careful, I finally whispered, and she said, Of what?

Down below.

She looked under the bed, she got down on her knees and peered into the empty space under the bed, and she told me that there was nothing there.

Still—she crawled into the bed beside me and curled her arm beneath my head. I was six years old. Back then it did not matter to me about her bathrobe or her terrible old-fashioned hairstyle or her physical closeness to me. What mattered was that she was protecting us both from harm. And that she did not have friends—this too I didn't mind, this too seemed right and fine to me. She was my mother.

She cooked for me when I was small.

She made cookies. Chocolate chip cookies and sometimes, many times, spaghetti for dinner. It was my favorite thing to eat. It was only when I started buying groceries for us that I realized the lifesaving cheapness of spaghetti and tomato sauce for dinner.

I'm starving suddenly. I stuff some more potato chips in my mouth. They're stale—too flexible. No chomp to them. I drop the bag on the floor.

I take two blankets off my bed and wrap them tightly around myself.

Then—I don't know what compels me, but I get down onto the floor and I pull myself slowly under the bed. I used to do this when I was young, when I needed the smallness of the space. I needed the protection. It's so dusty that I almost choke.

From my little hideout I shine the flashlight around the room and notice things about it that have not been touched since I was small: a jack-in-the-box that popped up for the last time ten years ago, hanging sadly forward, its cloth arms dangling and its crown lopsided. A coin collector full-up with coins. You put the coin in the little dog's mouth and it jumps forward and plop goes the coin into the barrel. A framed picture of a boy with a baseball bat. And many cutout pictures of Mike Piazza, John Olerud, Al Leiter. Other Mets players, everyone who led the team from 1998 until about 2008, when I stopped putting pictures of any kind on the wall. When I stopped coming home to her.

Over everything there is a layer of dust, thin near the floor and thick at the top of things, at the top of my bookshelf, where the books are gray with it. An old spiderweb sways in the corner nearby, abandoned years ago by the spider that made it. It feels as if I've been on a very long trip, as if this is my first time at home again after some journey, and if I close my eyes and try very hard I can go calm in the face, I can imagine that everything is still normal. That my mother is in her bedroom, or my mother is downstairs watching TV, and I am five or six or seven or eight and do not know what is in store for me.

I fall asleep this way. Under the bed, wrapped in blankets, the flashlight pointing its steady beam toward a blank spot on the wall.

This evening I was sitting on my couch watching Dr Phil when a little light knock came at my door.

O who could it be at this hour, I thought. Perhaps it was FedEx with one of the treats that I often get for myself: a book or a DVD or a shirt or, if I am feeling sorry for myself, a cheese basket from Harry and David. But it was almost seven at night.

I tried to peek out through the window behind me but whoever it was had pressed himself up to my door and I could not see.

I thought for a moment about not answering it but my curiosity prevailed and I trudged over to the door & I opened it.

There, on the other side, was Yolanda. A little suitcase was in her hand.

I almost shut the door again out of embarrassment—for in the time that she has been gone I have let things get very bad.

This was the state of my house:

The remains of several feasts had stacked themselves up in piles on the big table in my room, & I had begun a project to organize the photographs in my parents' albums that I had then abandoned, & I had not taken the garbage out in nearly four weeks, & I had gone on an online ordering spree and ordered many things I did not need such as a couple of pieces of large-ish workout equipment and some posters, & I had recently begun writing out lists of my possessions, a lonely morbid self-pitying act. So I had reams of paper on the table as well, lists and lists of things I haven't held or seen in years.

I closed the door partway to prevent her seeing, and I said, "Oh!"

"Hi," said little Yolanda. Her belly was swallowed up by her coat but her face looked softer, her cheeks fuller.

"I've been worried about you," I said.

"Sorry," said Yolanda. She was just standing there.

It was black outside, that winter blackness. The wind was gusting down from the park & the whole front of me got cold just from opening the door. On the street it was quiet. It felt like snow but it was not snowing.

She said nothing else. She was shivering so I put aside my pride & asked her if she wouldn't come in for a bit.

She put her little suitcase down just inside the door.

I squeezed my eyes shut tight and then opened

them again. I didn't know what to say about the state of things. Every excuse I had sounded limp & contrived. So I said nothing at all.

She looked as if she were trying to comfort herself—she had her arms wrapped around her, and she was rubbing her arms vigorously.

She would not say a thing.

Then I realized quite suddenly that I was angry with her. For her to just *disappear.* For her to befriend me and then *vanish.*

But I could not say as much so I told her she should sit down & asked her if she wanted something to eat or drink.

"No thanks," she said, but I wanted to feed her so I went into the kitchen and brought back with me some nice cheese, a Jarlsberg I've been ordering once weekly, and nice rosemary crackers.

"Look," I said, but before I could say anything more Yolanda said "I had an idea."

I did not want to hear it and I did. I thought, in my anger, that it was going to be something that was meant to take advantage of me. I could tell she was going to ask me for something that I would be wise to say no to—something with money, I thought—but I knew that I would not be able to. All of my life has been like this. I cannot say no. When I am fond of someone I can't say no to her.

"Where have you been?" I asked, to stall her.

But she would not tell me. She has a habit of

going quiet when I ask her things about her life—I do not do this frequently, but when I do . . . she folds her hands and looks at them and looks up at me eventually with a tight little smile. Or she tucks her hair behind her ear and shakes her head slightly from side to side.

"I had an idea," she repeated.

"What is it?" I asked finally. I cannot move her. I cannot make her do what she won't, or talk to her as if she were a friend. & this is what brings out the worst in me—the part of me that thinks she is only humoring me and does not hold me in any kind of esteem.

"I was gonna ask if you still needed help," said Yolanda, & here she looked about the room as if to prove her point. "And if you do, I was gonna see if you needed, like, someone to live here, and I could do that, I could cook for you and stuff, and clean, and I could do it for free. Or for, like, not much money."

I stared at her. What she was suggesting sounded at once so appealing and so horrifying that I could not find my words.

"You can think about it," Yolanda said quickly. "Obviously."

I was doing just that. I was thinking rapidly about everything that would be wonderful about Yolanda living with me: her young laughter, her company, the feeling that I have when she is in the house—one of possibility and some sort of a future for myself beyond a slow steady dying. But I was also thinking about what else her presence would mean . . . & how I would eat, & what would happen if I needed her to leave. & what would happen if I committed some embarrassment in front of her, the type that I used to save for when she was not in the house. & where she would sleep, & what would happen when she . . .

"When are you due?" I asked her.

"Three months," she said.

"Who is your doctor?" I asked her.

She shrugged. "I went to one when I first found out," she said. "He looked at the baby and said it seemed healthy."

Now I do not know much about babies but this sounded very wrong to me, & from the shows I watch I know it is important to go more often than that.

"Do you—know if it's a boy or a girl?" I asked.

"A girl," she said.

"You wanted to find out?" I said, because I have always thought that I would not want to.

"No," she said. "Nobody told me. I just know."

She had her hands on her belly. It was bigger than she was. She had on a dress that was too tight.

I wished that I could light a fire in the fireplace for her, for outside it was finally starting to snow. I could see it through my picture window and it turned my picture window into a scrim. She had come to me, I thought, like Mole & Ratty came to Badger in *The Wind in the Willows*. Which was read to me as a child. She had come to me very lost & the outside of the house was the Wild Wood, & the inside was Badger's very cozy & messy home.

"Now what will we do when the baby comes?" I asked her.

"I'll go to the hospital," she said.

"And after that?"

She shrugged. She had her brow all furrowed up, and I worried for a moment that she was going to cry, but she didn't . . .

"But will your parents worry?" I asked, and she shook her head. No, no.

"Well," I said, "you'd better stay here tonight, and in the morning we can talk about this." I thought a moment, and then added, "And in the morning you'd better go see a doctor."

It pained me not to be able to make her a bed. I didn't even know where the linens were for the upstairs rooms, but as it turned out, she did—and had washed them herself when she did my clothes. (I never let her wash my real clothes, but props that I had outgrown and kept.)

I walked her as far as the base of the stairs, and then I eyed her suitcase helplessly.

"Can I . . ." I asked her, and she said "No, I got

it," as she grabbed her suitcase and dragged it up the stairs behind her, leading with her belly.

I have never felt worse.

"Good night, Yolanda," I said, when she had reached the top of the stairs.

"Night, Mr Arthur," said the girl.

I stood at the base of the stairs with one hand on the banister for quite some time. I was just thinking. My first thought was to go into the kitchen & fix myself a great big meal, but something in me felt too tired. The effort it would take outweighed the pleasure it would bring.

So instead I sat down hard in my easy chair & put my feet up on the coffee table, looking with disgust at the several Chinese food containers that had begun their descent into rot.

I closed my eyes right there & drifted off, dreaming . . .

And suddenly she was before me, in her slippers and a pair of pajamas with rainbows on them, in a pink fluffy robe she had put about herself tightly.

I was nervous that I had been snoring.

"What time is it?" I asked her.

"Like midnight," said the girl. "Can't sleep."

"Well," I said.

She sat down on the sofa, her chin in her palm. Across from us the clock ticked softly. She looked up at me and raised her eyebrows.

"Glass of milk?" I asked her.

She declined by shaking her head without unpropping it.

Then she asked me something that she has never asked me before, & no one has since Marty died, & I think it was meant to change the subject, or perhaps it was something she had always wondered & she simply found the courage.

"Where's your family?" asked the girl.

It came at me very hard. It knocked the breath out of me. I did not speak.

"Your mom and dad," said Yolanda, as if to clarify.

"Dead," I said. Though only half of this was true.

"How'd they die?"

I shook my head.

"It's sad," said Yolanda. "I feel really bad for you. Sad to lose your parents."

I nodded.

"You never had kids," said Yolanda, & again I shook my head.

"Wow," she said matter-of-factly. "All alone."

"No brothers or sisters?" she asked me.

"None," I said, which was easier than explaining to her about William. I was feeling very sorry for myself.

"So I guess he's not your nephew," she said,

pointing to the picture on the shelf, & I had to admit that in fact she was correct.

"You remember your parents?" she asked me.

"Yes," I said.

"What were they like?"

But it was too much for me, & I felt a great mass of sadness welling up inside me, & so I told her that I would tell her about them another time.

"And what about your parents? Do you miss them?" I asked her, to change the subject.

"No," she said, "they're being stupid. They don't like Junior, so."

"And Junior is—back in the picture?" I asked her.

"*No,* crazy," said Yolanda. "But. When we got back together for a minute they kicked me out."

She looked down at her belly pointedly. "And I'm *pregnant.*"

"Terrible," I said.

She sighed loudly. "OK," she said.

"OK?"

"OK, I'm gonna get a glass of milk."

"Good," I said.

While she was in the kitchen I let down my guard for a moment and opened my heart and let in a great deal of grief that has tagged along beside me for most of my life, and I considered the fact that the men who come to excavate my house upon receiving complaints from the neighbors will find a fat old corpse who has no relations and nothing but a pile of papers to tell them: this was a human being and this was a man with a story.

What Yolanda brought back out was two pieces of chocolate cake that she had found in my refrigerator and two tall glasses of whole milk. She had put all of these things on a tray & she was balancing the tray on her stomach and grinning.

"Look at this," she said. "Built-in shelf."

I ate the cake as daintily as I could, but she had brought out dessert forks, and they always look ridiculous in my paws.

Her eyes were heavy by the time she finished.

"Goodnight again," she said, yawning, and again I told her goodnight, & then I got up and paced for a moment, which for me meant once to the door and once back.

When I wake up the flashlight's batteries have died and I have a plan. It is seven in the morning. I crawl out from under the bed and my spine is as stiff as a broom handle and I'm covered in dust bunnies. In daylight the house looks even worse, blue and abandoned.

I keep the blanket tight around me. I walk into the hallway and confront the closed door to her room. At least the note is gone. A scrap of it is stuck to a piece of tape, and I take it off very gently before turning the door handle.

I have to be very brave to do this. In my mind she will still be there, my mother, turned away from me on the bed, and in my mind I will fall to my knees and shout again. It happens in my mind.

But when I open the door nothing happens. The bedcovers are only a little messed up from where she was lying on top of it, but the bed is made. I see the little bit of vomit on her pillow and look away. I see the Cuba libre, partially frozen in its glass.

She's gone.

I haven't really been in here since I was a kid. I stopped coming in here when she got sick. She mostly didn't come in here either: she mostly stayed on the couch. It used to be a nice room, the only room in the house with a view of the Hudson over the tops of some roofs, but she let it get messy over the years, piles of shit everywhere, laundry everywhere. There's a little white desk against a wall where she used to sit to pay the bills. I sit down at her chair—it has a crocheted blue cushion on it that her mother made—and open each of the drawers in turn. In the first one there is garbage, mostly. Receipts and stuff. Pen caps, loose paper clips. One picture of her and Dee's mother Rhonda when they were in their early teens. They are wearing bright red lipstick and pretending to sing into spoons.

In the second drawer, files. I look through all of them, every one in turn, but all they have in them is tax returns from every year up to 2007. In 2007 she made 38,000 dollars total.

In the bottom drawer is a shoebox. Here we go, I think. I take it out. It's heavier than I thought it would be. I take the lid off. There's a brochure for the University of Phoenix, *An Online Learning Community!* Another for the Community College of Yonkers. Another for the Continuing Education programs of the CUNY system. Most of them look pretty new. I take them out and put them on the desk. Deeper into the box there are older ones. A 2003–2004 course catalogue for the New School. Flipping through it I see that she circled, in pencil, certain courses. *Contemporary Irish Literature. World Literature I. Introduction to Psychology.*

My whole life these things have been coming for her in the mail. College catalogues, brochures, envelopes with purple writing on them encouraging her to get an accelerated degree *in 2.5 years!* She went to college for one semester. I can't remember which college, which at this moment makes me very upset. I did not pay attention to her because she talked about it so much, her time at school—she would say it like that, *school,* as if she were so familiar with college that she could afford to be casual about it—and how it was the best thing she ever did for herself. I know it was in the city because she said so often that it was in the city. But I do not know which one it was and now I have no one to ask.

She was obsessed with college. She was obsessed with educated people. Unhealthily. I wonder for the first time if she dropped out because of me, because I was born. She never said she did. She could have gone back. I'm not prepared to think about it. I put the lid back on the box and leave it there on her desk. Half-heartedly I rifle through a few more drawers, but they are mostly filled with clothes and trinkets. Nothing I need.

Last I open a box on the floor next to the desk and inside is a folder. On it is written *Kel's 529 Plan.* There are a few statements in it. Apparently there is a college savings account for me someplace that has three hundred and twelve dollars in it. The last deposit was made in 1996.

The other stuff in the box is material from colleges trying to recruit me. That she was well enough to collect these things and put them in here is a shock to me. Some of them are from this year. It brings to me again a vision of what she did during the day, while I was at school and at practice. I shut this thought off.

I walk down the stairs to the first floor and then I open the door to the basement, where there are boxes and boxes of my mother's stuff that she never looked at or opened.

There is the little carpeted place. There, the couch facing the broken TV. I choose one box and drag it over to this area, and I sit on the couch and break open the cardboard, which is so old and stiff that it cracks like a wafer.

I can see my breath down here. It's as cold as outside. Weak light comes in through two windows at the top of the concrete basement wall.

The first box has only old clothes in it: bright purples and pinks and greens, colors that my mother must have worn when she was my age. There is a smell of perfume in them and I put them quickly away.

The next box I go through has books in it and nothing more. An anthology of world literature. A collection of some of Shakespeare's plays. My mother. At college.

I open the third. In it are baby clothes and a

rattle and a spoon and bibs. Mine. Some pacifiers, even. A lock of blond hair in a plastic baggie.

I dig down in. Under a baby blanket is a manila envelope, brittle with age, sealed shut. I think it's what I have been looking for. I open it with my heart thumping.

There are documents in there.

There's a birth certificate. Mine.

Under Child's Name it says: *Arthur Turner Keller.*

Under Mother's Maiden Name it says: *Charlene Louise Turner.*

Under Father's Name it says: *Francis Patrick Keller.*

I sit.

I hold the thing in my hands. It is relief that I feel. No Arthur Opp. And new information about the man I've always called father, whose first name, as it turns out, is *Francis.* I only knew him as another Kel Keller. *Kel* was what she called him. I don't know what to think. I don't know when my mother lied: on the birth certificate, or in her final letter to me. At least once, she was lying.

After the other Kel Keller left, from time to time she tried to call me by my real name. *Arthur,* she'd say, when I was misbehaving or on any serious occasion. But I wouldn't have it. She used to tell me this story all the time as an example of my stubbornness. *You'd point at your-self when you were four years old,* she used to say, *and go,* Kel! Kel! *So I stopped trying.*

All of these facts are floating around in my head. All of these memories.

But at least I have new information to use. Francis Patrick. His real name is *Francis Patrick Keller.* I'd only ever searched for Kel Keller.

I stand up and carry the certificate all the way up to my room. I sit at the table that serves as a desk and I open my old laptop, a hand-me-down from one of Dr. Greene's sons, and turn it on, praying that it's still charged.

Forty-three percent, it says. Enough.

I can still steal the neighbors' network. It's called *The Sappienzas* and I know them as a tight little family, happy and Italian, and I feel good about taking from them.

I open Google. It's slow.

Growing up, when I searched for *Kel Keller* and only got myself, it was like an echo. It was like sending out a hello and only hearing an echo.

Francis Keller, I tell myself. *Type it in.*

Type it in.

Francis Keller.

There is a Dr. Francis Keller from Texas. There is a 20-year-old Francis Keller on MySpace. A musician.

They are not my father.

I type in *Francis Keller Arizona.*

Nothing. Back.

On the third page there is a link to a hardware store in Queens. No explanation. I click it, and it takes me to a page with a fat smiling man with one arm wrapped around a trophy and another wrapped around a kid. His son, probably. *Connelly's Hardware,* it says. *Family-owned and operated since 1983.*

Farther down the page there are photographs of happy customers interacting with happy employees. Even farther down there are pictures of a softball game. Team Connelly's is playing Team Mike's Auto Parts. All of the pictures have captions identifying the players.

The very last photograph is a group of men in a bar. They are standing next to each other and each one is holding a beer. Under the picture it says *Jim Laughlin, Chuck Caliendo, Francis Keller, and Pete Howell after the game.*

I can't see their faces well. It's dark in the picture. But the man they call Francis Keller looks like he could be the same man in all of my photo albums. He's wearing a cap. He's skinny like my dad was in the pictures I have of him. He's got an arm around the shoulders of the fat man next to him. He's grinning, I can see that.

He's wearing a Connelly's Hardware T-shirt.

I'm still wearing the same clothes I was wearing yesterday. I haven't showered in almost a week.

I'm still wrapped in a blanket and shuddering with cold. I drag the tips of my fingers across my face and feel nothing.

I turn off the computer. I stand up and my knees feel wobbly and wrong. It feels like days since I've eaten a meal.

I make myself walk. Into the hallway. Down the stairs. I shed my blankets at the base of them.

I check for my wallet in my back pocket. I open it: no cash. I need gas for the car. It's part of my plan.

I have been in charge of my mother's money since she got sick. She gave me her ATM card so that I could walk to the machine and get whatever I needed, whatever we needed. Her disability checks went right into her bank account. The food stamps arrived in the mail. I got used to spending almost nothing on us. I got used to earning money in other ways. I'd deal a little weed when things got very bad. It was easy in Pells. I could get it easy in Yonkers, and then just charge a little more for my friends at PLHS. But doing this made me scared because of baseball. And all I spent money on was the electricity bill, the gas bill, gas for the car. She spent money on her rum and her junk food, the only stuff she ever left the house for. And to feed myself I lived off others, off of my friends and their parents. The credit card that Trevor or Kramer or Cossy would slap down at the end of a meal out—we went to one diner a lot, we went to Applebee's for a joke sometimes—became something we didn't acknowledge. My mother's disability checks were enough.

But now that she's—

What will happen.

My cell phone rang over and over again yesterday and I never answered and I won't listen to the messages either. Two calls were from her social worker. I won't listen.

I drive to the gas station on the corner, walk inside the little store.

Frank the owner raises his eyebrows at me.

Where you been? he asks, and I shrug and say nothing and pray that he won't ask the next question he always asks—*How's your mother?*

He doesn't. He leaves me alone. Maybe he's heard from the neighbors. I stick my ATM card—*her* ATM card—into the machine, not looking at the name in raised letters on the front of it, and take a deep breath.

I know exactly how much is in there since I posted bail. But a large part of me hopes for a miracle.

I request twenty.

The machine spits out a bill and a receipt. On the receipt it says there are eleven dollars and sixteen cents left in her account.

I give the twenty to Frank, put some gas in the car—squeezing the trigger over and over again, waiting for the last drop to fall out—and then get in and go.

Historians debate about the meaning of the word *Arizona*. It may mean The Good Oak Tree. It may mean Place of the Little Spring. It may mean nothing.

In my boy-imagination there were campfires in a great open desert and there were cowboys around the fire and my father was one. Kel Keller, like me. He was one of the cowboys, his horse was tethered to something behind him, he was singing old songs with the other cowboys and thinking of his faraway son. In my boy-imagination he got drunk sometimes and told his pals about the kid he'd had and left. The desert was cold at night. In my imagination. He wore a horse blanket. In the daytime it was so hot that he saw things. Saw me.

I had dreams about him. In between my dreams of ankle biting monsters I dreamt of my father. And every dream was of baseball: a great fatherly hand throwing me the ball from out of the sky, or my father as he looked in photographs waiting for my autograph after a game, or, once, playing with me on my team. *Catch* it, *catch* it, he was saying, but I couldn't, and I dropped it on the ground.

If he has been in Queens this whole time it will break something about me. If he is my father— and he has been so close.

• • •

The sky is gray now and everything is gray. Usually I don't have any cause to drive anyplace but Yonkers and Pells, so I am bad at going other places. In my hand there's a sheet of scribbled directions. It's shaking: I'm shaking. I'm driving badly I know.

I cannot get pulled over again.

The Bronx River Parkway to the Cross Bronx Expressway. I almost hit someone when I merge.

I've never been to Queens.

Where I am now there are factories, large brick-sided buildings with stray men standing outside of them in clusters. I duck my head down, I avoid their eyes. To me they are all my father. I am still clutching the paper in my hands, making turns off it. 295. Thirty-fifth Avenue. A young woman yells at a young man from inside of her car.

On Francis Lewis Boulevard I begin to scan. Connelly's is on this street. I drive past it once—big sign out front, cluttered storefront window full of tools and mowers—and then go around the block again. I park the car down the block. I'm finally warm and for a moment I leave the heat blasting and the car running. My stomach is still empty and it's making my hands shake but I have no money for food.

Stop, I think. Don't do it.

Suddenly I don't want to know anything: I want

to be an orphan forever and ever, I want to collapse into myself until I no longer exist, I want to live in my mother's house and never go out. I want to have things brought to me by mail and I want to have no friends or family at all, and I want to be my own family. I don't care about baseball or anything. I miss my mother. I am a little boy again.

I turn on *Sports Talk*. It is not Charlie Rasco but someone else. An impostor.

I sit there for half an hour, until I feel ill from the car's heat or fumes, until I notice that the gas tank is getting low again, and then out of fear of being stuck in Queens I shut it off.

I flip down the shade and I look at myself in the little mirror there. I am not me anymore. I am a different person altogether. Thin and frightening and old and pale.

It's eleven in the morning. I get out of the car and walk around to the trunk and open it up. Inside of it I have my life: some bats and balls and my glove and all the clothes I brought with me to and from Trevor's. I rummage through them looking for something better to put on than what I'm wearing: that gray sweatshirt, still, which is stiff now and stinks. Under it an equally smelly polo shirt. Below it jeans.

I come up with a button-down shirt, the other one my mother bought me, horribly wrinkled but better than this. Quickly I take off my shirts and fumble with the button-down, freezing again in an instant, standing there shaking with cold. My skin feels plastic. I have no coat.

By the time I'm dressed again I do not feel better. I look at my reflection in the car's window and try without much success to slick my hair down in back. I wipe at the corners of my eyes and mouth.

Finally I stuff my keys into my pocket and I stuff my hands into my pockets as well. I walk-run the half block to Connelly's. A little electronic bell goes off when I open the door. I hope there will be a crowd inside but there's no one, just me for a moment, alone in an empty store. There's a long counter to the right and no one behind it. There are aisles in the back and a wing that I can't see. The lights above me are fluorescent and too bright.

A heavyset man emerges from an office and walks toward me behind the counter. He's wearing a Hawaiian shirt and a thin gold chain with a cross on it. Connelly.

Help you? he asks, and I realize I haven't moved from my place three inches in front of the door.

I'm looking, I say—I'm just looking around.

My voice is a husk of itself.

Connelly raises his eyebrows and shrugs. He is not as nice as he seemed in his pictures. He is not moving, I can tell—he suspects something about me.

I turn to my left wildly and see a wall of gardening tools. Rakes and those flat sharp-pronged things propped up against each other. Gloves and stuff. I walk toward it.

You a gardener? asks Connelly, eventually, after I have stood there staring at things and not touching them for long enough.

My mother is, I say.

She never was though.

You looking for a Christmas present? asks Connelly.

I nod. I cannot speak.

Connelly comes out from behind the counter and asks me how big her yard is.

It's small, I say. Like, barely anything.

So she's got some little flower beds or something? asks Connelly. Some potted plants?

I nod.

He points to what looks like a miniature egg beater with sharp points. This is a great little tool, he says. Mixes up the dirt really good.

He looks at me when I don't reply. You OK? he asks.

Does anyone work here, I begin.

He waits.

Does anyone work here named Francis Keller?

You know him? asks Connelly.

Yes, I say. Because I do.

Hang on, says Connelly, and he goes back behind the counter where he can still see me.

KEL, he shouts. He's still looking at me.

I smooth my shirt. I clutch my hands together and release them.

I hear his voice before I see him.

The girl told me that I had to go for a walk.

She told me that she goes for a walk every day & so I should come with her once, just once.

It embarrassed me, thinking of this. Huffing & puffing away, laboring behind Yolanda, who, after all, is the pregnant one.

I told her that I would go for a walk if she would go see a doctor, & she said that sounded like a good idea, only she had no money to see a doctor.

"Don't you have insurance?" I asked her. Stupidly.

"Nope!" she said brightly.

"Well what about when the baby wants to be born?"

"I guess I'll find the money someplace," she said.

In my heart I know it is why she has come to me, for help, & although I know I should be upset I can't bring myself to be.

I told her I would give her the money. She made an appointment.

Yesterday she went out of the house at 10 in the morning and was gone for a very long time. Too long. By 2 I had told myself that she had left again & that was that & back to your old life, Arthur, but at 2:30 I heard her key in the lock & she came in carrying a bag of groceries.

"What are those?" I asked her. "You shouldn't be carrying anything."

"I got stuff for us," she said.

I saw carrots peeking over the top.

"Good stuff for the baby," she said. "Veggies."

At 3 I was watching television when she said, "Let's go."

"Where?"

"For our walk."

My pulse began racing before I had even moved.

"To where?" I said.

"To the park. It's nice out."

"It's December," I said.

"Yeah. Nice for December," she said. "Look at me, I wasn't even wearing a coat this morning."

"You should have been," I said.

"Come on. I love the park," said Yolanda. "So pretty."

"I have to tell you something," I said.

"What?"

But I couldn't speak.

"You don't have to tell me anything I don't already know," said Yolanda.

Prospect Park is less than 1 block from my brownstone. But the walk is an uphill one, and then there is Prospect Park West to cross, & then to get inside the park one must fight one's way across an interior road around which cyclists and runners come careening all day long & in every kind of weather. When I was younger I made this walk routinely, with Marty, who lived next door & would drag me out from time to time, or even, some very good & virtuous days, by myself.

But this morning it seemed like Mt. Everest. I imagined that traffic had increased substantially since the last time I had been there. I thought perhaps I would die if I tried to walk it but more than that I was afraid of being embarrassed in front of the girl. I can barely walk ten level steps, I thought to myself. I can barely walk from my couch to the kitchen.

"I gotta warn you," said Yolanda. "I'm slow right now."

The girl is a mind reader, I sometimes think.

"I'm slow," I said. "Too."

I don't think she knew the extent to which I had not been outside. But perhaps I am fooling myself.

I fetched my coat from out of the closet by the door. It was a coat I had not worn for years & I was afraid it wouldn't fit so I tried it on when Yolanda wasn't looking, & by some miracle it worked. It is a handsome coat & high quality. It is a nice gray trench that can be worn in the sun or the rain, and it has a tie that I let hang down by my sides.

Yolanda was the one to open the door.

"Yum," she said. "It smells like winter."

Indeed it did. When she had opened the outer door too I inhaled deeply and smelled the park from where I stood: the smell of cold air & fresh things dying. A lovely lonely smell.

"Come on," said Yolanda, and I looked into her sweet face & saw my own mother. So clearly that I almost wept.

"Really," I whispered, "I'm very slow."

She looked down at her belly and rolled her eyes. "You and me both," she said. "For real."

She walked down one step and turned around. I took my cane from where it was propped just inside the door: I rarely use it, for it is an outdoor cane.

"This for protection," I said. "In case of assailants."

It was a joke.

"Come on, Mr Arthur," said Yolanda again, & again I had a vision of my mother, inviting me into a swimming pool at somebody's house in the suburbs when I was maybe four. *Come, Arthur,* she said. *Come here.* The flick of the wrist. The echoing voice. The beckoning hand.

I stepped outside.

It was warm for December, just as she had said it would be.

Yolanda was waiting for me at the bottom of the stairs. She had both hands under her belly.

"Uf," she said. "I can feel her swimming around in there."

I walked down a step, cane first.

"She's healthy," said Yolanda.

I walked down another step, cane first.

"Who?" I asked.

"The baby," said Yolanda. "The doctor said."

Another step. My back, already, was crying out for mercy.

"Oh?" I said. "What else did he say?"

"She said it was a girl," said Yolanda. "But I knew that anyways, so."

"Did she," I said, stepping down again. "Did she tell you you were bad for not coming earlier?"

"Yeah," said Yolanda, looking chastened. "I felt really sorry about that."

I was walking. Outside my house. I looked up at it just out of curiosity—I had not seen it from here for so long.

"Do you think it needs work?" I asked Yolanda, & she turned to see what I was seeing, & together we looked up at the old house.

"How long you lived here?" asked Yolanda.

"That depends," said I. "I lived here once until I was eighteen. & again starting when I was twenty-six."

I thought about it. "I have lived here almost all of my life," I told her.

"Looks pretty good I think," said Yolanda. "Maybe the steps need work."

Indeed. The steps were in very bad disrepair. I had noticed on my way down. I told her she was smart, & that I'd hire someone.

In all the house looked happier than what I remembered. It looked noble & stately.

"Ready?" Yolanda asked, & she began putting one foot in front of the other very slowly, & I too put one foot in front of the other.

After five steps I was already breathing very hard, but fortunately Yolanda said she had better stop because her back was hurting her, so together we stood outside the neighbors' house for a moment, until we had caught our breath. & then we continued up the hill of 5th Street.

I believe it took us close to half an hour to walk as far as Prospect Park West, and crossing it proved to be the most difficult feat of all—for the first time there was a need to rush. Somebody honked at me and that was a very bad feeling but Yolanda said to him, "I'm pregnant, assh-le!" and the man behind the wheel raised his hands in apology.

By the time we had gotten across the street I had sweated through my shirt. It was one shade darker all over. I could feel small rivulets forming in the creases of my back. I stumbled once, terrifyingly, & thought for certain I would fall down hard on my knees, but Yolanda put a steadying hand on my arm & somehow I regained my balance. I waited for her to retract her hand in disgust but she did not, just said, "Careful," and only took it away when I was walking straight again.

I was worried about myself. I could barely speak in between breaths. & I had the whole way back to walk.

"Look how pretty," said Yolanda, & for the first time I noticed the outside of the park.

It was true. There was a barren kind of prettiness to it & I thought of my favorite of Shakespeare's sonnets, which I believe was my father's favorite too—I once found it typed amongst his things. Almost all of the trees were bare except for certain ones that clutched their leaves to them dearly. The Litchfield Villa was bright against the darkness of the trees & the cars in its parking lot reminded me of families. The sun was shining brightly & illuminating what it had selected for its focus. I put one hand against the stone wall that runs the perimeter of the park & waited there for a while.

"We could go back now," said Yolanda. "I wouldn't mind."

But suddenly I wanted to see inside it: Prospect Park is like a geode, hidden by a ring of ample trees, a jewel inside it. It was the inside that I remembered best.

This meant walking almost as far as I had already come, but a second wind was gusting in my sails, & so I asked Yolanda if we could go a bit farther. "Are you all right?" I asked her, and she said she was.

Perhaps because it was a nice day, there were more cyclists & runners than I had ever seen. In the 90s the park was not a place to go except for on bright summer days or weekends or peak times of the day. One would not go there close to dusk, which was what we were approaching by that time: we were under a darkening sky. Now, crossing the interior road was as difficult as crossing Prospect Park West. I had a near-collision with a cyclist who screeched to an angry halt. & again Yolanda was my protector, cursing at him & saying to watch where he was going, though in this case I believe he was in the right.

At last we reached a place where I could see the meadow. & I breathed in deeply. & Yolanda did too. It felt as if we were off in the country someplace or even in England, & I told her so, & she said I never knew you were from England, & I told her O I am not, but my parents were.

There were whole families gathered together under the winter sky. They were bundled up well and the little ones in strollers had hats on and mittens. It seemed to me that everyone was wearing brighter colors than I had remembered.

"You wanna sit down?" asked Yolanda, indicating a bench. "Because I do."

I said all right, tho when I sat I took up most of

the space between the wrought-iron armrests & Yolanda had to squeeze herself in to my right.

I thought what an odd pair we must make: me in my custom overcoat, the tie dangling; and the girl, almost forty years my junior, with a belly bigger than she was.

A family of four walked by us. They had bought nuts someplace, roasted in a cart, and the children —twelve and thirteen, maybe—were eating them out of white paper baggies. Their parents were stealing them from time to time. *"Dad,"* said the daughter, and swatted his hand from the bag. "Get your own next time."

Here is what I have always thought: that people, when they eat, are very dear. The eager lips, the flapping jaws, the trembling release of control—the guilty glances at one's companions or at strangers. The focus, the great focus of eating. The pleasure in it. I remember—when I went out more—I remember watching people in restaurants. People who ate alone, lost in the pleasure of it, O the pleasure of it. Digging for food in the bottoms of their bowls, guarding their fork, bringing the food to their mouths. Staring off into some middle distance while chewing. Thinking of things known only to them. To watch others eat is a thing of joy to me. & it is the only time I can forgive myself for what I have become.

We sat in silence until a big dog ran up to us,

free from its leash, jawing a stick, and Yolanda shied away from it. "I'm so scared of dogs," she said, and tho I'm not fond of them either I took the stick from its mouth and tossed it far away from us. The dog went running after it.

"There," I said. "There."

It was time to go back when there was only a bit of light in the sky. There was a nice purple sunset that we both noted.

Most of the families had gone home & I was thinking of the walk still ahead of me. I was thinking I could tell Yolanda, if things got really bad, that she could go ahead of me & I would meet her. I was also thinking of the steps up to my home, all twelve of them, looming in my imagination like the Empire State Building.

We started out as slowly as we'd left, stopping every so often to admire a bird or a tree. But I soon came to realize that the return trip was going to be much more difficult, for I believe my muscles had stiffened considerably after sitting for a while, and it had gotten colder too. My saving grace was that it was downhill for most of the way, & so I was able to use my own momentum to help me along.

It was fully dark by the time we reached the house. I paused for a moment, one hand on my railing, in preparation for my climb.

"What should we have for dinner?" Yolanda

was asking me, & I was trying hard to formulate an answer, when all of a sudden I noticed that the family who lives next door to me was coming toward us on the block. The father was staring at us intently.

"Your neighbors!" said Yolanda, delighted.

I was afraid & shy. I remembered the father approaching my door one day this fall & I was afraid he had something nasty to say to me.

Their little boys were bouncing around like jumping beans, & saying Daddy Daddy. His wife was looking at him too.

He had his key in hand, as if he were about to walk up his stoop and open his front door, but instead he came toward me.

"Hank?" his wife said.

I was a mess. I had sweated on the walk back & had a damp film across my forehead. I was quite badly out of breath.

"Hi!" said Yolanda, as the man approached.

"Hello," said the man, "sorry to bother you—"

"No bother!" said Yolanda, speaking for me, but in fact I felt it was a bother, talking to this man unexpectedly. I felt as if my knees were going to collapse. He had no idea what an ordeal I'd just been through.

"I'm—your neighbor there," he said, gesturing to his brownstone, which was not quite as nice as mine but still very attractive and perhaps better kept. "I'm Henry Dale."

"This is Arthur Opp," said Yolanda.

"I actually know that," said Henry Dale.

I assessed him. He was a young man, perhaps in his late thirties, but his hair was gray at the temples. He was as tall as I am but thin. He had a handsome face & a nice face. He wore tan corduroys & a blue oxford & a strange jacket the likes of which I had never seen—sort of a suit jacket in the shape of a denim one. & shoes that looked elfin and worn. His wife was blond & pretty & very thin & dressed in an outfit that reminded me of the gym.

"I work for a firm called Crandall and Stone," said Henry Dale. "Have you heard of them?"

"Architecture," I said. It was the first time I'd said the word aloud in years & years. I thought of Dad in a blue flannel suit he had. I thought of Mother.

Yolanda looked at me expectantly.

"When we bought the house from Marie Spencer," said Henry Dale, "she mentioned you and your family to us."

I said nothing. Henry Dale waited.

"Your father is one of my heroes," he said. "Architecturally."

I said nothing.

"You know there was a show—"

"I heard that," I said.

"At the public library," he said. "I went."

"It was great," he said.

315

I think Yolanda could no longer bear my silence so she chose this moment to speak. "You guys should come over sometime!" she said. It burst out of her.

We both looked at her.

"Well—" said Henry Dale. "I'd hate to impose."

"No, you should," said Yolanda. "I could cook." Then, upon seeing his gaze drop to her belly, she said, "I work for him." As if to clarify that I was not, in fact, the father.

At that moment one of his young sons ran up to him and tugged at his hand, & his wife came over too, pushing the stroller, holding their third boy by his hand, and introduced herself as Suzanne.

"Hello, Suzanne," I said. She had very nice eyes & a good firm handshake. I decided I liked her, & therefore I had to like Henry Dale, as well.

The best part of the day was the evening. I felt a sense of euphoria almost—perhaps it was endorphins from the exercise I had taken—& I was tired and calm for the first time in years.

Yolanda came downstairs wearing the outfit she almost always wears at night: sweatpants and a too-large hooded sweatshirt. I wonder if it is Junior Baby Love's sweatshirt & I hope that it is not.

I had a glass of wine & Yolanda asked if she might have one too.

"Not good for the baby," I said.

"But the doctor said," she replied. "She said I could have a little glass if I wanted."

"She just said that out of the blue?" I asked. "Or you asked her?"

"No," said Yolanda. "She just said it."

"You're too young, anyway," I said, tho it felt absurd to say this to someone who would soon be a parent.

"Nineteen," she said. "Almost twenty."

So out in the kitchen I poured her a little bit of Chardonnay in a juice glass, & then I splashed it with water.

When I brought it out again we sat there without the TV on. & even though we were quiet it felt fine, it did not feel uncomfortable, the silence.

"You ever put a fire in that fireplace back there?" Yolanda asked. She got up to peek behind the television.

"Not for many years," I said. Not since Marty, I thought. Marty was someone who liked a good fire.

"Can we put one in there?" Yolanda asked.

"I'd have to get a chimney sweep to come first," I said. "Who knows what's up there now."

"But why not?"

"Because it's dirty," I said. "Because it could smoke us out."

We sat there quietly for a while more. Until

Yolanda asked, "What should we make them for dinner?"

"Who dinner?" I asked.

"Your neighbors," said Yolanda. "What do you think they like?"

"They're not really going to come for dinner," I told her.

"Yes they are," she said. "They are."

I thought perhaps I hadn't been as happy since Marty died, & I thought Perhaps this will be my life now: full of Yolanda & her child, & walks, & watered-down wine by an imaginary fire. I could be happy like this.

The other Kel walks around the corner into view. I have spent years and years forcefully bringing him to mind, recalling whatever memories I have of him, turning them over in my head. His father face. He does not know me. He is smaller than I had remembered. When I was four he seemed huge to me. My father. My daddy. He doesn't smile and doesn't know me. His eyes are blank. He is no cowboy. He's wiping his hands on something when he walks around the corner of an aisle, going What is it already? to Connelly, going, I'm busy over here!

He has more of an accent than I remembered. *Heeeeeere.*

He has long hair—almost as long as it was in the pictures I have of him. I guess I'd always thought he would have cut it.

He's skinnier and more rascally-looking, someone who's been in trouble all of his life. Under his eye sockets his cheeks are hollow.

He looks nothing like a ranch hand.

Visitor, says Connelly, and tilts his head in my direction.

I'm holding a rake.

Help me, I want to say. It is all I want to say. *Help me.*

He's looking at me, waiting.

Can I talk to you for a minute? I ask him, but he doesn't hear me, and puts a hand to his ear to tell me so. He doesn't come closer.

I try again. Are you Francis Keller? I ask him.

Who's axing? he says.

Were you ever, do you know—Charlene Keller?

His face changes, the eyebrows lifting, the head tilting back. Connelly's watching us both, going back and forth with his eyes.

Holy, says Francis Keller, or Kel, or my father.

He tells Connelly he'll be back in an hour.

Oh yeah? says Connelly, looking at his watch.

Hang on, says the other Kel, and runs into the back. I prop the rake up against the wall and turn my back to Connelly. I'm having second thoughts about everything. I want to apologize to my ten-year-old self. I want to push this man away violently. I want to jump into his arms and say Daddy, Daddy. I want my mother back.

He comes trotting back out with a denim jacket, then holds the door open for me. I tower over him. I have half a foot on him.

I haven't been warm in days, and the cold that hits me when we're outside feels familiar. The other Kel walks to the right and I follow him. He's two steps ahead and he doesn't slow down. His denim jacket is so big on him that it swings like a bell around his waist. He lights a cigarette and offers me the pack and a lighter wordlessly, and I take one even though I don't smoke. Cigarettes.

It looks as though it will warm me.

After twenty yards he says, I always figured.

We keep walking.

How old are you now? he says.

Eighteen, I say.

—Jesus.

Did she send you? he asks.

No, I say, and start to say more—gone, tell him she's gone—but I can't do it.

We're both silent. I pull smoke into my mouth and then my lungs. I let it out slow. He turns a corner and then stops outside a little red door next to a garage. He pauses while we both smoke our cigarettes in silence. He looks at me, squinting, while he inhales.

You shouldn't smoke, he says. Bad for you.

But he seems like he's joking. His voice is growly, all smoked out.

He drops the cigarette and grinds it into the sidewalk. I notice his boots, black and scuffed on the toe. Ten years old. More. He could have had them when he lived with us. I try to remember.

He unlocks the door and ushers me in and then follows me, slamming the door hard behind him. We're in a stairwell that's almost pitch-black until he switches on an overhead light.

It reeks of garbage and cigarettes in here. It

reeks of staleness. Worse than my mother's house ever did.

This way, he says, and squeezes by me on the stairs, then leads the way up them to the only door, which he opens without unlocking.

G'wan, he says. Sorry about the mess.

It's one room. A bed in the corner. There are beer cans everywhere. Miller Lite. Tipped over on their sides or stacked on top of one another: on the floor, on the two tables, a couple on windowsills. There's a little kitchen with a bar separating it from the rest of the room. On the wall, there's a calendar open to a picture of a bikini-wearing girl on a motorcycle.

It hits me suddenly that he's young. Just a little older than Pottsy—in his thirties. That my mother too is young. Was.

You want a beer? he says, and I say no.

Good, he says. He walks to the fridge and gets one for himself. He cracks it and tells me I can sit anywhere. I choose a chair that's tucked into a table in the center of the room. I slouch in it, not knowing where to put my hands.

What should I call you? he asks me. He's leaning against the bar in the kitchen. He still has this look on his face like he's trying to recognize me.

Kel, I say, that's what everyone calls me.

Me too, says Francis Keller, and grins suddenly, shaking his head. How 'bout it, he says, two Kel Kellers walk into a room.

Then he looks alarmed. Your last name still Keller?

I nod.

Kel Keller, he says. Back to shaking his head and grinning.

I've just noticed that part of his ear is missing. The left earlobe, as if he were a dog who lost a fight. He fingers it absentmindedly.

How'd you find me? he asks.

Google, I say.

Google, says the other Kel. Jesus. I can't even begin.

He puts the beer to his mouth and tilts it for too long, until it must be almost gone. Suddenly I wonder if he's the one that did it to my mother. Got her drinking. Taught her how to.

You in school? he asks.

Almost done, I say.

—Gonna go to college? Gonna work?

Don't know yet, I say. And then for some reason I want to tell him—it's the rage in me that wants to—about baseball, about what I can have if I want it.

I play ball, I say.

Baseball! he says.

I nod.

You was always good, he says, and it's the first time he has acknowledged having memories of me. He must have millions. He must think about me. He must.

Are you my father? is echoing inside my head. *Dad, Mom is dead. Mom is dead, Dad.*

We used to have a catch in the backyard. Remember that? he asks.

No, I say. I'm lying.

—You don't?

I don't remember anything, I say, and he looks hurt, or else I am making it up.

—You any good?

I got the Mets looking at me, I say.

—No shit.

—I have a private practice this month with a recruiter.

On the 10th. With Gerard Kane and his clipboard and his sunglasses hanging around his neck. It occurs to me that I should eat, that I should practice, that I should find my strength someplace.

You grew up big, says the other Kel. You haven't changed much. Hair's darker. You was white-headed as a kid.

He puts his flat palm three feet from the ground.

Mets, huh? he says. Good thing we got you started early, I guess. Too bad it ain't the Yanks, though.

The Yanks. *But your things,* I want to say. It occurs to me that the box in the basement could belong to anyone. Believing the Mets things were his was very possibly a fantasy of my childhood.

Now I am waiting for him to apologize to me. If he is my father he will apologize to me, or offer an explanation, an excuse.

How is she? he finally says, and because I want to shock him I tell him, She's dead.

—No kidding.

She's dead, I say again, and it's the third time I've said it and the first time I've meant it: that she's gone, my mother is gone, I cannot ask her anything or tell her anything ever again.

Sorry to hear that, says the other Kel. That's a damn shame for you.

I shrug.

—Recently?

—Yeah.

She was a good lady, he says pensively. Now I'm gonna get emotional. You know I knew her from the time she was a girl.

He drains the beer, crushes the can, and tosses it on the floor.

When we was in school, he says, I wasn't good at anything. Not anything. And she was always nice to me, always had a nice thing to say to everybody when they needed it.

So you got anyone left? he asks.

Nope, I say.

Me neither, he says. Makes you feel any better.

Then he says, I guess. I guess you found me for a reason?

I freeze. I don't know what to say.

—You wanna know anything about her? You wanna ax me something? I'll tell you.

I say, No—it's not—

She loved you, he says. I remember how much she loved you. There wasn't anyone else she cared for.

It is not what I want to hear and I turn my head away sharply and look out the window.

How come you left? I ask him.

He breathes out hard. Well, he says. That's a tough one. I guess I got the bug to travel, and then I got the bug to be—my age, which was only a little older than you right now, you know?

I say nothing. It is not enough. I would not have left me.

Did you ever live in Arizona? I ask him.

He laughs loudly.

For about five minutes, he says. Too damn hot out there.

Then his face changes, as if he's realized something.

You're not mine, he says. Oh, Jesus. She must of told you you're not mine?

I breathe out. I realize I have been holding my breath.

She never did? he asks. She really never did?

No, she did, I say. She told me all that.

He clutches his heart, laughing now. Jesus, you scared me, he says. Thought I was gonna have to break your heart.

He opens a new beer. How'd she die? he asks me.

She—had cancer, I say.

—Sorry to hear that. Took my mother too.

He walks across the room and sits on a ragged black couch.

It was partly my fault, he says.

—What?

—Her telling you I was your dad.

I say nothing.

—I told her—before we got married, I told her—Charlene, if you have that baby it'll be mine too. I'll be supporting it. She was pregnant already. She probably told you.

I nod. I will not betray my mother to this man.

—We told both our parents it was mine and everything. Jesus. We were kids.

Yeah, I say. It is all I can think of to say.

—She was smart. She was in school. Going to college at night. Her parents were helping her and they stopped helping her when they found out. Told me she was my responsibility now. And we didn't have the money.

He looks at me. You know I did want kids, he says. Pains me that I never had any.

He laughs. Hey, never too late, I guess, he says.

I have to ask him but it takes all of my strength to. I swallow it like something bitter.

—There's something she never told me.

—What's that?

—She never told me who my real dad was before she died.

He laughs, loudly, one time.

—Ain't that a trip. Never told me either!

He sips his beer and shakes his head some more. Never would tell me. But I loved her so I took her back. She was funny, wasn't she? he asks me. She was an odd duck, but I loved her. Never met anyone like her again.

We was broken up when she got pregnant, he says. In case you were wondering. Hadn't seen her in a year.

I want to leave. Every part of me wants to leave. My right knee is jogging the way it does in class. I look around his apartment. If he knew the places I've been. If he could see Trevor's house or Lindsay's house for one minute. He wouldn't believe the school I go to. He wouldn't possibly believe the friends I have. And their parents who love me.

Before I get up I ask him, Have you ever heard of Arthur Opp?

He squints some more. Arthur *Opp?* he says. Arthur Opp. Nope. Never have.

Then he says, Is that who you're named after?

I don't know, I say. I think so.

She never would tell me, he said. I was the one called you Kel. I told her Arthur was a bad name for a kid. I got Francis, he says. I know how it is.

When I tell him I have to leave he says Hang on a second, and he goes to a little table by his unmade bed. He opens it and reaches his hand way in and then comes out with an envelope.

He takes out money from it. A hundred-dollar bill.

Take, he says, walking over to me. Go ahead.

I can't, I say, and he says, Please. Please take it. G'wan.

So I take it, and stuff it in my pocket. I take it without saying thank you and then I walk out the door and down the stairs, letting the door slam shut behind me.

Last night the girl called her parents. I heard her even though she was all the way upstairs. She was shouting at them in Spanish. I wished I could speak it. Her voice came out in hurt waves. The conversation was not long.

Whatever she was saying, it sounded very angry & very tearful. I imagine it was about JBL.

I tiptoed to the base of the stairs to listen harder & I swear I heard her say his name. Ma*ma,* she kept saying. Ma*ma.*

Like her baby one day will say to her.

Is it wrong of me to say that I hope she stays? I want the best for her: I want her to be happy. But since she has been here life has opened for me like a flower & I feel I could be content with her forever. I want to meet her child. I want to be in its life. I asked her last night about buying things for the baby, a crib or some clothing or diapers, & she looked at me strangely & said Don't worry about it.

Instantly I felt absurd. How could I think. How could I say that.

This morning she went out for a walk & did not ask me if I would come. I wouldn't have anyway

—the last one was very hard for me & today every part of me aches—but it would have been nice to be asked.

When she was not back after an hour I began to watch for her out the window & I saw that she was talking to Suzanne Dale, whose three boys were buzzing about them as well. Suzanne had the baby on her hip & I saw Yolanda ask to hold him. When she took him in her arms her face changed: it became softer, & I saw she would be a good mother.

When the girl came in again I pretended to be reading.

She sat down across from me.

"Nice walk?" I asked her, very casual.

"Yup," said Yolanda.

Then she said "Suzanne told me about your dad."

My heart pounded.

"What did she tell you?" I asked her.

"About your father."

"I see," I said. I closed my book very gently. I cannot even remember what it was. I may have been holding it upside down.

"He's famous," said the girl.

I looked her in the face. She is very very lovely, even more so with the baby now. I think it is bringing out in her something wise & ancient. She put a hand under her chin. "You don't like to talk about it," she said.

"He is quite famous," I said.

"You don't talk to him?" said Yolanda.

"I do not," I said.

"I don't blame you," said Yolanda, and here she rolled her eyes as if to say *Parents,* which would normally have been charming.

"He is an old man now," I said.

"How old?"

"I suppose—eighty-four," I said.

"Old," Yolanda agreed. "Where does he live?"

"I believe he lives in London," I said. "The last I read."

Yolanda pondered this. She made a little *hmm,* and sank back in her chair.

"What happened to your mom?" she said at length.

But I could not bear it anymore, & I remembered once again the pleasure of solitude, & I remembered why I had chosen it years ago.

"Bedtime for me," I said.

"You're bad," said Yolanda.

"I'm sorry?"

"You're bad," said the girl again, & I knew what she meant.

I wished I had something in my hands to hold. I wished I had something warm to hold & drink from. A mug of tea. With cream and sugar. I felt that would help me.

She had opened something in me. I was bleeding.

• • •

Listen, I wanted to say to her.

I wanted to say to her, Yolanda: This is the house I grew up in. I left it for years. I went to college. I went to graduate school. Far away from here, in places as pastoral as a dream. Massachusetts, Vermont. I met Marty. I thought I would never come back.

I turned twenty-six. I had no parents, but I still had the house—empty then. I took a job in Manhattan and I had no other place to live. So I returned. I came back to it to find an inch of dust on every surface. Dust in clumps. And all the things my mother left behind, and, longer ago, my father, were still there—my mother never removed his things. Their outdated clothing, their books, my mother's cigarette case, the ancient cigarettes inside. *ACO,* her initials, inscribed upon it. I opened it. I tried to smoke one but it was too old. The kitchen was empty: I had cleaned it out before I left, mustered inside myself some adolescent reserve of strength and responsibility. I had cleaned it out completely. But their plates were in the cabinets, still. My mother's plates that she had chosen when they were first married. The towels and sheets were in the linen closet. The things of my father's that she had saved, sentimentally, pathetically. His reading glasses, stowed in a drawer. It was a house for ghosts. My mother said it and it was true. Every picture still

333

hung on the wall. There were photo albums in the library. There were rugs rolled up in a corner. The neighborhood was different.

I got a new television. I filled the kitchen with food. I convinced Marty to move in with me and then to rent the top floor of Marie Spencer's house, next door. Things were cheap then. Apartments were so cheap. You wouldn't believe it. She lived there for the rest of her life. I slept in the room that was once my parents'. In their bed. I bought new sheets for it. When I had company— I had company in those days, I had quite a few friends—they gasped when they came in at the beauty of my house. All of us were hippies, all of them were poor. Marty was over all the time. We both got jobs at the same university. First she and then I. She recommended me. I thanked her. It was her pleasure, she said.

I taught for almost twenty years. I had a job & I was normal. I used to go to concerts. I used to go to movies.

I met Charlene & fell in love with Charlene & then Charlene disappeared. I used to wander. I used to go for long walks all around the neighborhood, even late at night. I used to lie on the floor, spread out like a starfish, & gaze at the ceiling of my huge empty home & wonder why I had been chosen for the life I was living. Why I was chosen to be so alone. For a while, in my forties, I used to think I would marry Marty & we would have children. We got along so well. But I never once asked her for a date. She told me she was in love with a woman. Hilda. Who left her without a thought, who broke her heart. The women who were meant for me never seemed to know it. They were there and then gone. More people in my life have died than I believe is fair. About this, about everything, I used to wonder why, why, why. I used to feel things would certainly change someday. I used to wonder when they would.

I suppose I had been silent for quite some time.

"Anytime you wanna talk about it," said Yolanda finally, "you can."

& she patted my hand as she stood up.

Don't leave me, I wanted to tell her, *don't ever leave.* But in my heart I knew that this, also, was not fair.

I am nobody's. And I have no place to go. It is one in the afternoon. I get into my car and put my head down on the steering wheel. I could turn the car on and sit there until the car runs out of gas. I could find a cliff and drive the car off it.

Instead I start the car and drive straight until I find a gas station, and then with twenty dollars of the hundred-dollar bill that I have I fill the tank almost halfway up. When I pay I buy the cheapest things I can find to eat: a pack of peanuts, a bag of Cool Ranch Doritos, and a huge Arizona Iced Tea, each for ninety-nine cents. I open the peanuts while I'm pumping gas and I down them in three mouthfuls.

I get back in the car and blast the heat. This time the car is warm and I feel better, actually, I feel better about life. I have food and fuel and slowly my body is thawing. A great mystery has been solved for me. There is another in its place.

Halfway back, I stop at a McDonald's drive-through because I still feel weak. This time I let myself get whatever I want: I get a Quarter Pounder, two Quarter Pounders, and a large fries, and a large Chicken McNuggets with honey and barbeque sauce, and a large vanilla shake, and a large Coke. I pull into a parking space and let the car keep running, the heat keep blasting, and I turn on the radio and there is my friend Charlie Rasco, talking about what's been happening with those Giants. I'd call in but my phone is dead.

This is the most delicious food I've ever tasted in my life. I feel as if I've been off in a desert someplace. I feel as if I've been stranded until now. I eat it as slowly as I can, tasting everything, feeling everything, letting it in, and memories and memories, too: how McDonald's was a special treat, how after baseball games we got McDonald's. On sunny days.

By the time I decide to go to Lindsay's my hands and feet have already made the decision for me. I'm turning down the road that goes to her house, the long wooded road with the nicest houses on it. They are tucked back there behind the trees, their chimneys and gables showing, sometimes a front door or a fancy car in the driveway. This is what my mother wanted for me, I think. Not baseball. This.

I see the garden down at the end of Lindsay's driveway—bare, just a low scrubby plant left—and drive slowly past it. Field hockey's over for the year. School ended an hour ago. If she's not at a friend's house she'll be here.

There are no cars in the driveway, but hers could be in the garage. This is what I tell myself.

Her parents won't be home. I know their schedule now.

I drive up the road a little farther and pull over in a place that isn't visible from Lindsay's house. I don't want to be presumptuous. In case she has told her parents. I can't bring myself to park in the little spot reserved for me by her sisters, last time I was here—it is not mine anymore. I imagine that I am back in that time and that my mother is home, drunk but at home, waiting for me to return and feed her something. My mother, a baby bird.

Why I never took her anyplace I do not know.

I do know but I don't want to know. It was that I was embarrassed of her, of the way she looked and acted.

But I could have said, Mom, do you want to go for a drive?

And then she could have said, OK.

Then I could have taken her to the secret places that I am fond of going to, the nooks and crannies along the Hudson that I have rooted out with my car.

I open the door and get out, avoiding my reflection in the car window. I'm still wearing the cotton shirt I put on to meet my father, who was not my father. I'm instantly freezing. I still smell bad. I find a wool winter hat under my front seat and put it on: it's the best I can do. I walk back up the road to the driveway and then I walk up the driveway.

The Harpers' house is big as ever. I keep waiting for alarms to sound, or for the front door to fly open.

I look up at the row of windows along the top. Again I wonder which is Lindsay's. I walk onto the porch. An old wooden swing creaks over to my right. Its pillows are off for the winter. I ring the bell.

Let it be Lindsay who answers, let it be Lindsay, I think. I whisper it too, out of superstition.

I wait.

After one minute I ring it again.

But there is nobody there.

I sit on the naked swing over to the side of the porch. I am planless again, so I decide to stay.

After ten minutes there's a crunch on the driveway and Lindsay's Lexus comes rolling up the slight hill toward the house. I freeze. I do not know whether it is better to sit or stand. I'm shaking a little from cold. I have both arms wrapped around me. My breath is coming out in quick small puffs of gray cloud.

Lindsay is dressed for the weather, wearing a down vest. She hasn't seen me yet. She shuts the door and grabs her backpack from the passenger's seat, throws it roughly over her shoulder. She coughs. She does not know I'm there. I want to disappear. She slams the car door and walks toward the porch, swinging her keys on the end of a lanyard you can buy at the Pells merchandising table set up after school every day, in the gym wing. I have one too. I want to watch her forever from a distance, just like this. She swings them around and around until the lanyard is wrapping her hand.

Lindsay, I say, but it is too quiet.

Linds, I say.

She's on the porch now, trying to let herself into the house.

She jumps backward, dropping her bookbag. Both of her hands fly to her chest.

Oh my God oh my God, she says. You scared me so much.

She looks at me. *Kel?* she says. Are you OK?

I shake my head. Not really, I say.

Where's your coat?

I shrug.

Hang on, says Lindsay. Just hang on a second.

She fumbles with the door again and then it is open. I stand up.

She shuts the door behind her again. Oh.

But then she comes out, says, Sorry, I had to put in the alarm code, and gestures with her head for me to come inside.

Where's your car? How'd you get here? she asks.

It's parked on the road, I say.

Weird, says Lindsay, and it makes me almost laugh for the first time in almost forever.

I come inside. The house is warm and tight. Our voices bounce off the sides of things. It's large but enclosed: it feels safe, a fortress.

Angelo and Maxie come bounding toward us and Lindsay kneels down beside them and says Hi, hi!

I have never been good with dogs so I stay back, but one of them sniffs at me and I pet him on his head.

C'mere, says Lindsay, and makes her way into the kitchen. Sit down, she says, pointing at a stool.

You want a smoothie? she asks, and I almost say yes until I see it is a little joke. She's joking about her mother. Let me make you a smoothie, she says again, but in her mother's voice.

Lindsay puts her elbows on the island and looks at me.

What happened to you, where have you been, she says. Everyone's been talking about you.

She shakes her head. I can't believe you punched Matt Barnaby, she says.

But I can see that she is laughing a little. I smile too, thinking of it. The look on his face: like *This is so unfair.*

You know it wasn't even him? she says. It wasn't even him who told me.

It wasn't? I say.

—Nope.

—Who was it?

Just some girl, says Lindsay. Some girl that

Christy's friends with from gymnastics. She was at the party you guys went to.

Shit, I say.

Poor Matt, says Lindsay, laughing. Then: Whatever. He probably deserved it. For something else.

She turns away from me, toward the fridge, and I look at the glossiness of her hair, her healthy girl hair, brown and straight, in a ponytail.

I'm starving, she says. She pulls pounds of food out of the refrigerator: cheese and apples and leftover pasta with tomatoes and olives in it. Then she goes to the pantry and gets chips and Oreos and peanut butter. She pours herself a glass of milk. She takes a spoon and heaps some peanut butter onto a cookie, then dunks the whole thing into a glass. She bites it. Yum, she says. Oh my God, I was so hungry.

She looks at me. Take something, she says. Whatever you want.

I feel the weight of her offer. I slide around the island and pass her. I open the fridge for myself.

Oh my God, you stink, she says, laughing. Where the hell have you been?

When I have made myself a sandwich we go into the living room and sit together on the same couch. But we're both facing straight ahead. We're not looking at each other.

I eat my sandwich slowly.

Kel, says Lindsay, I'm still mad at you.

I know, I say. I'm sorry.

Is it your mom? asks Lindsay.

Yes, I say.

All she knows about her is that she's sick. Thinking about all that has happened in the past week makes me tired.

Do you want to tell me? asks Lindsay. I think you should tell me.

Yes, I say.

But I can't find the words to begin with.

OK. Do you want to take a shower? asks Lindsay suddenly. Would that make you feel better?

It would. It does. Lindsay brings me upstairs and gives me a towel from her parents' linen closet. It's green and soft. You can shower in my bathroom, says Lindsay. Her bathroom is just off her bedroom, which we walk into together. It is just as I had imagined it, green and good smelling: a dark wooden desk against one wall, her laptop shut on top of it, a peace-sign sticker slapped over its logo. Yesterday's shirt hanging over one post of her canopied bed. The heat in this house makes a low comforting hum, a rush of air.

The bathroom off of Lindsay's bedroom looks like something I guess you would find at a fancy hotel. The shower has a bench in it. The shower-head is as wide as a sunflower.

OK, says Lindsay. All yours.

I shut the door behind me and unbutton my shirt. The smell of me. The sight. I'm a skeleton. My hip bones stick out over the tops of my jeans. I have a full beard.

I turn the shower on as hot as it will go and watch the water for a while, pulsing and turning, making patterns on the glass.

When I step into it my knees go weak and I have to sit down on the bench. I lower my head. I let it wash over me.

Lindsay only has girl things in here. Girl shampoo and conditioner, which smell exactly as she does, like lemons and winter. Some kind of lavender soap with little rough things sticking out of it. Girl shaving cream and a pink gummy razor. I use them all: I want to. I even shave my face while I'm in the shower, lathering up with the flowery shaving cream, cutting myself all over.

I don't know how long I'm in there.

I smell like a girl when I emerge. The bathroom is full of steam. I wrap a towel around my waist, not wanting to get back into my bad smelling clothes.

I crack open the door. Lindsay's lying on her bed, gazing up at the ceiling.

Linds, I say. For some reason I'm whispering. *Do you have any clothes I can borrow?*

For a minute she blanks. Then she says, Hang on, and leaves the room.

I come out of the bathroom. Just to be in her room without her. Just to pretend, for a moment, that I can be here whenever I like.

When she comes back she's holding a T-shirt that says PELLS LANDING HIGH SCHOOL and sweatpants. They are boys' clothes. But they are not mine. My stomach lurches at the thought that they might be Matt Barnaby's, and I almost say his name, but I don't.

Instead I say, Whose are these?

My brother's, she says.

I have nothing to say to this. I want to touch her but I can't.

You shaved, she says. You're all cut up.

I touch my cheek and my fingers come away bloody.

Lindsay looks at the rest of me, standing there in her parents' towel. Oh my God, she says, you're so skinny.

I feel very embarrassed when she says this. I cover my skinny chest with my arms.

Here, says Lindsay, and hands me her dead brother's clothing.

I go back into the bathroom to put it on. It only seems right. The pants are too big at the waist and too short and for the first time I imagine Lindsay's brother as a person.

I sit on the bed. Lindsay sits on the bed. I feel warm and relaxed. I feel safe with her.

Tell me, Lindsay says, in a voice that sounds tired of asking.

So I do, and it feels like the reversal of a hundred-year-long spell. It feels like waking up. It feels like the shower did. I lie down on my side, facing her, and she lies down on her side. Facing me. When I cry my nose runs onto her comforter and I wipe it on the back of my wrist. Lindsay touches me again: a hand on my upper arm, a squeeze.

When I am done, I turn over, toward the wall, so she can't see my face. I bring my knees up to my chest and I hold them.

Why didn't you tell me before? asks Lindsay.

Because I didn't want her to think of me as a bad kid. Because I didn't want her to feel sorry for me. Because I was embarrassed. Because I wanted to be part of a club that she was in. Because I wanted her parents to like me. Because I didn't want her to think I was complicated, that I would burden her.

I say, I don't know.

What are you going to do? asks Lindsay.

I don't know, I say again to the wall.

I can't take care of you, she says. I'm too young.

I know this. I knew it to be true before I told her. But something in me hoped she would adopt me: she and her parents, together, would decide that I was too good and worthy to be alone in the world, and they would take me in, and all of us could take a family photograph. I could be in the next photo on their wall. I could play soccer with her sisters in the yard. I could fix things around the house.

I know, I say to Lindsay.

Let's talk to my dad, she says, and I say, No way.

It's his job, says Lindsay. His whole job is helping students.

She gets a look on her face like she is protecting her family's honor, so I say OK, maybe.

Good, she says. When he gets home.

Maybe, I say again.

What about college? she asks.

I'm not smart enough, I say. I know it is a self-pitying thing to say.

But Lindsay doesn't object. Well, she says. What about baseball?

I have a private practice with a scout for the Mets, I say, a little proudly. But after I say it I despair.

When?

Next week, I say.

Lindsay looks at me pointedly.

When's the last time you threw a baseball? she asks.

I shrug. I've been playing football all fall, I say.

You better eat something before next week, says Lindsay. A lot of things.

Then her face changes suddenly and she says Kel, Kel.

What?

I'm sorry. I'm so sorry for you.

Later, we go downstairs to the kitchen again. You should start eating now, says Lindsay.

Pasta, I say.

No, meat. Lots of meat, she says. Like, eggs and whole milk and meat.

She gets out what she can find from her fridge and puts it all in front of me. OK, go, she says.

She watches me.

After a few minutes she says, What about Arthur Opp?

Yolanda & I have begun to read the obituaries together. I read them aloud to her or she reads them aloud to me. It is not as morbid as it seems. Yolanda saw me looking at them one day & asked me what I was reading. I told her.

"Why?" she asked me.

& I told her I thought of it as an act of service, a way of commemorating & respecting. To think of each person individually, just for a moment, & to contemplate each life. The lonely ones especially, the childless or the left behind. It is my church—because I do not go.

"Who died?" asked Yolanda, & this was how it began.

This evening, I was reading them aloud to Yolanda as she chopped carrots in the kitchen. Every now & then I would pause to open a cabinet & close it again. I was very hungry but I was embarrassed to eat anything in front of her. I still have not grown used to it. She had been chopping carrots for a very long time.

"What do you want?" she asked me, finally.

"O nothing," I told her. But I stopped wandering & I stood in the doorframe instead. I could feel both sides of it pressing into me. Comfortingly.

"If you eat too many carrots the baby will be yellow," I said.

"No she won't," said Yolanda.

"She will indeed," I said.

"Fine," said Yolanda, and she went to the refrigerator & got out a cucumber, & chopped that all up as well. "Can you order some more cucumbers next time?"

"Yes I certainly can," I said, & I thought of all the things that can be done with cucumbers, including salting them & pickling them & putting them with cream cheese on a sandwich or a bagel.

Yolanda turned to me and wiped her brow with the back of her wrist & then put her other hand on her back & stretched like a cat. She made a little groaning noise as if she were in pain & I asked her was she.

"Just my back," she said. "I can't sleep well anymore."

At this I became gravely concerned & embarrassed at once. I wanted to offer her someplace else to sleep, for the mattresses in this house were bought in the 1960s and the sheets & pillows are just as old. But I had no offer to make, so I did not make one.

"I talked to my mom again," she said, and suddenly I saw her for the little girl she was, for her face sort of crumbled as she said it, the way anyone's does when one is talking about one's mother.

"What did you talk about?" I said.

"The baby," said Yolanda. She looked at me as if to say *What else.* Then she said Come on, and walked swiftly toward me carrying a plate of carrots and cucumbers, & I backed up out of her way, & she stomped firmly into the dining room, placing her snack on the table.

We sat down there. It felt formal & appropriate. I felt she had something to tell me. She ate her vegetables & offered me some & I declined at first but not for long.

"Would you like to tell me about it?" I asked. This is what I used to say to my students. They would sit across from me just as Yolanda was sitting. They would cast their eyes downward when upset or embarrassed. It is amazing what students will tell you. Everything. I felt at times like a priest or a therapist. I loved it. I miss it now, the feeling of being confessed to.

"Why would I?" said Yolanda. "I don't know anything about you." & she said this very gloomily & propped her head up on her little hands.

It stung. We both ate a carrot & let her pronouncement linger in the air.

"I'm sorry," I said. "I'm not very good at such things."

Marty had been the only one to drag it out of me. & Marty was gone.

Yolanda shrugged. We sat together silently until

the room was full of silence & I was afraid to say anything for fear that I would break something. I was still as a flower.

Finally Yolanda spoke. "My mother was thirty when she had me," she said. "She was old. She didn't think she could have kids even."

"Not *old* . . ." I said.

"Whatever, she didn't think she could have kids. She prayed for a baby every day. When I was born it was a miracle. Then she never had any other kids after me."

"An only child," I said.

I asked her where her parents were from. "Argentina," she said.

"Buenos Aires? Rosario? Córdoba?" I asked, with a wish to be connected to her past. When I was a child I was obsessive about geography and what I learned then has, with surprising consistency, remained intact.

"In the country," she said. "In the mountains."

She said a favorite uncle brought her mother and father over when they were young and in love and newly married. The uncle got her mother a job cleaning houses, which is still how she makes a living. But for Yolanda she had wanted something different.

"What did she want you to do?" I asked her.

"I don't really know," said Yolanda.

"Go to college?"

"I don't really know," she said again, sadly. She

was wearing her too-large sweat outfit that I hope is not Junior's and she put the hood of it up and played with the drawstrings of it, pulling them taut until only her nose was showing. She was jigging her legs up and down, which she always does when she's sitting.

"I met Junior through a friend," she said, muffledly. "I never brought him around because I knew they wouldn't like him. Then when I got pregnant I had to bring him over and I was right. They didn't."

"Do you?"

"Not anymore," she said. "Not even at all. I don't know why I ever did," she said. She was tying the drawstrings of her hood into a bow, blindly. Her whole face was obscured by the gray fabric. She looked like a helmeted knight.

"When I told them I was pregnant they said that's it. They said, you're an adult now and you have to work now. They took me out of school. I was about to be a senior in high school. I would have graduated this spring."

"O no," I said.

"I deserved it," said Yolanda. She nodded through the hood. "I did."

I began eating carrots to have something to do. I crunched them very brutally. I did not want to think that I was doing Yolanda a disservice by having her here. But things were coming into focus.

353

"My mom got me a job at Home-Maid and the first place they sent me was your house."

I swallowed the carrots before they were fully chewed.

She undid her hood, slowly, and then took it down from her head. Her hair, which is normally pulled back tightly, was loose and slightly fuzzy. Like a chick. In general she reminds me of a chick. It is in how she moves & in her general greenness, her dearness. She is something to be cradled.

"Do you want to go back to school?" I asked her.

"Maybe someday," said Yolanda. "I don't care. Maybe."

"Once the baby's born?"

"Maybe," she said again, & then I could tell she was done with the subject. She looked at me with her eyebrows raised then.

"Go," she said. "Your turn. You have to go now."

She was looking at me fiercely. I could tell she was waiting to be betrayed.

So I had to do as she said.

"I was born here," I said.

"Here in this house?"

"Here in Brooklyn."

"How old are you?"

"Fifty-eight years old."

"Go."

"I was not a happy child. I was not well liked."

"Why not?"

"I did not know how to act like the people I went to school with."

"Why not?"

"Because they all had parents that had grown up here too. And grandparents."

"And your parents were born in England."

"Yes."

"So they had accents?"

"They did indeed."

"Why did they move here?"

"For his work."

"He was an architect."

"Is. Yes."

"Go ahead."

"My father was not kind to my mother. He was very infrequently home, and when he was he was berating her in one way or another."

"Berating?"

"Insulting."

"For what?"

"For her weight, mostly. She was large."

"As big as you?"

I paused. It stung. I let it sting. It was her honesty.

"No. Not as large as I am. Still large. She was always trying things. Mail-order brochures for calisthenics programs. The lentil soup diet. The grapefruit diet. She was always stuffing herself into dresses that didn't fasten."

"What was her name?"

"Her name was Anna."

"Pretty."

"She was pretty. She had a face that looked like the moon. When I was a child I would look up at it and think about the moon."

I ate a carrot.

"What was school like for you?" I asked her.

"Fun," she said. "I liked it."

But she would say no more. This is a standard Yolanda answer.

"She called herself Anna Ordinary. Or she called herself Mrs. Tubbs," I said.

"What did she eat?"

"Everything she could think of. My father was away on business much of the time. When he was gone we would have special treats. The night before he came back she would stand in front of her mirror and force herself into her corset and then force herself into whatever dress she planned on greeting him in. Often I was in charge of fastening it, and often it would not go."

"What would she do?"

"She would buy another dress."

A teakettle whistled in the kitchen and Yolanda got up to answer it. I hadn't known she had put any on. She doesn't drink tea. I realized that it must have been for me, & the great weight of my appreciation for Yolanda settled into my gut.

She returned with a mug of it and a quart of milk. I thanked her kindly.

"Go," she said.

"My father left us."

"They got divorced?"

"No, he left. I was eight years old, almost nine. They never divorced. He said he was going to work on a building in England so he'd be over there for quite some time. He never came back."

"Did you go there?"

"Once. Much later."

"Did your mom want to move back?"

Yolanda has a very charming habit of, when she is asking questions, looking absolutely fascinated with your responses, her chin on her hand, leaning toward you slightly, smiling when it is appropriate, widening her eyes, gasping in horror, clapping, even. She shakes her head in disgust when things disgust her. She moans, "Oh no," when she hears something she does not like.

"I believe she would have liked to, yes. But she would not allow herself to."

"Why not?"

"It would have meant that she had failed. She came from a good family. They both did. My father continued to support us from abroad. He still supports me."

I paused. There were parts of this story that I had never articulated. Perhaps not even allowed myself to think. But in that moment Yolanda seemed a safe vessel for them.

"She—my mother—always insisted he would

return. Even after he stopped calling altogether. She would dress herself up sometimes as if she expected him to walk in the door. When she wrote to her relatives she always referenced him, and the projects he was working on in England, as if he had told her about them."

"When's the last time you saw him?"

"Just after my mother died. I was eighteen. He wrote to me—it was the first letter I'd had from him in almost a decade—and said he was very sorry to hear about Anna, and would I like to come see him in England."

"So you went?"

"I went on the *QE2*. A big ship. I used a suitcase that was my father's, one that he had left behind. When he left he did not pack most of his things, so they stayed in this house for years until I threw them all out in my twenties."

I became embarrassed suddenly. I pressed one hand to my cheek and felt its hotness.

"I thought perhaps he would recognize me by his old suitcase. If he did not recognize me by my person, which had changed quite a bit since I was ten."

"You got fat?"

"I did. Yes."

Yes. I did. Not as fat as I am now. But fat all the same. It got very bad when I was a teenager. On the *QE2*, I spent a week at sea avoiding the formal dinners they had because I was too embarrassed to eat how much I really wanted to. Additionally I was by myself and the concept of being thrown together with a group of strangers every evening was too much for me to bear. So instead I requested dinners in my room. Dinners that would have been enough for three. For six. In the daytime sometimes I went up on deck and looked out at the vast sea & felt sorry for myself. Or I read. But most of that trip I spent holed up in my room, eating.

I had brought light blue bell-bottom pants, a sort of turtleneck sweater, & brown suede shoes. I had saved this outfit for the day I would meet my father. I imagined that this was a very smart outfit. I had long hair then. Down to my shoulders. It was 1971. The day of our arrival, I panicked: I realized that I could hardly button the pants. In a week I had gained enough weight to make them tight. I squeezed & squeezed myself into them. I thought of my mother doing the same thing, years ago, before my father left. I strained the fabric, I forced myself into them, & finally the button went through the hole. I couldn't breathe out. I felt trapped.

I wanted to tell her this. Instead I said, "There was my father, waiting down at the bottom of the gangplank with hundreds of other onlookers. I recognized him but he looked older."

He looked at me & then away. He looked at me & then away.

He stood up from where he leaned against the railing.

At ten feet away I said his name. *Arthur.* I could not bring myself to call him Dad.

He looked at me again, & he did not smile.

I was close enough now for him to shake my hand, but he didn't. He reached out and put one hand on my shoulder.

"My goodness," he said.

"What was your father like? When you saw him again?" asked Yolanda.

"He was the same but different. We drove together from Southampton, where the ship had come in, to London. He was quiet, you know."

He had an Aston Martin. I could not fit in it well. It was a two-hour drive to London, & we stopped once along the way for lunch. He sat across from me & ordered a prawn cocktail. Then he ordered steak and chips & I ordered the same.

"You look like Anna," he said. "Almost exactly like Anna."

My mother had always told me I looked like him, but I did not say that, I could not imagine saying that. Instead I said, "People used to tell us that."

"I was so sorry to hear about her death," said my father.

"She's better off," I said, which was & was not true.

"What are you going to do with yourself now?" asked my father.

"I'm not quite sure," I said. "College. I don't know."

"Have you applied already? Have you gotten in?"

"Yes," I said.

"Where?"

I had applied to Harvard, Yale, Princeton, Dartmouth, Stanford, Amherst, and, as a backup, New York University. Of these, I had been admitted to Amherst and New York University.

"Amherst College," I told my father.

"Amherst," he said, looking off into the distance. "That's in Maine?"

"Massachusetts," I said.

"It's very good?"

"It's very good," I said.

"Excellent," he said. "Congratulations."

I did not eat much of my lunch. I was starving but embarrassed. We were quiet for most of the rest of the trip.

"Would you like to take a detour through Maidenhead on the way into London?" he asked. "It's a bit out of the way, but."

"OK," I said.

I vaguely remembered parts of it from a visit in my early childhood. I had gone with my parents to visit my Granny Conan. He pointed out to me the places that would have been important to my mother: her childhood home, Granny Conan's home; a park she loved; his house, his favorite store, which still existed. The church they both went to with their parents.

I didn't say anything, but I happened to know that it was at this church that they had met. At a dance. I had heard the story over & over again from my mother. My father had been the most handsome boy in the room. Her friend Lorraine had pointed him out to her specially. My mother hadn't thought he could possibly notice her. But then he did, he did. He came walking over. He was wearing a beautiful suit. He had asked her to dance. Not her friend Lorraine, who was considered a beauty, & who had been sitting right next to her. Not Lorraine. My mother.

"There's my school," said my father. I could only see a glimpse of it from the road. The sign in front of it said St Piran's, which was a name I knew from the tales my mother had told me about my father's life. "I spent a number of terrible years there."

"Did my mother?" I asked—for I realized suddenly that for all the time my mother spent describing my father's childhood, she had never told me much about her own education. Or else I had forgotten. Already I was beginning to forget.

"Heavens, no," said my father. "It was for boys then."

•••

When we got to London everything changed. The women were dressed in what looked like costumes to me: bubbly dresses or striped tight pants. The men as well—brightly colored suits and ruffled shirts and polished boots. We pulled into a parking lot below a very fancy stone-sided building with turrets and gables and crenellations. He jumped out without parking his car and wordlessly handed the keys to a boy about my age. I had a harder time getting out & it took me a moment to regain feeling in my legs. They had been mildly asleep for half an hour. I got my suitcase out of the trunk and held it awkwardly. Behind us, the boy parked the car like an expert. I couldn't drive. I still can't.

"This way," said my father.

The lobby of his building was polished. Every surface looked as if it had been rubbed with a soft cloth until it gleamed. There were fancy women walking back and forth in fancy ridiculous hats. Their boots clacked across the floor. There were little dogs in little handbags.

When we took the elevator up I think my father was nervous about being in it with some-one my size. An Indian elevator man said, "Good afternoon, Mr Opp." But my father said nothing about who I was.

His apartment was the penthouse. The elevator opened directly into it. It was large & spectacular

& modern, & I was very surprised. I had thought —it was an integral part of my ideas about my father—that he preferred old things, that his taste ran toward antiques & dark wood & brass. This was what our house was like in Brooklyn. Our brownstone that he had chosen especially for us, his family. My house was my father's house, always—my mother always told me how much he loved our house.

But this apartment was open & airy, with a wall of windows that looked out on the city. Modern art covered the walls. A plush zebra-striped carpet covered a large part of the floor. There was a giant vase with tall white branches coming out of it like crooked fingers.

"Here we are," said my father. "Let me take your luggage." He took it before I could say anything, & it was only then that he finally looked at it.

"I recognize this," he said. But it was too late.

I was alone. I shifted awkwardly from foot to foot. My pants cut into my belly. My shoulders strained against my silly turtleneck sweater.

I heard tiny footsteps walking down the hallway to my left, & when I turned around to look there was a little boy, five or six years old, redhaired & tiny & knobby-kneed. He was wearing short pants like the ones my mother had put me into on my first day of school.

My heart dropped.

"Hello," I said.

"Hello," he said.

"What's your name?" I asked him.

"William," he said.

"I'm Arthur," I said.

"I know," he said.

He sidled toward me. He was very serious. He had his hands in his pockets.

"Where's all your things?" he asked me.

"My father has them," I said. & realized then what I should have said. I felt huge. I felt I was an imbecile.

He looked at me.

"You're from New York," he said.

"Yes," I said. His accent. Before I got to school and had it beaten out of me, I used to have an accent like his. When I was a very small boy and spoke mainly to my mother and father.

"Daddy used to live there," he said.

"Yes, he did," I said.

My father's girlfriend's name was Alexandra. She had red hair like her son. It came down to her waist. She was younger than my father, but not by all that much. She was very beautiful and very kind. She scooped William up when she found him talking to me and turned him upside down like it was nothing.

"Oh *Arthur*," she said. "We are *so glad you're here*."

Her eyes filled with tears and she smiled in such a way that it looked like she was frowning.

My father came back into the room and said "Ah, well, you've all met each other."

We went to dinner that night at a very fancy restaurant where they all knew the chef. I sat across from them, my father and Alexandra, and William sat next to me, except when he was up & running about the restaurant. Alexandra asked me lots of questions about New York and said she had a number of connections there, & that the next time she visited she would be sure to look me up & we'd have tea. I'll be at college in Massachusetts, I thought, but I said nothing. She asked me if I'd been to several restaurants in Manhattan that I had never heard of. It meant to me that my father had been in my city without calling me. The chef came out after the meal and knuckled the head of young William, who grabbed his wrist and clung to it & tried to hang off it. Alexandra swatted her son playfully. "Monsieur Molineux," said Alexandra to the chef, "*C'était tres bon. Trop bon.*"

My father worked all the next week. I saw London. I stayed out of the house for as long as I could. When I had visited every museum & every neighborhood that I wanted to see, I sat on benches in Hyde Park & wrote in my diary. I was sad. I missed my mother. William, by this point, had figured out that we were brothers, of a sort, & referred to me constantly as such. The differences between us made me very embarrassed. I wished I could be more natural around him. But I didn't know how to be.

Once, Alexandra told me that it must have been difficult growing up the way I had, and that she understood because she'd had a mother like mine. "Still," she said. "What a terrible loss. I'm so sorry."

It wasn't Alexandra's fault that she said those things. I still don't think it was her fault. My father had probably lied to her.

On Friday evening he sat down across from me—I had been lying on a sofa, thinking nobody was home, and when he entered the room I sprang to my feet—and asked me, "Arthur, have you given any thought to when you'd like to leave?"

I hadn't. I was not sure what to say.

"I suppose you have plans for the summer?"

I did not. I made something up. A job that I did not have.

"Here's the rub," said my father. "The three of us are going to the shore next week to visit Alexandra's parents. I'd invite you, but I thought that."

He did not finish.

"Anyway I've bought you a return ticket," said my father. "Different ship. You can exchange it if you like," he said. "I don't mean to rush you.

Stay as long as you like. Use the flat while we're gone."

I decided that I wouldn't.

On the day I was to leave, my father asked if I would mind terribly if he sent me to Southampton on the bus—he had a work obligation that he simply could not escape. Alexandra said, "You must come back and visit us anytime you like. William will be so sad if you don't."

"He had a family over there," I said to Yolanda. "A different family."

"Oh *no*," said Yolanda.

"Yes, he did."

"What about your mom?"

"He wasn't married to the woman over there. They just had a son together."

"You got a brother, then," said Yolanda. "You told me you didn't."

"I suppose I do," I said.

"What's his name?" said Yolanda.

"William," I said.

"You don't talk to him?"

"No," I said. "I don't talk to any of them."

I never saw them again in my life. I know that my father married Alexandra after my mother's death, for in his biography it says so. I do not know what William is doing. I know that my father is still alive, for I get Christmas and birthday cards from him—this tradition began upon my departure from London & has not ceased—along with the money that he puts into the fund he established for me as a boy. But I know nothing else about him beyond what I read in the papers. The three of them exist in my mind as a hallucination or a mirage. That week exists in my mind as the week I lived somebody else's life. Not mine. Certainly not mine.

I told the girl none of this. I said, "Thank you."

"Yeah," said Yolanda.

She paused. "How long you been inside here?"

"Here inside this house?"

"Yeah."

"Ten years."

"Till now," she said.

"Why now?" I asked her.

"Because we went for a walk!" she said triumphantly. "We went outside."

"You're right," I told her.

She went to bed not long after that. She put her sweatshirt's hood up again. Ascending the stairs, she looked like a gnome, or like somebody's good-luck charm.

I talked to Lindsay's dad. He got home before Lindsay's mother. Lindsay and I were sitting in the living room. Lindsay said, Dad. We need your help.

He sat down across from me on his couch. I was in an easy chair. I hadn't seen him since the Thanksgiving football game, and I don't believe I had ever looked him in his face before. It was a nice face. It looked like Lindsay's. Open. I told him everything I could tell him. I see, he said, over and over again.

He said, This must have been very hard for you.

I can see why he is a good superintendent and probably a good father.

I could see him thinking about his son. I do not know his son's name. Lindsay's brother's name. I felt bad for her. She was looking at the wall next to my head, and it was very clear that she was remembering him. It occurred to me that it was wrong of me never to ask her his name and never to tell her to put her head on my shoulder and cry.

Mrs. Harper came home later with Lindsay's two sisters and looked surprised to see me. Do you guys want pizza? she asked, and there was nothing I wanted more, but I told her I had to go. Mr.

Harper shook my hand when I left and held it.

Kel, he said. You're going to be fine. OK? OK? You're going to be fine.

When I walked out I forgot where I had parked my car for a minute. On the street, said Lindsay, from inside the door. When I turned around she was a dark shape in the window. Behind her was her brightly lit house.

I went to Dee's. I tried to call him on my way but he didn't answer. So I just went and rang the doorbell. Rhonda answered the door. She had dyed her hair blond and there was a purple streak in it. There was a new gap in her teeth that you could see when she smiled. She's known me since I was born.

Oh, baby, she said to me. Oh, you poor kid. She put both big arms around me and then put one on the back of my head. It wasn't awkward, it felt good. She hummed to herself. She was always fucked up when we were kids, always with a different guy. My mother used to say she had a reputation in high school. When I slept over at Dee's, sometimes we heard her fighting loudly with whatever man she had over. Dee would cover his head with a pillow. I would pretend I was asleep so he would not be embarrassed. I would not tell my mother for fear of her not letting me stay there anymore.

Dee told me she'd found Jesus, and sure enough there was a big cross around her neck, and when she told me to come in I saw a poster on the wall that said *Footprints.* It was about God carrying people around.

Dee's not home from practice yet, she said, but he will be soon. Sit.

She gave me a turkey sandwich.

Thanks, I said. My mouth was full.

Then I spilled my guts for the third time that day, and Dee came home in the middle, and I just kept talking.

Dee's mom was crying now, she was a mess, and Dee said Mom, Jesus, wipe your nose, and his mom said Don't say *Jesus,* baby.

I said, In her note she told me that my father wasn't my real father.

I expected her to cover her mouth in astonishment, but instead she nodded sadly and said, I know that. I knew that.

I sat. I felt betrayed. I put both of my elbows on my knees.

Kel Keller, she said, as if she were thinking about him.

I wanted to ask her the most important question I had but I felt like I was losing my breath. So instead I asked her a secondary question. How did you know? I said.

Well, said Rhonda. Right around the time she got pregnant, she called me up scared. She didn't wanna tell your grandparents. I said, Is it Kel's? And she said, No, I haven't seen Kel in a year. They dated in high school but they broke up after that.

Rhonda was sitting on the sofa across the room from me. There was stuffing coming out of it. She was covering her belly with a cushion. She was still teary-eyed. Dee got up suddenly and went into the kitchen and came out with two Yoo-hoos, one of which he tossed to me.

Oh, Charlene, said Rhonda. We were just kids back then. I had already had this one, she said, jerking a thumb toward Dee, who smiled and shrugged.

—She called me and said, What do I do, Rhonda? I said, Whose is it? But she wouldn't tell me.

You don't know? I said. I was relieved and disappointed all at once.

—She would never tell me. Wouldn't tell Kel Keller either. But he had always been in love with her so he took her back. It was a big secret that you weren't his. I mean he must have known, but he acted like you were his son. She told her parents you were. He told his parents. They got married in Atlantic City. I was maid of honor. When he left your mother she was sad but not that sad. They weren't right for each other. I always told her that.

OK, I said. OK.

Dee was looking down. He tossed his bottle of Yoo-hoo into the air and caught it out of the air. I was so angry with my mother suddenly that I didn't know what to do. I wanted to yell at her the way I used to when she was alive. To be honest, that's what I wanted to do. Or to grab her and shake her by the shoulders. Which I never did, never except for once, when she was passed out, when she was acting like a child. I shook her hard.

Have you heard of Arthur Opp? I said.

Arthur Opp, she said. She started to shake her head slowly but then clapped her hand to her mouth. Arthur Opp! she said. She laughed. That's a name I haven't heard in years.

You have? I said.

—Just after we graduated, she went to college for a semester. You know that?

—Yeah.

—Arthur Opp was one of her professors. She had a crush on him, said Rhonda, her face still lit up with the memory of what it was like to be young. She used to talk about him all the time. My God, Arthur Opp.

I paused. I did not want to say it yet. I wanted her to go on.

—We made up a song about him. We were being silly. I can't remember how it went.

I thought of my mother at my age. It was hard.

—You know what? said Rhonda. They used to write to each other. They were like pen pals. After she dropped out of school she wrote to Arthur Opp to thank him for teaching her, and then he wrote back. She was real excited. She showed me the letter. They wrote to each other for a while.

—I know, I said. I used to see his letters.

I wanted to tell her the rest but I waited for a long time. Something about it felt so personal and strange that I didn't even want to bring it up. I felt like I was opening my mother up for teasing.

Your mother was different than all of us, said Rhonda. She was always falling in love with these guys. God bless her.

I said, She told me.

Dee and his mother waited.

—That Arthur Opp was my father.

My face got hot and I looked away from everyone, out the window, into the dark street.

Rhonda sat in stunned silence for a minute and then did the worst thing she could possibly have done: she burst out laughing.

Mom, said Dee. Jesus.

Good for her, Rhonda said. Sorry. But good for her.

She could have been lying, I said.

Maybe, said Rhonda.

I'm named after him though, I said.

Arthur? said Dee. Your real name's Arthur?

Yeah, I said, Arthur. At this point I was almost laughing too. I don't know why but it felt good to almost laugh.

Arthur, said Dee again. And the laughter burst out of him too in a holler. He lowered his head over his knees to laugh.

And then we were all laughing, and Rhonda the hardest, patting her own cheeks, wiping her eyes, gazing off into the distance someplace, remembering things about my mother that I would never know.

Later she asked me did I want to stay there, and I said just for a couple nights, if she didn't mind. But I have been there ever since. I've been sleeping on the couch, buying my own food with the hundred dollars that the other Kel Keller gave me.

Next I went back to school. Mr. Harper said he would talk to the principal and to my teachers, and I think he did a good job, because they have all been especially nice to me. Matt Barnaby still has a bruise on his cheek, still has a black eye. Trevor still won't talk to me, but Kurt will. At lunch I sit with Kurt now, and with some people he is friends with.

Lindsay sits with me now too. Her friends, I think, are still mad at me. In my opinion this means they are good friends.

It's nice in a way not to be going out with her. I miss her but it's nice to have her as a friend, as a very good friend, it's nice that for the first time she knows who I am and I know who she is. It's important.

Pottsy made me stay after class and said Anything you need, Keller.

Thanks, I said.

Anything you need, he said again.

Thanks, I said again.

I'm not allowed to play basketball this winter.

I'm sorry, said Coach. It's just not in my power to let you.

I imagine that Matt Barnaby's parents had a hand in this. But I don't particularly care. Dee and I play basketball together on the Warburton court when he gets home from practice. It's usually dark already and it's usually very cold. We play until our fingers freeze, until the inside of our ears burn from the panting. Only streetlamps light the court. Anyone else would be scared to play at night. But we're not: we're huge, we're bigger than everyone else. We could kill anyone who tried to hurt us. We live here and this is our neighborhood. We play and play for hours. Sometimes he lets me make a shot.

I have been telling people. I have stopped lying or being very silent. I have been telling everyone the truth. I have been letting them help me. They all want to help me and so I am letting them.

Lindsay told me that when someone in your

family dies you have to let people think they are helping. It is kind to. It helps *them,* she told me. It helps them to think they are helping.

So I've been trying. For Lindsay.

I have to do something about my mother. A woman from the hospital called and told me that she was sorry, but I was going to have to do something about her body immediately. Apparently they've been calling a lot.

I talked to Mr. Harper about it and he says I am the one that has to make the decision.

When we—he said. Have you thought about cremation? he said.

I never had. I always thought my mother would be buried. It's what happened to people after they died. But something about cremation made sense to me. I feel as if my mother spent her whole life being buried. I feel as if she should be released somewhere.

Mr. Harper said he would call the woman and talk to her about it.

I have to sell the house. It isn't mine, anyway. I'll never go back into it. Only for my things. Only for her things. And I need the money. Mr. Harper says he can help me with that too. His sister is a real estate broker in Scarsdale. I imagine my mother's will be the shittiest house she ever sold.

I wrote an obituary to put in the paper. I didn't have to, but I wanted to. Pottsy helped me write it.

Yes. I keep letting people help me. I feel like I am opening, but also like I am dying.

I talked to Gerard Kane's assistant on the phone. Sarah. She still sounded pretty. I put on a deep voice when I talked to her. I felt powerful for the first time in a very long time.

I said, Can Gerard still do Saturday the 10th?

I called him by his first name. Like a man.

She said, We're on.

So that's when it is. I don't feel ready, but I have to be.

I looked up Arthur Opp on the computer at school. There is only one Arthur Opp in New York City, and he lives in Brooklyn. There was no information about him. It seems like he does not teach anymore. Just a phone number and address. I wrote down both on a little piece of paper and put it in my wallet alongside my mother's letter.

Late at night, after Dee and his mother were both asleep, I called him. I let it ring once and then hung up.

In some ways I feel that I am everyone's son. That I have many parents now.

Pottsy and I wrote this about my mother.

379

Charlene Louise Turner Keller of Yonkers died Monday, November 28, at the age of 38. She was the mother of Arthur "Kel" Turner Keller and the daughter of Paul and Barbara Turner (both deceased). She worked for five and a half years at Pells Landing High School. She was a good person and she loved to have a good time. She had a long struggle with a lot of different illnesses.

May she rest in peace.

I thought you just sent the obituary to the paper and they put it in, but Pottsy said no, you have to pay. I panicked a little but Pottsy said he wanted to pay for it. That he'd be in charge of it.

No, you don't have to, I said. I don't have to put one in for her.

But in my heart I felt she had spent her life not being noticed. So I wanted to tell someone—I wanted strangers to read it and to think, She was too young—and to shake their heads. And to say her name in their heads.

So I was relieved when Pottsy put a hand on my shoulder and said Keller. I want to.

"So many of them are young," said Yolanda. It was her turn to read the obituaries. She was leaning forward in her chair, her ankles hooked around its legs.

Just as I realized who it was Yolanda reminded me of, she read a name aloud: "Charlene Turner Keller."

I said, "What did you say?"

"This woman," said Yolanda. "She was young. She had a kid too." She touched her own stomach.

Before a game, when I was young, my mother would say, Don't be nervous! and I would say, I'm not, and she would say, Me neither. Then she would say, You look nervous, and I would say, I'm *not*.

The thing is that she was right. I was nervous. I was always nervous and only she could see that. I was shaking in my cleats, I was fucking terrified. A little kid. But I'd walk onto the field like a pro, tossing the ball in the air, grinning at the other team if I wanted, chucking the ball hard back and forth with someone to warm up. A little sound like *hup, hup* would come out of me when I was really throwing well.

She took my hand in the car. When I let her. And I did let her, because I was nervous, and she was the only one who knew it.

I wake up dreaming of her and this. It's the first nice dream I've had about her, and I take it as a good sign. I have slept in my lucky socks, the ones I've been wearing the night before games since I was about ten. I hit my first grand slam wearing them. No one is up in the house yet. It is my job to wake Dee up, and I shuffle down the hall and knock lightly on his door. No response.

Yo, I whisper. I do not want to wake Rhonda up.

I knock again, louder, and then crack open the door to Dee's room. He has heavy dark blinds that make the room black even though the sun is up. I see him in the light of the hallway, asleep in the same twin bed he's always had, his feet hanging a foot off of it. When I used to sleep over when we were kids we had a rule: whoever woke up first would wake the other one up. I usually slept later than he did. I'd be in my sleeping bag on the floor and a basketball or a pillow or a sock would hit me in the face, and Dee would say, Get up.

Now I walk over to him and give the bed a shove with my foot.

He opens his eyes.

You up? I ask him.

I am now, he says.

He's driving me to my workout with Gerard Kane. Just before we walk out the door, Rhonda comes flying down the hall. Good luck, she says, I prayed for you!

Thank you, I say, and we close the door.

Behind us, through the closed door, we can hear her talking. I'm still praying! I'm praying now, she is saying.

I could drive myself but Dee offered and I let him. It's at a giant practice facility in Eastchester, and we take the parkway to get there, and on the way Dee puts on the radio. He doesn't ask me if I'm nervous and I'm grateful.

Instead he tells me things about the girls we grew up with. Who is pregnant and who is in jail and who dropped out of school. All of the girls he tells me about are girls I hooked up with when I was younger, or smoked with, or drank with, or kissed on a cold park bench in a bad bad park. Remember Denise? he asks me, and I say I do. Dead, he says.

—How?

Overdose, he says.

He looks straight ahead of him and never at me. I do the same.

All the girls he tells me about were four years younger and full of ideas when I knew them. Denise Torres wore a bright green jacket every day in the winter and her laugh started with a *K*.

I have been trying to imagine what my mother was like when she was young. She would have been small. She would have been quiet unless she was nervous. If she was nervous she would have talked too much. I know she had one or two friends because Rhonda was one of them but I don't imagine she had many more. I know she did not get along with her parents. They were not much in our lives and then they died. They did not like her husband, the man who used to be my father. She would have shuffled head-down through the hallways of her school. She would have found heroes to worship because she always did. She would have had crushes on teachers and senior boys who did not know her. All the girls I know from Yonkers, all the girls who will never leave, she was like them.

I wanted her to wait until I could take better care of her. I wanted her to wait until I was old enough to fix her, make her well again, put her someplace warm and tight.

I can see the practice facility over some trees while we are still on the parkway. A white bubble like the top of a circus tent. I feel a tug in my gut. I've been working out all week with Coach Ramirez, who told me how stupid I was not to call him sooner. But still. I've been eating eggs and steak and vegetables. I've been lifting but not enough to make me sore. I've been drinking protein shakes. One of my teammates told me he could get me juice from a guy he knows but the good scared and superstitious boy inside me told him no.

The facility looks huge when we pull up outside it. It's as big as a warehouse. Both of us look at it.

What's it like inside? I ask Dee.

There's a field inside, says Dee. With bleachers and a wall and everything. Nice turf.

Did you play here? I ask him.

Nah, he says, and he looks embarrassed. My

mom brought me here to see some preacher last year. They used it for a church. People falling down in the aisle like—

And he mimes a seizure, his eyes rolling back in his head, hands going up. He laughs.

You need me to stick around? asks Dee.

I say no. Lindsay has offered to pick me up. I pat the roof of the car when he drives off and then I am alone.

I wasn't sure what to bring with me so last night I emptied out a small athletic bag of mine and cleaned it because it smelled bad. Then I carefully put everything I could think of into it. My cleats are inside the bag. My glove. Four bottles of water. A bag of trail mix. I don't know how long I'll be here. A cell-phone charger. I don't know why. A copy of this highlights video that Coach and I put together at the end of last season. My wallet. Inside of it is my mother's note to me. I carry it around everyplace I go.

I'm wearing my summer-league uniform, the Cardinals' uniform, which I now think might have been stupid. Over this I am wearing a sweatshirt and sweatpants. I take a long slow breath in and out. The air is freezing. The glass doors to the inside are covered in frost from the cold. I open the one on the right.

When Yolanda went to bed last night I sat up for longer than I usually do. I did not move from my chair. I leaned my head back and looked up at the ceiling, & then I looked all around me at my world. The dark wooden shelves loaded with books. The television, O my joy & comfort. The musty old couch.

I lifted up my shirt and looked down at my belly. I used to do this when I was young.

I thought of Charlene and how I had betrayed her. For really I felt this way: that I had betrayed her & myself. That somehow I had a hand in her death.

Before she called me this fall, before Yolanda came to me, in the ten years I spent with myself and no one else, I had ways of consoling myself. Yes there was food, but there was beyond food this idea I had of an oversoul of loneliness. A connectedness among the world's lonely that I could turn to when I was very low. There was a delicious romance in being utterly alone, & I told myself I was nobler for it, & that there was a purpose to my solitude, O there must be.

I would pray. I no longer pray as much, now that Yolanda is here. I would pray first thing in the morning and last thing at night. I would remind myself of how many people there were like me, & how many people fall into the despair of loneli-ness, every day it happens, I would say, every day someone loses his connection to the world & then becomes the noble hermit, becomes connected to himself, the snake eating its tail, & then he must look steadily toward the lonely oversoul for help, he must or he will die. And then he becomes like I am, and the oversoul grows and expands lovingly, generously, and welcomes him as a member of its secret club. All of the people in the world who are lonely or sick or very sad.

Before everything, before Marty died—Marty, my dearest friend in the world. While I was still teaching, & even before. When I was a child. When I was unborn. I felt destined for solitude, very certain that one day it would find me, so when it did I was not surprised & even welcomed it.

Throughout my life I have met only one person with whom I felt a certain kinship in this regard, and it was Charlene Turner. From the moment I met her I thought—you too? And I could see by the look in her eyes that she also felt it. She was more lonely at the time than I, I could sense it, and it made me love her.

Last night, in my sorrow, I went into the drawer of my bedside table for the ten-thousandth time & from it I took out her stack of letters. Then I found what I was looking for: the letter in which she first suggested that we meet. & I allowed my mind to drift back through years & years, to the sense of possibility I felt when I first received that letter, the glimpse into a future very different than the one that, as it turned out, lay before me. I recalled our dinners together, our lunches, the glory of sitting across a table from a woman. Each time I saw her, I felt more & more convinced that she understood something about me, & I her.

This feeling in me was solidified the first time we went out for dinner & she ordered several things & ate them unself-consciously. It was roast beef she was having, & she cut it into little precise squares first, & dipped them into their sauce, & then chewed them with her mouth open sometimes, looking all around the room. She drank too much. She had three rum and Cokes. It seemed like a childish drink to me. I was having water. I've never drunk very much. I was having water and shepherd's pie that at first I tried to eat delicately, but she was so oblivious to me, still, that I relaxed.

She became quiet halfway through the meal. I asked her was she upset about something but she would not tell me at first. Then after a while she took her glasses off—I can see this motion still, hazily, as if in a dream—and put her fingers on the bridge of her nose. Then she turned her face toward me & put both her hands up to it. One on her forehead. One on her cheek. Her hair was down around her shoulders that night and lazily it slid off of one of them & down her back.

"I'm invisible," she said to me. "I'm really invisible." A very fat tear rolled down her cheek, the saddest tear I've ever seen, & I had and resisted the urge to touch it.

What do you mean, I asked her. But she shook her head & she would say no more. Instead she talked about school & work & how she planned on balancing the two, & how she had never been happier than she was now in her life, coming to school in the city, starting her life in the world. It was what she called it. Making her life in the world. I knew what she meant.

She stood up shakily at the end of the meal and raised one finger in the air as if testing the wind & she pointed it at me smiling.

I have always loved aggrieved & unbeautiful women. I have always loved beautiful women too, but it is the unbeautiful ones that haunt me & find me & abide, whose images I see before me when I go to sleep. My mother was unbeautiful. Charlene was unbeautiful. Marty.

None were invisible to me. Furthermore I don't believe I was invisible to them, & this has remained, for me, an anchor in the world. Charlene, in her letters to me, told me things about myself I had never been told before. She made me feel noble & worthy. She told me once that I was a hero of hers. For years, our correspondence allowed me to feel connected, still, to Charlene Turner. Even after she stopped responding. Even then. I thought of her, & remembered her fondly, feeding the ducks, sipping her drink, walking swiftly wherever she had to go. I thought of her & I felt she was surely also a member of my club. & so I did not blame her for losing touch. I really didn't blame her at all.

When, years later, she called me, it was a surprise but I realized that I had been expecting it all along. My innermost self had been expecting it.

She said to me, He'll call you. And so I began to hope. I did not hesitate to. I did the foolish thing of imagining a life with Charlene & her son. This led me to Yolanda. & Yolanda broke my spell of solitude. I feel somehow, I can't explain it, that my diminishing loneliness caused Charlene's to increase. I have felt, always, that we are connected by that thread.

She named her son Arthur. It breaks my heart. It touches me deeply & yet I feel that some chance has been wasted.

The first time we met for coffee, the fabric of her purple down coat got stuck in the teeth of its own zipper. I helped her. I moved her hands away from it with my own & I pulled the fabric loose without a tear. Thank you she said.

They're there when I arrive, Gerard Kane, his assistant Sarah—not as pretty as she sounded, a little plain—and another kid, a black kid, about my age, maybe a little older than me. I don't know who he is. A few other men stand around chatting with them. They could work for the facility, I'm not sure.

They're all sitting in the lobby, a large plain room with rough carpet. Like the lobby of a church, high-ceilinged, skylights letting sun in. Mr. Kane is drinking coffee. He's leaning forward in his chair, his arms resting on his knees. Even in the winter his sunglasses hang around his neck on a string. His face is sunburned except for around his eyes. His mustache is as neat as I remember, his forearms as huge. He's wearing a pullover windbreaker with the sleeves pushed up to his elbows.

Kel! he goes, when he sees me. How are you, kid?

He stands up to shake my hand and I set my things down.

This is Marcus Hobart, he says, indicating the kid sitting down next to him. He'll be pitching to you today.

When Marcus stands up I see he is even taller than I am. Definitely stronger.

How's it going? he asks me, and suddenly I realize he's there for the same reason I am.

Locker room's there, says Mr. Kane. Come on out when you're ready.

Marcus and I go in together. He pulls off his jacket and his tear-away pants and I see that he's wearing a summer-league uniform too. This makes me feel better.

You play for the Jays? I ask him.

Played, he says.

Cardinals, I say, pointing pointlessly to my uniform.

Cool, he says. You in school still?

Yeah, I say.

Where at?

Pells Landing, I say. But I live in Yonkers.

I got you, says Marcus. Like he doesn't care at all.

How bout you? I ask.

Played in college for the Gators for a season, says Marcus. But I hated it. Now I'm trying to make this happen, he says, patting the air on either side of him, indicating Gerard Kane and everything that goes along with him.

Before I leave I take out my mother's note and look at it. I want for it to comfort and inspire me, but it doesn't.

The main area of the facility is perfect. It's strange to be enclosed by something so large.

Sound bounces off things here. I can speak quietly and still be heard.

They have us toss the ball back and forth for a while. Farther and farther away from one another, to see what kind of carry we've got. It's something I've always been proud of: I can throw the damn ball as far as I want to. And precisely. Always I've been able to do this.

I chuck it to Marcus and it's high and right. He chucks it to me and it's perfect, it stings. Within a few throws I can feel my right shoulder warming up and then aching dully. It is not something I have felt before.

A mattress in the backyard. A mattress with a red bull's eye on it.

Marcus can throw the ball too—better than I can, maybe. It stings to catch a ball that this kid throws in from the outfield. I can feel it for seconds afterward. They have video cameras on us. They're recording what we do.

Warm up, Kel, says Gerard Kane, and hands me a weighted bat. He takes over what I was doing and throws the ball with Marcus for a while. I imagine what he's feeling: the sting of Marcus's arm, the winging ball hitting his glove and stinging.

The ache in my right shoulder gets stronger while I'm swinging the bat.

Several boys from a local team, there early before a game, pile into the bleachers to watch us. They are twelve or thirteen. The age I loved playing the most. They tumble over each other, getting into the bleachers; they shove at each other's backs and heads. *Go!* says one to another. They are very happy, they are thrilled with life.

At end-of-year banquets she sat by herself and I sat with her, not my friends. I was good then and guilty.

She didn't let me paint the door. They took pictures of me with the door all peeling. Junk in the yard.

A kid from the facility is the catcher. He's excited, you can tell. He squats behind home plate, mask on, mitt on, kind of bouncing on his haunches. I feel I am not ready yet. I keep swinging and swinging the weighted bat. Marcus Hobart walks to the pitcher's mound and stands there, even taller than he was when we met. Very casual.

Ready, Kel? asks Gerard Kane.

The man who used to be my father gave me a baseball glove for Christmas. The last Christmas he was with us he gave me a glove but he didn't tell me to oil it and he didn't put a ball in it and wrap it around with string. I had to learn that on my own. I had to learn everything on my own.

Gerard Kane says, Hang on a sec. He walks up to one of the guys standing around watching us: one of the managers, maybe, someone who works here.

You mind clocking this for me? he asks, and hands the man a clocking gun.

I drop one of the bats and walk toward the plate. When I was little I had this superstition: I had to step into the box with my left foot first. I had to, or I wouldn't get a hit. Then at twelve I forced myself to break this habit in practice, over and over again until it didn't scare me anymore. Today I step in with my left foot. Just in case.

I try to remember how it was when I first began doing this well. When I first began getting attention for hitting. There were times when I just *knew*. I *knew* I would knock it out of the park. I try to feel this now but it won't come.

Marcus winds up and releases a pitch that I misjudge. I don't swing. It's a perfect strike. I stand and shake my legs out.

Ninety-six! calls the man clocking it.

Hoo, baby, says Gerard Kane.

My mother used to come to all my games. Every single one. She was there for every single one until she got sick. Sitting by herself in the stands. Wrapped up in a blanket if it was cold. Wrapping me in a blanket on the drive home.

Marcus pitches again and I swing and catch a piece of it. It flies up behind me and hits the wall.

After six pitches I finally hit one: a grounder between second and third base, closer to third, and I think that if I had been standing on that base I would have dived for it and chucked it hard to first. I'm a good fielder.

At this point I would have struck out already and it fazes me. Marcus's pitches don't let up. His best pitch is his fastball.

I used to cry when we lost until a coach told me not to. I was nine or ten. Don't do that, he said. Coach Laughlin was his name. Don't do that, Don't cry, he said to me. I never did again.

On the twelfth or thirteenth pitch I hit a homer. Well, what would be a homer on a regular field. Here it hits the back wall with a little *thup*.

There you go, Kel, says Gerard Kane, and I think maybe, maybe I still have a chance. If I don't fuck up anymore. Please let me stop fucking up.

But I swing so hard at the next one, and miss so hard, that I almost hit the ground. I stagger backward, trying to catch my breath, trying to stand up straight.

Gerard Kane walks over to me and puts a hand on my shoulder. Kel, buddy, he says. You nervous?

No, I say. Just—football, you know? I've been playing football all season.

You'll stick with baseball, if you know what's best for you! he says.

On the pitcher's mound, Marcus tosses the ball up in the air and catches it.

How many hours have I spent in my life doing that. Just doing that with any type of ball I could find. Baseballs and basketballs and footballs. Rocks when there were none. Marbles. Pennies. Flipping quarters. Throwing books in the air and catching them. Just tossing things. I think it is what I have done most in my life. Lying down on my bed or standing up or out in the little back-yard or on the street or on the way to or from school or in practice or at recess or on the neighborhood court. The clean release of a sphere into space. The muscle behind it. The force from your legs, from your gut, from your back, from your shoulders and biceps and elbows—the sling of the elbow, the catapult—and then the flicking wrist, and then the loving palm, and then good-bye, goodbye. The dance off the fingertips and into the air. The skipping spin. The last loving touch and then it's gone, gone, and you know when you've done it right and when you've done it wrong. There is certainty and there is justice in it. You know when you say goodbye to it with your skin. Whether it will go right or left, too high, too low, you know. You know. You know.

I swing. I miss. I wait. A strike. A ground ball. A strike. It's not terrible—I take a piece out of a lot of them, and I hit one more home run—but I'm not here. I fail. I don't hit my stride and I can't get used to Marcus's pitching. He is better than I am. I know it to be true. A better player. More deserving. Once I allow myself to have this thought I can't shake it. I can't unthink it. I want to feel sorry for myself, but I almost feel relieved.

The last thing we do is a sixty-yard dash. Mr. Kane gives us a while to warm up. I run a lap around the bases while they measure the distance and set up cones. Normally I can do it in 7.1. That has always been my speed. But I know, today, that 7.1 won't be impressive, that I must dig into all of my reserves and come up with something better than that. So when I run it I tell myself that I am on fire, that I am running from a murderer. I used to run up the stairs to my room as quick as I could when I was little because I always imagined a bad guy running up them after me. So I picture this. And when I'm done, Gerard Kane looks at his watch and says, Seven flat.

But Marcus Hobart runs it in 6.93. I should be faster than him. He pitches. I should have been faster.

Thanks, guys, says Mr. Kane. We'll be in touch with you, OK? Good hustle today.

He shakes both of our hands. I look again at his sunglasses, hanging around his neck on a cord. *Take me with you,* I want to say.

Sarah says, Bye! Very cheerfully.

Then both of them grab their things and go.

I almost run after them. I almost say to Mr. Kane, *You have to give me another chance. You have to let me show you—in the spring. I'm so much better in the spring. Let me work out and then let me show you again. Let me eat right for a month.*

But I don't. I sit on the bleachers—the twelve and thirteen-year-olds watch me but don't say anything—and take off my cleats. I pull my sweatpants back on, shivering a little because I'm sweaty and cooling down, and then I pull my sweatshirt on and then my sneakers. I haven't called Lindsay yet, but I don't want to hear her voice because I think it will break me. So instead I send her a text. *Done.*

Marcus Hobart comes out of the locker room.

Nice meeting you, he says, and he shakes my hand. I'll see you around, OK?

But I know that I won't. See him again.

While I'm waiting I tell myself that maybe it wasn't so bad. That maybe they need us both. We play different positions, I tell myself. Maybe it's fine. But in my heart I know. I know it's not good enough. What I did, how I played. I know it's not nearly good enough for the majors.

When Lindsay picks me up I think she knows before I get in the car.

Hi, she says. She doesn't ask questions. This is why I like her: Because she is an athlete. Because she understands.

Do you want to come over for the afternoon? she asks.

OK, I say.

And I sink into the seat of her father's Lexus, smooth inside, leathery and soft, a whisper of a car. Comforting in ways it shouldn't be.

My mother drew the bull's-eye. She propped the mattress up and drew the red bull's-eye on it for me. My mother, wearing sweatpants and a robe, her feet bare in our grassless backyard, and there I was behind her, tossing a baseball into the air. And catching it. Oh I caught it. Oh I always did.

"I'm gonna be back," said Yolanda.

"Very good," I said.

I was sitting in my armchair & *Cash Cab* was on. I would not look at her.

"You look thinner," said Yolanda.

I shifted but did not reply.

"They want me there when the baby comes," said Yolanda. She was holding her bags.

"Of course," I said.

"My mother apologized," said Yolanda. "For the things she said. My father too."

"That's good," I said.

"They even said I could go back to school if I wanted," said Yolanda. "If I can keep working. They'll help watch the baby."

"Excellent."

"I can work for you on weekends. I can bring the baby with me."

"Perhaps."

"Am I still invited to your dinner party?" asked Yolanda.

"Don't," I said. It was too much for me.

"What?" she said. "You're having one. The Dales are coming. Don't stand them up."

But I knew when she left that she would not be back. No one comes back you see.

"See you then," said Yolanda, & opened the door.

Before she left she looked at me for a minute. "What are you going to do?" she said.

"O you know," I said, but even I didn't.

"There's fruit salad on the counter," she said, & then, finally, she left.

It was the first time I had been alone for the night in a couple of weeks. After she left, the house let out a sigh of relief & settled into itself somehow. I could hear things I hadn't been noticing. The heat went on. The radiators clanged. I wandered a little bit for no reason, peering into corners & out of windows. I went into the bathroom & looked at myself in the mirror. I turned my head from side to side & decided that Yolanda was right: I did look thinner. I went out of the bathroom and stood at the foot of the stairs & looked up them into the dark stairwell. I turned the light on & off again. I walked to the piano and ran my finger over the black of it, just as Yolanda had done the first day she came to me, & found no dust there. I lifted the cover off the keys and played a C-chord. It has not been tuned in more than a decade but it still sounds almost right. It was a gift from my father. When I was a boy I played seriously & I practiced all the time.

Then I put on the radio. Then I walked into my bedroom & tried to remember it as it was when I was a very small boy, when my parents lived there. I have a memory of climbing in bed with them in the morning, one of the few times they were happy together, O I must have been very small.

Then I walked to the wardrobe & opened it & remembered all of my mother's dresses, how they hung in there from small (on the left) to large (on the right), & how she would lovingly finger the small ones & in misery tell me which events she had worn them to. Anna Ordinary.

Then I walked into the kitchen automatically, my brain was telling me to, the other-Arthur that lives in there. But when I opened my refrigerator I could not muster the energy, I simply could not, & so I closed it & leaned against it & wondered what would become of me. I felt anchorless. But also in some ways I felt weightless.

The fruit salad that Yolanda had made was sitting on the counter. She'd made it out of fruit that she ordered online. It was huge & beautiful. She had put two salad spoons in it. & a smaller bowl next to it so that I might serve myself.

So I did: I filled the bowl with beautiful fruit. Apples & pears & bananas & mangoes & grapes, red and green. Kiwis like stars on the top. Blueberries & strawberries & oranges & grapefruit. I went to the couch and almost turned on the television but I stopped myself. I sat with it instead. I put one blueberry in my mouth & closed my eyes. Inside of my mouth it burst & popped. Its blue flavor. Its juice. I swallowed it neatly & chose an apple piece next.

Outside the street was quiet.

When I was a boy there would have been shouting of one kind or another. A boy to another boy. A mother to her child. I miss these sounds.

A banana. I had forgotten bananas. Their warmth & charitable nature.

When I had finished I went to bed and realized that I could feel a rib if I poked hard enough into my stomach. I could feel one rib someplace deep inside my flesh.

In the morning I woke up later than I had in years. It was ten o'clock. Normally I get up at sunrise & I cannot go back to sleep. I lay in bed for a while listening for Yolanda, to see if she had returned—I had no basis to believe she would, but I listened nonetheless—but the house was silent as it had been the night before, & the windows rattled. There was a gusting wind out-side. It was colder than it had been all month.

I read for a very long time & then I made lunch & then read some more. I put on the television & turned off the television.

I stay at the Harpers' all afternoon. We play Wii with Lindsay's little sisters in the basement. Over and over again they beat me at tennis. They kill me. Mrs. Harper comes downstairs and says Kel, would you like to stay over tonight?

They know about my practice this morning. Lindsay told them. They probably feel bad for me.

OK, I say. If you don't mind.

I could go back to Rhonda's but it's warm here.

Their house is like the Cohens'. They give me a room of my own. Lindsay says, It was Andy's.

This was his name: Andrew Harper. It's the first time I've heard Lindsay say it. His room is light blue and dark blue.

I change before dinner and then I start down the stairs and then I hear Margo and Mrs. Harper talking in the kitchen.

How long is Kel staying here? Margo asked.

Just for tonight, says Mrs. Harper.

Why is he staying here?

Mrs. Harper pauses. He lost his mama, she says finally.

His *mama?* says Margo.

Yes, says Mrs. Harper. The way we lost Andy. He lost his mama.

Oh no, says Margo.

• • •

Oh no. I stand still in the hallway for a while after that. Lindsay finds me and says Coming? She puts a hand on my back. Burgers, she says.

When we go downstairs little Margo is looking at me worriedly with her two fingers in her mouth. A habit her family tells her she is too old for.

After dinner we go into the living room, where the Harpers have set up a tree, and we all watch a movie that Margo and Kayla have chosen, an animated version of Rudolph the Red-Nosed Reindeer that I too watched when I was a kid. The girls laugh and laugh and laugh. Lindsay laughs at them. I laugh at Lindsay. Their tree has little lights on it, every color. It has ornaments and some of the ornaments are silver-framed pictures of each of the Harpers. The fact that Christmas is in two weeks has not even crossed my mind until now. I should get Lindsay something beautiful. I should get her something she will look at and hold in her hands and put on her body someplace, on her neck, on her wrist. In her long hair.

Before Margo goes to bed she hugs me.

The Harpers go next and then Lindsay and I look at each other, and then we go down to the basement.

I think of a time not that long ago, oh just a

couple of months ago, when I would pick Lindsay up from this house and drive her places, when my mother was at home. When she was alive, when she was a wreck but alive. When I had the option of going home to see her. When I didn't—when I never went home to see her.

Stop, says Lindsay. Stop thinking what you're thinking.

We lie down so she's at a right angle to me on the curved sectional couch. Our heads are touching. I kissed her down here.

We're silent for a while. I wait for Lindsay to talk. She is like this: quiet, quiet, until she builds up the courage to say what it is she has to say.

Are you going to call him? she says, finally.

No, I say.

—Why not?

—I'm going to write to him.

—Why?

It's what my mother would have done, I say.

I dig in my back pocket for my wallet and take out her good-bye note to me. I hand it to Lindsay. It is the most trust I've ever put in anyone.

When she is done reading it she hands it back to me without saying anything.

She was a shitty writer, I say, and I laugh. It's not funny though. I wish I hadn't said it.

No she wasn't, says Lindsay, firmly. And Lindsay is the best writer I know.

I take something else out of my wallet next. It's the piece of paper with the phone number and address of this man Arthur Opp.

I hand this to her next, over my head.

Brooklyn, says Lindsay.

I'm gonna mail it to him, I say.

The whole note? says Lindsay.

The whole note, I say.

You don't want to keep it? says Lindsay.

No, I say.

In fact I want to get rid of it very badly. As soon as I can. The week after she died, I read it all the time because I missed her. But after a while I got sick of it, sick of regretting, sick of remembering it all. Finding her. Calling the goddamn ambulance. Sitting in the goddamn hospital. I want to drop it in the mailbox and be done with it. It seems easier to me than calling him and explaining the whole situation. It seems right.

Lindsay gets up suddenly and walks to the supply closet. She disappears inside it and comes out with an envelope and paper.

Here, she says, handing both to me.

She helps me write the note to go along with it. I make her write the address on the envelope because her handwriting is nicer than mine and I want to make very certain it won't be lost in the mail. She looks at me when it is time to write the return address and I tell her I guess she should use her own. It's more likely to find me here now.

I hold the sealed envelope in my hands and look at it. I look at her.

We can mail it now, says Lindsay. If you want.

Very quietly we tiptoe out of the dim house. The only light in the entryway comes from the tree. Outside it is cold and still and I can see every star. Lindsay lets me drive her car, and we both try not to slam the doors. At the Pells Landing Post Office I leave the car running and get out and walk up to the mail slot on the side of the building and drop it in. I close my eyes for a minute. Just a minute.

When I get back in Lindsay has turned on the radio and I smile at her for the first time in what seems like years. And I feel like a kid for the first time in years.

Do you mind if we go someplace? I ask her.
—Where?
—Do you mind?
—No.
So I drive up the Hudson to the beach I know, and there are little lights on the dry-docked boats, and a train whistles by in the distance. This is where I came the night I kissed you, I said. After Margo broke my taillight.

Why did you come here? she asks me.

I wanted to think about you some more, I say.

And I was avoiding my mother, I say, but I laugh, it's a joke.

We talk for a very long time and I ask her if it gets easier and she says not really, just different, a different duller kind of hurt, the kind that doesn't surprise you anymore. I ask what her parents were like when it happened and she says they have never been the same. We fought all the time for two years after it happened, she says. But not so much anymore.

After a while I turn the car off so we don't waste gas and it's so warm that we fall asleep there, facing the boats and the dark river.

I dream of many things, among them the old man who helped me and my mother get to the World Series, the old man from Pennsylvania who, years ago, paid for our car to be towed. I think of him when I need relief, when I need to feel that the world is not after all very bad. In my dream he is driving in his truck with my mother beside him. They are singing along to the radio. They're smiling. I am there and not there. I am outside and they are in.

When I wake up I am shivering with cold. I look to my right and Lindsay is crying. She pushes her forehead into my shoulder like a child and says, I miss him. Oh. I miss him.

Dear Arthur Opp,

My name is Kel Keller. But my real name is Arthur Turner Keller. I think you know my mother Charlene Turner Keller. I am sorry to tell you this, but she has died.

I am very sorry to be the one to tell you, in a letter.

Why am I writing to you, you might be wondering. It is because of something she wrote to me actually. I have enclosed her last letter to me. It is important that you have it. You will see why.

I have put my address and my phone number on this envelope. I hope that you will be in touch with me if she was telling the truth. Which I don't know if she was. She wasn't well when she died. Or for a lot of her, most of her, life.

Yours truly,
Arthur "Kel" Keller

I did not see the letter until a day after it came. Since Charlene died, & since Yolanda left, I had not been checking my mail as eagerly as I once checked it. It seemed to me that everything that happened this extraordinary autumn was over & done with & I was finished hoping for more. The mailman came every day and pushed the mail through the slot & I let it sit there. If I walked by it I'd pick it up. But since it was always junk, I usually let it lie.

Then on Wednesday I mustered up some effort and scooped up the whole pile & began the nasty process of sorting. When I came across his letter I put everything else down.

The letter was written in three different hands. My address, and the return address, were written on the envelope in very neat proper handwriting. The first page that I pulled out was written in a boy's messy handwriting. And the second and third pages were written by Charlene. O I'd recognize her handwriting anyplace.

Now. What the letter said I am still repeating in my head. Over & over again like a mantra. I must have read it thirty times in utter astonishment. I wanted to make sure I hadn't gone mad.

My first reaction—I am weak—was to take the blessing that had been bestowed upon me & swallow it greedily & never look back.

To tell him: *Yes, yes, it is possible you are my son, you, Arthur, were named for me, & therefore you are my son, my very admirable son, fully formed, absolutely perfect, my son. My long-lost son. Arthur.*

But I couldn't do it. It wouldn't have been right to deceive him. It would have haunted me forever & ever. I would have taken it into the afterlife with me. I would not have rested easy in my grave.

I walked into my bedroom & got out Charlene's letters & leafed through them to find my favorite one of all. It is my one love letter. It was sent in the midst of our courtship. In it she said many things (O I could name them all) but the one that is most important to me now is something she said that I found peculiar then.

She said that in her wildest dreams we would be married & I would be the father of her child. At the time I took it as something hypothetical, but I wonder now if she already knew. If she was pregnant when she wrote to me. If she stopped seeing me because she was pregnant by somebody else. *You would make a very good father I am sure,* she wrote to me then. *You're smart and you respect people.*

• • •

We were never intimate. Occasionally we held hands. Occasionally she took my arm. Occasionally. Nothing more. The closest to Charlene I ever felt was the very first time we met outside of school—the one time I helped her with her coat. If I could have helped her with her coat for hours, for the rest of her life, I would have.

I sat on the bed and read her old letter over and over again. & then I read the new one I held in my hands. For one whole day I pondered what to do.

Finally I allowed myself to call Yolanda, though I had promised myself I never would, not until she called me first. It was important & I had no adviser. Fortunately for me she answered.

"Invite him to your dinner party," she said, after I told her my strange tale.

& I felt somehow that this was a very good idea. & I felt that now Yolanda would come too.

My task then was to write back to the boy.

I am deeply sorry to hear about your mother's death. I knew her when she was about twenty years old. We had a special sort of friendship, but I regret to tell you that, although you do have a father—everyone does—he is not I. I wish with all of my heart that I could tell you differently. I hope this doesn't bring you any sort of despair. Fathers aren't all they are cracked up to be. For example I know who my father is, but I also know he isn't a very good one, and I probably would have been better off without him. All my life I have heard it said that you can't choose your family, and all my life I have lamented this fact as true & unfair. But I think it is possible to look at things differently: I believe we can choose to surround ourselves with a circle of people we love and admire & they can become our adopted family. For example I had an adopted sister for many years. Her name was Marty. & I seem to have found a daughter to adopt along the way as well, & her name is Yolanda, & I hope you will meet her someday.

And then I invited him to my dinner party, & told him about all the letters I'd had from his mother over the years, & that maybe I could tell him about his mother when she was young, & I encouraged him to bring whomever he pleased.

I opened my front door & put it in my mailbox and I tipped the happy little red flag up.

At last I walked to the shelf & took his picture off it & studied him closely. I stood there, very still, until my knees hurt. Suddenly I thought I saw in him a certain resemblance to my father,

416

when he was young. Something about his eyes & ears. His stern worried expression. O yes, I thought, he could look like my father.

I imagined, one day, telling the boy the story of our name. My mother used to tell me it was a name for kings. When I was growing up this embarrassed me because I thought of myself as very far from kingly. But looking at his picture —Arthur, who was named for me—I reconsidered. Maybe all along it suited me, if only so it could be given to him.

Last night, a thought occurred to me that I had never had before, and the thought was of Arthur Opp's letters to my mother. All of the letters he sent to our house. At times they were separated by weeks or months, but they always came, and my mother always brightened and smiled and took them into her bedroom to read. He was a sort of magic in her life, and in a way he was magic for me too—the mysterious Arthur Opp, who in my childish dreams was a rich benefactor who would one day appear and marry her.

I was sure she had saved his letters. I was sitting at dinner with the Harpers when I realized this and I nearly jumped up from my chair and then I sat back down again.

Everything OK, Kel? said Mr. Harper, and I said yes it was, but I had forgotten about something.

You need to go someplace? said Mr. Harper.

Yes, I said, hoping he would not ask for an explanation, and sure enough he did not, and so for the first time I felt like a man instead of a boy.

This time it wasn't so bad going into my house. Mr. Harper's sister the real estate agent has gotten some people to make it look nicer to get it ready to sell, and the electricity is back on. When I flicked the lights on inside the front door they went on merrily and the furniture was all neat with nothing on it.

I did have to take some deep breaths before going into her room, but her bed had different sheets on it and it was made up nicely, and so it was better. For a moment I was worried that maybe they had thrown things out, the real estate people, but I yanked open some of the drawers in her desk and all of the documents in there still seemed to be in place.

I had already searched through her desk once so I knew Arthur Opp's letters wouldn't be in there. I went to her bedside table instead and opened the one little drawer in it, and there they were, right away, no trouble at all to find.

All the letters were flattened and unfolded in a stack. Next to them was a stack of envelopes. She had thrown nothing away. Gingerly I took out the letters. They were on paper monogrammed with *A.C.O.* at the top. It looked classy. They went in order from latest to earliest. It was a heavy pile of paper, thick as a book. The top one was dated September 12th of this year, and I did not want to read it right away. I tried to think about what was happening September 12th but I couldn't recall.

So instead I read the oldest one, from December 20, 1992.

Dear Charlene, it began. *Thank you very kindly for your thoughtful note.*

I only let myself read that one. I sat there for quite a while. Then I tucked all of them under my arm, and walked down the stairs, and into the living room, and into the kitchen, and out of the door, turning every light off as I went.

When I got back to the Harpers' it was late and the little girls were asleep. Lindsay's parents were someplace else in the house and I could hear their quiet voices going back and forth in a murmur. Lindsay was waiting up for me.

Hi, she said. She was holding something in her hands.

What is it, I asked her. She held it out to me. It was a letter from Arthur Opp, addressed to me.

This came today, she said. My mom just gave it to me.

I began to laugh.

What, said Lindsay. What's funny.

I showed her what I was carrying. Then I put the latest letter from Arthur Opp on the top of the pile, and thought of taking it into another room to open it, but I did not want to be like my mother, so instead I tore open the envelope right there in front of Lindsay, but I didn't take out the note inside it.

I was trying to breathe slowly. For inside I knew there would be some sort of answer.

What do you think, said Lindsay.

I don't know, I said.

If you had to guess, said Lindsay.

But I didn't want to guess anymore.

Together we read his letter. We read it seven times. He was not my father. I wasn't crushed. I felt no badness or anger. I was not sure what I had wanted. He sounded like a teacher in his letter. I liked him. I tried to picture him and couldn't, so I pictured someone backlit by the sun. He could be anyone. Anyone except my father, according to him. All of my life I thought this about my father: that he could be anyone I passed on the street. On the street I looked for my father in every man I saw. I looked for him in my sleep. Now I know there are two less people my father could be. Two less for me to wonder about. The rest of the world remains.

I feel like people are only really dead once you stop learning about them. This is why it is important to me to keep learning about my mother, and what she wanted, and what her life meant, what she meant by the life she led. Then she will be alive, somehow, and her wish for me will have come true. My vow is to learn more about her. To see her as she saw herself.

So I like that Arthur Opp knew my mother the way he did. That he had a connection to her, outside of me. I like that she had a secret. I like that she had some little thing to think about, someone separate from me and my life. I wonder if she was in love with him. I can see her being in love with him, from the letters of his that I have read. She always had heroes, from the time I was little: I was the main one, the great hero of her life, but there was Dr. Greene, and the rich people from Pells, and my coaches, and my teachers. She liked hearing about them from me. She would have loved the Harpers. She liked smart people. She wanted me to be smart.

I am not mad at her for lying. I think she did it so I would be sure to meet him. I can see her doing that. I can see her giving us to each other as a gift.

I haven't heard a word from Gerard Kane. I didn't think I would, but—there was a part of me. The little-kid part, the part that felt like I couldn't possibly fail at the one thing I was ever good at. I guess I could keep trying. I still have the spring ahead of me. Maybe I'll play better than I ever have, and maybe some other scout, some other recruiter, will notice me. Maybe. All of these are maybes. And then I think about the Marcus Hobarts of the world, the people who play like they are magic, the people who play like they were made for baseball and baseball was made for them. Sometimes I think that I am like this too, like I am part of this, but there are days, more and more, when I'm not sure. And I think you have to be sure. I think the Marcus Hobarts of the world are positive.

So I've been thinking about what Ms. Warren said, which I kind of can't believe. It isn't too late. It's not like I don't have college coaches still interested in me. I talked to Lindsay's dad about it and he said, I think that's a really good idea, Kel.

Of course he did.

But really I'm considering it. Now that my mother's gone—I guess I can do whatever I want. This is a thought that makes me feel happy and sad all at once. It is what I spent two years wondering about: how I would ever leave her, how I could possibly hope to have a life outside of Yonkers or Pells. Now I can go to school wherever I want. Alaska, if I want to. California. Hawaii. Arizona. Anyplace in the wide world.

When she first died I thought to myself, I could have prevented it. And this was the most painful thing to think. She wasn't hit by a train. It wasn't a clean even death like that. I could have stopped her. I could have reasoned. At first when I thought of these things I would shut my brain off, just as I do before games. I would stop myself from thinking anything at all.

But today it seems possible—just possible—to think about her in all her states, drunk and sober, tidy or messy or anything. The times she was a good mother, because they existed, they did exist, and the times she was very bad.

This was what happened the first time I realized she was really in trouble. She hadn't gone to work in two weeks but she hadn't yet been fired. I was a sophomore. I was fifteen years old. I took the train home and then got on the bus and by that time it was already very late. I don't know what I was thinking of. I don't remember much from those days. Already I fed and clothed myself. I made money for myself any way I could. I stopped at the corner store at the gas station and said hi to Frank and bought myself a roast beef sandwich and bought my mother a turkey sandwich. I bought us both chips. I was happy about something that I don't remember anymore. Basketball practice maybe. It was winter. It was cold out. I was thinking maybe I could sit down with her and reason with her about going back to work. Everyone's been asking about you, I would say. Dr. Greene keeps asking when you're coming back. This was not true, but it seemed to me then to be the surest way to lure her back to work.

But when I walked up to the house it was all dark inside. No lights were on. I put my key in the door and turned it and said, Mom? Mom?

I was a kid.

I tried to turn the lights on but no lights would come on and I realized that once again she probably hadn't paid the electricity bill. Shortly after that I would start looking for it in the mail and paying it myself. But that day I fumbled for the flashlight on the wall and used it to find my way into the living room and she was sitting there crying. She was wearing her robe and looking out the window and she was sitting in a chair slumped forward.

What's the matter, I asked her, already very weary.

She shook her head and would not answer.

I got you a turkey sandwich, I said, and took it out of the plastic bag and put it in its white butcher paper on her lap. Set it down there without knowing what else to do.

She didn't touch it.

Eat it, I said. You should eat that.

Then I had an idea, and I went into the kitchen and found a couple of birthday candles and some matches, and stuck them into a potted plant and lit them up. Then I put the potted plant on the hearth and I said, Look, Ma. A fire in the fireplace. Remember? A fire in the fireplace.

Come with me, I say to Lindsay. Please. I can't go by myself.

But you should, says Lindsay.

But I can't, I say.

Arg, says Lindsay, and her face puzzles up in exasperation. He'll be like, who's this girl?

—Then I'll say Hi, Mr. Opp. This is my girl-friend, Lindsay Harper.

She rolls her eyes at this but she also almost smiles.

You really want me to? she asks me.

He said I could bring whoever I wanted, I tell her. And I want you to.

Because I'm out of gas, I say, and she thwacks me hard in the back.

I'm nervous, says Lindsay.

I'm nervous too, I say.

She puts on a dress to go to Arthur Opp's house. It's the first time I've ever seen her wear one. To school she wears jeans or her sports uniforms. She looks like a woman. I tell her so and she acts insulted.

In a good way, a really good way, I tell her.

Ready? she asks me, and I say yes, because I am.

Yolanda arrived this morning & has been helping me all day. Her parents are coming tonight
from Queens.

"Oh my God," she keeps saying. She whispers
it under her breath. She is nervous for me to
meet them. I imagine them as male and female
versions of Yolanda. Thirty years older. I imagine
them in hooded sweatshirts. I imagine them
nervous, like she is.

We went for our walk after she got here & we
saw the Dales & their sons. "See you tonight,"
said Henry Dale, & I nodded rather smartly &
casually, & then marveled over how natural it
felt—the Dales are coming over for dinner.

Then we came back and made lasagna, a recipe
that Marty taught me that I'm now passing on to
Yolanda. Once it was in the oven Yolanda and I
both cleaned the house, & she gave me orders
like "Go get a cloth from under your sink. Dust
that shelf. Throw out those containers. Jesus."

I think things look very nice now, especially
since Yolanda ordered flowers from the Internet,
& they came this morning. Lilies & roses &
mums. She was the one who answered the door
& she pretended like they were for her, saying to
the deliveryman, "O this is so sweet! O I can't
believe it!"

After she shut the door she went into the kitchen & put them all in a vase & then put the vase in the middle of the dining room table. "See? Look how nice," she said.

In a fit of sentimentality & self-pity, I asked her today if she would let me meet the baby after it was born and she asked if I was firing her. I took this as a very good sign. I told her that I liked the name Anna for a girl. I don't think she does but she was polite about it anyway.

Then she went upstairs to her old room to lie down for a bit before the guests arrive. Including Kel Keller, who called me three days ago to tell me he would come. Hearing him speak to me was miraculous. He was tentative & shy. He was quieter than I'd imagined. He did not sound like his picture. I told him how sorry I was & he said thank you. We talked briefly about his mother & he revealed the nature of her last few years & of her death, which I had suspected, but it was very sad to hear it confirmed. He asked me only one question and I was able to answer it in a way that seemed to please him. When we hung up I went to take his picture off my shelf—I feared that he would think it strange for me to have— but then I changed my mind. Charlene sent it for a reason.

I have had several bouts of nervousness thinking about his first sight of me. I wish I could be obscured by something when he first sees me, hiding behind a plant or a sofa. I wish I could be shadowed by something larger than I am. But I can't be, so instead I will throw open both doors as wide as I can, and I will stand there in full sight of him, and I will welcome him into my home.

For an hour, while Yolanda was napping, I sat in my chair, looking around this room, pondering the life of Charlene Keller since I had last seen her, & how it could have been different—how my life too could have been different. Both of us stuck in our homes, curled into ourselves in loneliness. Both of us alone. It could have been different, I thought. Quite different. I did not linger there.

Instead I walked to my front door & opened it. I peered out into the world. The street was quiet & nothing moved. I opened the glass outer door & walked out onto the stoop. A car rolled by, looking for parking, & for a moment I grew nervous & excited but it was not the boy. I stood very still then & put my arms about myself.

O what will happen now, I asked. But I was alone, and I found I could not answer.

About the Author

Liz Moore is a writer and musician. Her debut novel, *The Words of Every Song*, was published in 2007, and her short fiction and nonfiction can be found in print and online. She is a professor at Holy Family University in Philadelphia, where she lives.

Center Point Large Print
600 Brooks Road / PO Box 1
Thorndike ME 04986-0001 USA

(207) 568-3717

US & Canada:
1 800 929-9108
www.centerpointlargeprint.com